I0579353

TRAILS THROUGH TIME

TRAILS THROUGH TIME

LARRY ENGELS

Deeds Publishing | Athens

Copyright © 2020—Larry Engels

ALL RIGHTS RESERVED—No part of this book may be reproduced in any form or by any electronic or mechanical means, including information storage and retrieval systems, without permission in writing from the authors, except by a reviewer who may quote brief passages in a review.

Published by Deeds Publishing in Athens, GA
www.deedspublishing.com

Printed in The United States of America

Cover design by Mark Babcock.

ISBN 978-1-950794-26-3

Books are available in quantity for promotional or premium use. For information, email info@deedspublishing.com.

First Edition, 2020

10 9 8 7 6 5 4 3 2 1

*For my son Bret who hiked the trails with me,
climbed the peaks, and found the gold coins.*

Contents

1. A Father's Treasure Map   1

2. Into The Forest Of Time   23

3. Those First Days, "1894"   39

4. The First Trail   59

5. A Winters Work—Snow   69

6. Prospecting For Gold   75

7. Molly Arrives   87

8. Life At The Chalet "1896"   105

9. A Warm Cave   121

10. The Teahouse   131

11. The Tallest Peak   145

12. Changes With The Century—A New Chalet   165

13. Bankhead   181

14. Exciting Years 1904—1910   197

15. Let It Snow   215

16. Our Son For A Summer—1911   225

17. Goodbye Sweet Molly   243

18. Lost Years / A Final Diary Entry   265

19. The End Of The Trail   281

About the Author   293

Acknowledgements   295

1. A FATHER'S TREASURE MAP

"Good luck, Craig," Professor Stanley quietly responded as Craig placed the exam paper face down on the professor's desk. "Thanks, Doctor Stanley, I really enjoyed the course," Craig responded. Hallelujah, he couldn't believe it; his last exam was over. No more school for three whole months. It felt as if the weight of the world had just been lifted from his shoulders. With a burst of energy, Craig Bristol flung open the front door to Stanford Hall. He took one deep breath of the jasmine scented air and then ran all the way to his car in the remote freshman parking lot. There wasn't a second of his summer vacation to be wasted.

Driving back to the apartment, he wondered if his roommate, Bill, had gotten back yet. They had a lot of last-minute things they needed to do before they left on their trip the next morning. He ran down the list in his head … let's see: take their school stuff over to Tony's house for storage, get the car serviced, finish packing, buy film, and buy picnic supplies. Craig and Bill had decided that they would picnic and camp some on the trip to save money, a precious commodity for both.

Craig tingled with excitement as he thought about the adventure that lay ahead of them. Striking out with his best friend to explore new places…well, it was about the most exciting thing he could think of. They were starting out on a three-week trip of over five thousand miles. Sure, he had taken trips before to places like Florida, but this was really going to be an especially fun trip. On this trip, they would set the schedule; no parents telling them what to do, or when to do it; complete freedom.

His mother and several friends had been out to the Rockies before. He had heard their stories of the great snow-capped mountains, stories of snow storms in July, and some pretty incredible adventure stories involving bears. In Boy Scouts he had camped in the mountains of North Carolina in some awfully nice spots. He wondered if he would like the Rockies as well. Certainly, he expected it would be cooler than it had been recently there in Alabama. He was counting on that.

Aside from being a good time of the year weather wise, he had been told that the campgrounds probably wouldn't be too crowded this early in June. Maybe the winter snows would still have the peaks covered. He hoped so. Snow was to be one of the treats for this southern boy who had seldom seen snow. Craig remembered having heard someone say the mosquitoes might be bad in June. Better make sure to add bug repellant to his list, he thought. Certainly a few mosquitoes wouldn't put a dent in their plans.

The tingling excitement he got from thinking about the trip was diminished from time to time though as he remembered the emotional event that had led up to the trip. He knew that had it not been for his father's letter, he would not be making this trip. At times, he was angry and resentful that his mother had kept the letter from him all those years. She had said she wanted him to be mature enough to deal with the "upset" the letter might cause. Craig suspected she delayed so long in part due to her own pain over losing his father. She had also said that she thought that delaying it was the way his father would have wanted it. She had waited until Christmas, after his eighteenth birthday, to show him the letter.

Craig thought how wonderful it would have been to have had a father like Bill's. All those years when he was growing up, he missed not having a father. Even if his father had been killed in an auto accident years ago like Kerry Dawson's father, it would not have been that bad. To have a father who up and vanished had been hard to accept.

In his early years, Craig often felt an outcast, wondering if people weren't talking behind his back saying "poor little boy, his father had run away and deserted him." He remembered one bully in particular, David Rockwell, who taunted him in grade school. Maybe that was true; maybe his father had been some jerk who deserted' his family. He couldn't really believe that and somehow, he knew his father was not at fault. One thing he did know, it sure had been hard on his mother. For years she held out hope of some word from him.

That letter had made him see things a little differently. Maybe his father had really loved him, he thought. He must have Craig reasoned. Why else would he have gone to the trouble to hide treasure for him if he hadn't? Small though the treasure might be, it said something about his love, didn't it? Imagine leaving buried treasure for a two-year-old, complete with a treasure map. Maybe his father had just been crazy. He wondered how many fathers did something like that for their kids.

He thought of the modest treasure. Quite soon after reading the letter, he found a coin book in the library and looked up the value of a twenty-dollar gold piece. According to the coin book it might be worth about five hundred dollars, not bad he thought. Considering his middle-class upbringing five hundred dollars was a tidy sum.

Craig remembered having heard his mother say that gold was not a very good investment. He also remembered his mother saying that his father was not very good with investments. Luckily, his mother had been an investment whiz, otherwise the financial difficulties associated with his father's disappearance could have been devastating.

If his father had really been crazy, then money probably wasn't important to him, he reasoned. In any event, the thoughtfulness of it made him feel special. Thinking about him too much brought tears to his eyes. Craig had read the letter over and over in his mind, having by now memorized it thoroughly. He cherished each word since there had been so few to remember his father by.

"Dear Craig, since you are reading this rather than me telling you of your surprise, it is reasonable to assume that I am dead. Don't be sad. Hopefully, I have gone to a better place. I am sorry though, because I had hoped to share so much with you." Craig stopped and thought about that. If he were planning to run away, surely that passage would have been worded differently, he thought.

The letter continued, *"I had wanted to share with you the experience of the beautiful Canadian Rockies. This land out here is my favorite place in the entire world. I somehow feel more alive here than anywhere else. This place has a strange power over me that I do not fully understand. I feel a part of everything here like I somehow belong here. I want you to have the experience of exploring these mountains as I have.*

"As a bit of incentive for you to hike some of the trails through the marvelous backcountry, I have carefully placed a twenty-dollar gold coin under a rock for you to find. Enclosed is a map, instructions, and pictures of the hiding place. I hope to continue this practice every year in a different place. Enjoy this wonderful world as much as I did. May you be happy always. Now go find your gold. Love, Daddy."

"Hey man, you ready to travel," Bill shouted as he burst through the door?"

Craig jumped, as he was thrust back from his daydream to present reality. "I sure am," Craig half-heartedly said while hiding his tear-streaked face from Bill.

"Seven a.m. will come soon," Bill chimed in. "It will be a long day getting to that big McDonald's arch in St. Louis."

"Say, we need to get our act together. Did you remember to get me that film?" Craig asked Bill. The question came too late as Bill had disappeared into the bathroom.

When Craig was planning the trip, he had decided on two things immediately. First, he would invite Bill along, and secondly, he would attempt to retrace a similar trip that his father had recorded on a road map years ago. Apparently, his father had made a trip out West with his college roommate following his junior year. Bill and Craig would make the trip following their freshman year.

The route would take them through St. Louis, Kansas

City, Denver, and then up through Yellowstone and Glacier Park. They would continue north into Canada, stopping at Banff and ending up at Lake Louise, where with a little luck the coin would be found hiding under a rock on a mountainside.

The trip, they calculated, would take them about five thousand miles all total. This distance in three weeks would be a stretch for the pair. By sharing the driving, they planned to put in long days of travel out and back in order to maximize the amount of time in the mountains. Craig remembered the promise he and Bill had made to Craig's mother. They had promised not to drive too fast and to stop when they got tired.

Craig's first view of the mountains came just at sunset on June 5th, their second day out. They were about forty miles outside of Denver. At first, he thought they were clouds on the horizon. Soon he began to recognize the subtle difference from the clouds. He could see immediately even in that faint light that these mountains were much more magnificent and rugged than the mountains of North Carolina. Though he could hardly believe it, they looked as though they were covered with snow.

"Wow, look at all that snow," Bill kept saying the next morning as the two made their way thru the recently plowed Trail Ridge Road. They had arrived in Rocky Mountain Park and it was really something. They were lucky as the road had just opened a few days earlier. The two young Southerners were really not prepared for the vast amount of snow that lingered, clinging to the peaks. More amazing to the pair were the twisting canyons of snow the snowplows had carved out and that they were maneuvering their car through.

The snowcapped peaks kept getting even more spectacular as they traveled north and camped in the wildly romantic Tetons a couple of nights later. They laughed as they read the highway plaque explaining the name Tetons, was a name chosen by French trappers since they thought they resembled a woman's breasts. Bill declared himself to be an experienced climber of the mountain's namesake. Craig laughed, "In your dreams, Bill old boy."

They explored the fascinating wonders of Yellowstone, all the time complaining, like most visitors of the pungent rotten egg smell. They gawked at their first bear in the wild, a somewhat mangy looking old black bear that was at one of the numerous turnouts near Old Faithful. "Well, Bill, I guess I sure underestimated how much film to bring. At this rate we will be out before we hit Banff," Craig lamented. "Yellowstone is some place; I hope these pictures turn out. I really want to show these pictures to the girls," Craig added.

"Canadian Border One Mile" the sign read. They were quite excited. "Just think, our first time out of the good old USA. Hey, Craig, do you think they will check our suitcases?" Bill asked.

"Don't know, probably not," Craig piped up. "You don't have any wild weed do you, Billy?" Craig asked half-laughing, knowing that Bill was straight as an arrow when it came to drugs.

"No, you fool, and you better not either," Bill admonished Craig.

To their astonishment, the border crossing was a snap. They were expecting some big deal. Instead, a long once over by a plump middle age customs lady was about it. She did stare at their long hair in a most disapproving way. Craig thought about making a smart comment to her, but wisely thought better of it.

It didn't take long for Craig to see why his father liked Banff so much. The town was touristy with all its shops, but it somehow had an old west small town feel about it as well. Of course, the fact it was in a different country added to the mystique. All the different nationalities made it quite interesting. Walking along the street, they heard a multitude of different languages being spoken. Of special curiosity was the large number of Orientals they encountered.

Banff was a quaint little town set in a valley beneath magnificent peaks. It had a beautiful river called the Bow that flowed through it, cascading over a magnificent waterfall. Adding to the scenery were the numerous lakes and meadows that were part of the valley hosting the little town. As for the sense of smell, the smoke from the many fireplaces and the wonderful smell of balsam filled the air. Their sense of sound was stirred with the lonely train whistle as it made its way up the valley.

The old hotel was such a grand building. It sat there on a heavily wooded knoll overlooking the spectacular Bow River Falls. This hotel was definitely something out of another er*a*, Craig thought.

"I wonder what things were like back then?" Craig asked Bill.

"Don't know; reckon they had indoor plumbing or just a row of out-houses?" Bill mused.

"Now Bill, can you really imagine this grand place and a row of Porta-Potties lined up beside it, you fool," Craig responded. They both laughed at the absurdity of such a sight.

During the planning for the trip, Craig had found that there was a campground 'atop' the mountain. Rather than some great mountain, it was just a rather large hill adjacent to the town site. His mother had said that she remembered it as having quite a nice campground. That is where they had decided to spend their first night at Banff. The campground was in fact the nicest one yet on their trip. It was a short but steep hike up the road from Banff, requiring a bit of an effort.

The campsites had marvelous views of the town and valley below. Wildlife was abundant around the campground. The large nagging birds, they soon learned, were magpies. The small red squirrels were a bit nosier than their southern gray cousins. When they had checked in at the campground gate to get their campsite, Bill had asked if they needed to be concerned about bears. The ranger had said probably not, but cautioned them to keep a clean campsite. Though they were looking forward to seeing more bears, they weren't too excited about viewing one from their flimsy tent.

When they got their campsite set up for the night, they were famished and hiked down the mountain to town and an early dinner. Choosing a restaurant from such a wide assortment was quite a decision. Soon, they came upon one place that seemed perfect. It was called "Wild Bills." Craig joked, "Hey, Billy, they must have known you were coming, sounds like just your kind of place." Buffalo burgers, they discovered, were really not too bad.

After dinner they did what most 19-year-old males would do; look for some girls. With all the shops, it certainly wasn't hard to find the girls. Bill struck up a conversation with one girl he met while they were getting ice cream. Craig decided to make himself scarce for a while. "Bill, I'll meet you back at camp later," Craig said as he headed off up the street.

Craig again walked up the path by the Bow River to the old hotel. He gazed in awe at the grand old building. He wondered which room his parents had stayed in when they had visited here. He even wondered if he had been conceived here since his birthday was about nine months after his parent's last trip here together. This certainly was an enchanting and wonderful place; no wonder his father had loved it so.

Craig's thoughts then turned to Julie. He would really like to bring her here. He realized that he suddenly missed his girlfriend very much. Maybe it was this romantic setting; perhaps he would call her later that evening. Bill and Craig had talked about bringing their girlfriends on this adventure. Bill had been reluctant, saying the gals would limit their hiking and that they would be wanting to stop and shop, or potty every five miles. Craig wondered if the real reason Bill was reluctant was that he wanted to be able to 'cat' around, he being the more sexually adventurous of the two. In any event, Craig now regretted the decision.

Walking back to the campground, Craig thought what it must be like to stay in that grand hotel. He thought that he would probably feel uncomfortable even if he could afford it. Besides, it was probably filled with rich old snobs. Thanks to his mother, he and Bill would get the chance to find out about such a place. His mother had arranged for the two to stay in a grand hotel when they got to Lake Louise.

The sun was just setting at nine o'clock as he made it back to camp. Craig thought how strange it was for the sun to be setting so late. He really enjoyed the extended daylight. Boy had they been lucky with the weather so far; no rain, just sunny and cool. After all the excitement of the day, sleep came easily that evening. The cool breeze played through the tent flap and eased all cares.

Craig was awakened early by sounds outside the tent. Fearing it might be a bear he cautiously peered outside and was surprised to find a herd of about six very large deer grazing nearby. As he soon learned, these new animals were really not deer at all, rather they were elk, and he was to see many more in the days ahead.

They decided to drive down to Banff for breakfast. The little restaurant they chose had a very friendly and attractive waitress. She appeared a little too old for them to 'hit' on but she did seem to possess a wealth of knowledge about the area and provided some good suggestions as to places to see. "You really should see Lake Minnewanka, and the ruins of the ghost town at Bankhead are interesting," she said. After receiving directions, Bill and Craig opted for a drive up toward Lake Minnewanka, some four miles from Banff. Seeing the sign for Bankhead along the way, they decided to stop there on the way back from the lake.

Lake Minnewanka was all the lady in town had promised, a beautiful blue lake surrounded by high peaks on three sides. One odd thing they noticed was scuba divers near the dam. Craig finally decided to ask one of the guys putting on his wet suit near the road what they were doing diving in ice cold water. The diver went on, quite excitedly, about there being the remains of buildings, a regular little village down below. Wow that does sound interesting, Craig thought.

As it turned out they ended up eating their picnic lunch at Bankhead. This place was really amazing, he thought. Their waitress had certainly been right about this old ghost town. It was fascinating. The more he read about it on the plaques, the more exciting it seemed. He was really charmed by the place and wanted to explore all of it. Craig was now torn between exploring Bankhead and continuing at once on up to Lake Louise to find the coin. He decided that they would go immediately to Lake Louise, find the gold coin, then come back to Bankhead and spend the time they had left exploring and hiking around there.

Taking in the scenery that surrounded them as they approached Lake Louise, Craig thought to himself that the area was even grander than that around Banff. His father had thought it was the prettiest spot on earth. From the little village of Lake Louise, just off the Trans-Canada Highway, the pair made their way up the two-mile drive to the lake. When they saw a sign for parking, they turned in, not realizing that the Chateau entrance was just a bit further.

They walked down the little path from the end of the parking lot, through a bit of forest, and came out on the famous viewpoint for the lake. They both agreed pictures they had seen certainly did not do it justice. Bill kept saying, "I can't believe the color of the water." Craig commented too on the blue-green mirror that lay before him, reflecting every bit of the spectacular scenery. He was taking pictures like crazy. In the late afternoon sun, the glacier on the mountain at the end of Lake Louise glowed a beautiful golden color.

Off to their right, stood the large stately hotel, the Chateau. They walked toward the hotel, across a little stone arched bridge over a stream coming from the lake toward the hotel. "Wow, this is sure going to beat a tent," Bill kept saying.

Craig said, "Bill old boy, don't get too spoiled." Once they entered, they were astounded by the elegance of the place. Neither young man knew quite how to act when they went to check in. If not for the generosity of Craig's mother, they would never be staying in such an elegant and expensive place. She had insisted on paying for two nights at the Chateau. Craig guessed it was at least partially out of sentiment, since that was where she had stayed with his father whenever they had vacationed at Lake Louise.

Their room was in the center with a wonderful view of the lake. His mother had certainly reserved an excellent room. He even wondered if his mother and his father had stayed in that very room. A wonderfully fragrant breeze lifted the drapes beside the open window. Some three floors below the window lay the perfectly manicured lawn ablaze with spectacular colored flowers, Iceland Poppies, according to the sign. "You know, Bill, if I could turn you into Julie, this would be about perfect," Craig said longingly.

"Bet we can pick up some substitutes. I saw some cute gals as we were checking in," Bill announced. "Do you think those spoiled rich chicks will give us the time of day? Besides those blondes are probably from Sweden or some such place and probably don't even speak English. But you never know, we will check them out later, my horny buddy," Craig added.

"You were right, this will sure spoil us for camping," Bill lamented as he flopped down on the bed closest to the window.

"Yep, the ground never felt this good," Craig commented while trying out the other bed. After a brief rest, the two opted for a walk around the lake before dinner. A cool breeze was coming across the lake from the Northeast. Craig gazed off toward the North; thinking to himself, up there somewhere lies the coin, just waiting for me. Then came the somber thought that out there somewhere might lie his father's bones. He quickly tried to put that thought from his mind.

There sure should be trout in this lake. "That's what I believe I am going to have for dinner," Bill announced, "There should be trout in this lake. That's what I believe I am going to have for dinner."

"You know, I am getting pretty hungry right now," Craig responded. They agreed at that point to cut short their walk and return to the hotel for dinner. On the way back to the Chateau, they were briefly detained by a pair of playful porcupines foraging for food beside the lake. "Better not get too close," Craig kept cautioning Bill. Had these two creatures not been accustomed to people, this could have been a bad experience for the pair.

"Wow, we saw porcupines," Bill kept saying, having been more impressed by the yellowish-brown porcupines than the bears of Yellowstone.

As they talked during dinner, Craig nervously tried to think of some polite way to tell Bill that he wanted to go alone the next day to find the coin. For some reason he thought that this experience should be his and his alone. He had never really known his father and the experience was becoming a very emotional one for him. Most definitely he would not want to show tears in front of Bill.

Craig finally found what he thought was the right moment and interjected, "Bill, you know it may take me several hours to find the coin tomorrow. There is no point in you wasting all that time. Tomorrow why don't you check out some trails and areas to camp? I will get up early, go find the coin, and meet you up on the mountain at that Teahouse place for lunch. According to the map, it should not be too far away."

The plan was fine with Bill. Surprisingly, Bill did not seem too disappointed not to be going on the treasure hunt. Craig suspected that Bill understood his need to go alone. Though quite crazy at times, Bill did have an understanding nature about him, Craig thought to himself.

After dinner the two embarked on a half-hearted adventure to find female companionship. Quickly they discovered that girls meeting their specifications were not to be found. The only ones of appropriate age appeared to be well attached to two other guys. They finally yielded to their exhaustion and headed back to their room.

Lying in bed that night, Craig had trouble going to sleep, despite his exhausted state. He kept thinking about his father, the father he never knew. If only he had known what had happened. How could he have disappeared without a trace, without any clues, just no explanation? Craig agonized again over this just as he had so many times before.

Craig remembered the stories that his mother had told him over the years whenever he had asked about what happened to his father. When he was about ten years old, she told him all she said she knew. Sure, she had left out the coin treasure; he wondered if there were other things, she had failed to tell him. His mind wandered back to her words: "It was the end of August 1982. For several years your father and I had been making summer trips to the Canadian Rockies. He enjoyed backpacking in the mountains around Lake Louise. That year, even though I couldn't go, I encouraged him to go anyway. I was fearful about him going alone. I couldn't bring myself to leave you, Craig. I have often wondered how different things might have been had I gone, but who knows; then you might not have had either parent.

He was going to be gone nine days and was supposed to fly home from Calgary on September 2nd. I was there to meet his plane but he was not on it. A search was started. I went to Canada and joined in the search. The search involved the Park Rangers and the Mounties. Search planes were used to no avail. No trace was found of him. Finally, after two weeks, the search was called off. I didn't give up hope that someday he would be found, or come back.

Apparently, he left his cabin at Moraine Lake the morning of August 26th and he was last seen getting on the lift at Whitehorn Mountain near Lake Louise. Oddly, no one remembered seeing him get off the lift. It had been stormy that day and it was felt he might have fallen from the lift. A thorough search beneath the tram revealed nothing."

Craig really felt sorry for his mother. While he was growing up, she really had to struggle. She was determined that he was to have it all. His mother had enlisted his uncles as surrogate fathers. She had them take him camping and teach him sports, all the things she felt his real father would have done. Though that had all been great, still he would rather have had a father. Craig wondered if his hunt tomorrow would turn up any new clues. He didn't really expect any since the coin was hidden a year before his father disappeared, now seventeen years ago. Wouldn't it be something if he could find out what happened, he thought?

Sleep finally took him from these thoughts of the past, folding into dreams, the dreams ended abruptly by the 6 AM wake-up call. It jolted both Craig and Bill from their sleep. Craig pulled back the drapes and looked out at the early light glowing off the distant Victoria Glacier. Little did he know that by sunset that day his life would be forever changed.

During the past several weeks, Craig had memorized his father's map and the pictures of the rock under which he was to find the gold coin. The letter had said that the coin would be found in a film container. The coin was to be an 1870 gold eagle. Assisted by the good topographic map he had brought along, it should be an easy matter finding the spot, or so he thought.

It was one of the speediest breakfasts he had ever eaten. The waitress even commented on Craig's rapid devouring of his food. "My, son, you must have a mountain to climb today, but surely it can wait for you to eat," she commented as she handed him the bill. "No, just buried treasure to find," was Craig's honest but unbelievable reply. She laughed; obviously thinking he was joking. Little does she know, he thought.

The morning air had a frosty chill to it. The little thermometer hanging from Craig's backpack showed thirty degrees. The sun filtering through the forest foretold of a beautiful day at hand. About a mile up the trail, Craig and Bill parted company. Bill went on north toward Lake Agnes while Craig headed up the steeper trail leading west up the sparsely treed flank of Mt. St. Piran.

Craig soon learned that with the passage of seventeen years, things had changed a bit. The location of the trail to the pass had changed. He knew from his experience in Scouts that it was not uncommon to shift the location of trails every ten years or so. In heavily used areas this helped control erosion. It certainly was a stroke of good luck that he had brought along an old trail map his father had used on one of his trips. By comparing the old map with a new one, he was able to correctly locate the faint outline of the old trail's route.

Following the overgrown trail took some degree of effort, but it soon paid off, for there straight ahead were the unmistakable rocks he knew so well from the picture. The spot was just as his father had described it. The rock outcropping, he saw consisted of a number of very large boulders in the middle of an otherwise quite barren slope. Craig thought this to be a bad location to hide anything valuable, since it appeared the area was in the path of frequent avalanches. Not far below were patches of deep snow intermingled with freshly downed timber, a sign that there had been an avalanche there last winter.

It was nine that morning by the time he arrived at the rocks. Craig thought he would have plenty of time to find the coin and get back to the Teahouse by noon. He guessed the Teahouse to be some two miles by trail from his location. He and Bill would probably get a sandwich up there. They had planned to spend the afternoon hiking around Lake Agnes.

To think that seventeen years ago that same week his father was standing in this very location thinking about him and trying to find a place to hide a treasure for his little boy. Craig was gripped with emotion. His eyes watered as he thought about the father he never knew and all the years that had passed.

A gray plastic film container was sure going to be tough to find amongst all the rocks. Then a frightening thought occurred to him. What was the prospect of finding a snake under one of these rocks? With great caution, he began the search, using his eyes to explore every crack before venturing in with his hand. Luck was with him, because before long, he found the little gray object of his search. The container was in a large crack under the rust colored boulder. It was partially concealed by a smaller rock, which had been placed in the crack. Craig was amazed at how easy it had been to find. As he bent over to pull out the film container, a shiny object caught his eye. It was something buried deeper in the crack.

Anxious to open the film container, he quickly ended any further exploration. Snapping off the lid, he found a little plastic envelope containing a nearly perfect 1870 gold eagle coin. Folded neatly with the coin was a small note. It read: "*Craig, I love you, little boy. I hope you have enjoyed finding this coin as much as I have enjoyed hiding it for you. This is a favorite spot of mine. I hope you grow to love these mountains as much as I. Love, Dad.*"

Craig could no longer hold back the tears. So, his father really had loved him. Surely, he didn't run off and leave him. Oh, how he wished he were here. He reread the note, thinking about every word. Some minutes later, after regaining his composure, Craig took a drink from his water bottle and was preparing to leave. It was then that he remembered the other object he had seen in the crack. Searching the crack again, he determined that it was some kind of jar. The jar was firmly embedded in silt that had washed in under the rock. He could tell that it had been there for some time. Using a stick, he worked to unearth the jar. It finally yielded, and Craig pulled it out with his hand.

It appeared to be a rather large old fruit jar. It had a glass top to it. The top had been held on by a wire, which had rusted in two. The top, however, remained firmly attached to the jar. Apparently, it had been sealed by some sort of glue he thought. The jar was so dirty that he had difficulty telling what was inside. Shaking the jar produced the unmistakable sound of coins. Craig's heart raced with excitement. Surely this was not from his father, he thought. This looked way too old for that. What other treasure had he stumbled upon? Craig wondered.

Feverishly using his trusty Swiss Army Knife, Craig worked around the lid until, at last it came loose. Quickly he dumped out the contents. There were three coins and a rather thick folded notebook.

Though slightly disappointed at there being only three coins, his disappointment was brief. He quickly realized that two of the coins appeared to be gold, and likely very valuable. Further examination of the coins yielded another great surprise.

The first coin was gold, and similar to the one his father had left in the film container which was dated 1909. The second coin wasn't gold after all. It was an ordinary quarter dated 1977, but how was that possible; the jar looked older than that. The last coin was the oddest of all. It was rather crude, looking almost handmade. It sure looked like gold. The word Timberstone, and a date of 1982 were stamped on one side. Turning the coin over, it was stamped Lake Louise 1894.

This mystery, coupled with the excitement of more gold, was almost more than he could stand, and to think these coins might be worth a thousand dollars! He now turned his attention to the notebook. Maybe it would explain these strange coins. He casually lay down on the large flat rock and began to seriously examine the notebook.

The notebook seemed to be an assemblage of quite a few pages, held together by some sort of wire. It looked like a crude handmade book. It had been folded in half to fit it into the jar. Opening the book and flipping through the first few pages, he found the writing to be small and hand printed. The pages were yellowed and brittle. Surely this must be very old, he thought. It looked to be some sort of diary. Within the pages were several black and white photos.

A sudden chill came over him as his mind began to take in what he was reading. The words quickly put him firmly under their trance. *"Dear Craig, I hope you are the one reading this. My dear little boy; how I do miss you. There has not been a day in my life since we last parted that I have not thought of you and your mother."* So, it was from his father, Craig thought as he looked up, taking a deep breath. How truly wonderful! he thought. The chill he felt quickly returned and was stronger than ever as he read on. *"Craig, I hope you are sitting down, and I hope you have a strong heart, for your sense of reality is about to be shattered, as mine was years ago.*

"I have decided to write down some of the events in my life these past years so maybe you can understand why I never returned. God willing, I will keep this diary up for as long as I live here. I have placed this jar behind the film container in hopes of your finding it, and after reading it you will finally know me and my story.

"To begin with, I have had a very exciting, wonderful, and yet very tragic life. A life I could never have dreamed of. Let me start by telling you that I am writing this to you on the seventh day of August in the year 1896." Quickly Craig reread the date, looking for a correction, and, finding none, Craig abruptly looked

up to the heavens. His poor father had lost his mind; thinking oh, how sad. Soon though, his eyes returned to the pages, and he read with renewed concentration. Yes, it did say 1896. No way, he thought, as he became totally immersed in reading the diary.

Craig's Rock

2. Into The Forest Of Time

The morning of August 26, 1982 had an ominous look right from the start. Fog drifted slowly up from the valley, making the cool morning air seem even colder. I checked out of my cabin at Moraine Lake thinking to myself, right on schedule. Looking again at the sky in that early hour, I was hoping the weather was just bluffing, as it often did this time of the year. I knew it was quite common to have a few clouds in the morning and then clear later in the day.

My adventure on the Sawback Trail had been planned too long to let this spell of weather spoil it. The plan was to drive the rental car up to the trailhead at Dolomite, drop it there, and then hitch a ride back to my starting point at the base of Whitehorn Mountain. Generally, I would not have considered hitching a ride. In a national park, somehow it seemed alright. I had seen a lot of people doing it, though most had been younger than me.

From a previous trip, I knew that there was a gondola lift that traversed the distance from the base of Whitehorn Mountain up to a point near the intersection with the Sawback Trail.

By taking the gondola up, I would save a hard climb and more important, precious time. Time was the one thing I had too little of on this trip. I knew one of the guide books I had read professed that going to the summit in such a fashion was akin to cheating, but I didn't care.

The journey through the rugged Skoki Mountain Range on the Sawback Trail was to take three days and would include an overnight at what sounded like a most pleasant little lake called Larch Bow. I would arrive back at the trail end on Thursday and pick up my car. With a little luck I could make it back to the Chateau in time for a shower before catching Jenny Dolan's last set in the Alpine Lounge that evening. Yep, I had it all planned, I did.

The fifteen-mile drive to the drop off point went very quickly. Shouldering my pack and wincing under the weight, I thought of all the dumb things I was carrying. Did I really need that little TV? The reception was likely to be poor at best, and the camcorder, it was pretty heavy as well. What the heck, I joked to myself thinking that the extra weight on my back would take some of the weight off my belly.

No sooner had I left the shelter of my car and started walking down the road than the sky began to darken and became more threatening. A wiser man would undoubtedly have turned back, but no, not I. My gortex gear would have to keep me dry, I reasoned. And so, with reckless abandon I pressed on.

After sheepishly giving the hitchhike sign to two or three vehicles, a blue Honda slowed to a stop. I hurriedly jogged over to the car. The preppy looking young couple asked me where I was headed and on learning I was going their way, and deciding I looked harmless, they offered me a ride. Their names were Tom and Sally Key. They were both schoolteachers from Wisconsin who were out here on vacation.

They asked about the hike I had planned. I described my route along the top of the Sawback Ridge and then down to a campsite in the valley behind Mt Whitehorn. "That sounds like a great adventure. Tom, what do you think, do we have time to take that hike?" the energetic Sally piped up. For a minute I thought they might just want to join me and give me some company on my trip. After a bit more discussion, the pair determined that they didn't have the time since they were due back at their jobs in less than a week. As we neared the junction of the road to the lift terminal, the threatening clouds further dissuaded them from joining me.

They wished me well as I got out of the car. They insisted on giving me their address, requesting I send them a note about the trail so they would know it was something they should plan on their next trip. I have often wondered what became of that couple. Oh, what an adventure they missed.

I continued on the half mile to the terminal, thinking all the time about the threatening weather and that I soon might be wet and cold, despite my modern gear. It was 9:15 am as I arrived at the lift terminal. I had feared that the lift might be closed but I was pleasantly surprised to find it running.

It appeared as though I was about the only one foolish enough to go up that morning. The lift operator was grumbling that he hoped the wind would get up soon so he could close down and go home. I joked saying, "Man don't leave before you get me to the top." With those parting words, I got into a single gondola by myself. A sudden jerk and the swinging little gondola whisked me off up the mountain.

I had ridden the lift once before several years earlier. I well-remembered that it was one of the longest rides of that type that I had ever taken. As I remembered, it took about twenty minutes to get to the top of Whitehorn Mountain. I kept thinking that by riding up rather than hiking the trail which ran below the lift it would save me nearly half a day. I also felt the scenery along the mountain ridge would be more spectacular than that of the thick forest.

Almost immediately as my gondola started up the mountain, I saw a flash of lightning off to the West. The sky had now turned an eerie shade of yellow, reminding me of my one experience with a tornado years before. They didn't have tornadoes in the mountains, of that I was pretty sure. Good thing I had packed a rain-suit and pack cover. The enclosed gondola would keep me dry until I got to the top; once there I might have to hang out at the upper terminal until the storm dissipated. For some incredible reason, I did not worry about being in the gondola during a storm, why I shall never know.

1894 Gold Coin

I started thinking about you, Craig, and the gold coins I was going to hide for you to find. Taking out the film container containing the coins, I looked at them, all three. The one that seemed extra special was a twenty-dollar gold piece dated 1894. As I held it, I stared at the coin. I wondered what this grand land might have looked like before man had its way with it.

As the gondola passed tower number seven, I could see what I knew to be the road that leads to the Park Superintendent's cabin. I remember wondering what it would be like living there. As the cabin came more clearly into view, my eye caught an odd sight. There in a clearing appeared to be a large array of communication towers and satellite dishes. I wondered if the tram might interfere with reception. Surely this obtrusive piece of modern technology seemed very out of place. At least they could have attempted to screen it a bit better, I thought. That was the last thought I remember before a brilliant flash.

As I opened my eyes, there was a blur above me. Everything seemed a mass of mingled colors, blue, green, and white. Those first few moments were cloaked in a foggy mist. I remember my head throbbing. I seemed to be drifting with the clouds in and out of a dreamlike state. Gradually I realized that the motion I felt was not that of the tram. No, I seemed to be lying on the ground.

The ringing in my ears was gradually replaced by the gentle whining of the wind through the tall pines that surrounded me. The pleasant fragrance of fresh cut balsam filled the air. There was blue sky above. The storm had passed. How long had I been unconscious, I wondered?

I looked around at the forest floor where I lay. Apparently, I had been knocked out of the tram by the wind or a bolt of lightning, I thought. How could I have survived that? I soon began to realize the shocking absence of any sign of the tram or the car in which I had been riding. The wind must have blown me some distance and the lift must be close by, I reasoned. If I had fallen such a great distance, I must be severely injured.

I lay there another minute or so, pondering what had happened. With some effort I managed to get to my feet. Still being quite dizzy, I leaned against a tree for support. It appeared as though I had suffered no broken bones. Another good sign, I spotted my pack lying nearby and it also appeared to be intact. I thought how amazing to have survived such a fall. My legs were trembling just thinking about it. But with each passing minute I had a greater concern, quickly turning to panic and setting my stomach to churning…where was the tramline?

As I searched about, again to my surprise I found the film container of coins that I had been holding. Opening it I discovered two of the coins were safe. It was good luck not to have lost those, but then I realized the 1894 one was missing. Realizing I was thirsty, I searched out my water bottle, which was still securely stored in my pack. After drinking, I splashed some water on my face in hopes it would cause me to think clearer.

I kept telling myself; don't panic; there is a logical explanation for this. I then proceeded to start searching for the tram in earnest. The forest was very dense. In a systematic attempt to find clues to the mystery, I tried to walk in a circle of about fifty yards. There simply was no sign of the tram or the trail beneath it.

Again, trying to deal with the situation rationally, I dug into my pack and pulled out the topo map of the area and my compass. The map clearly showed the tramline and the service trail that accompanied it. Since I knew about where I was along the line when the storm hit, it should be simple to locate it, or so I thought. I checked my bearings with the compass.

I thought it also should be simple to find the road to the superintendent's cabin. After walking about a hundred yards in what I perceived to be the right direction I found no sign of it. I remembered a small stream I had seen from the gondola. I reasoned that if I could locate this stream then I could follow it back down the mountain and it was bound to cross the tram line, or if not that then the road leading to the station.

I followed what my compass showed to be a westerly direction for about ten minutes and then stopped to listen. Sure enough, above the sound of an annoyed jay, in the distance I could hear the sound of running water. In a couple of minutes, I was standing beside a very pleasant little stream. Finally, I had something to follow.

Consulting the map again I found that the stream should cross the tram line road about a half mile from where I thought I must be. The map also showed the stream continuing on down toward the valley, eventually emptying into the Pipestone River at what looked on the map to be another mile from the tram line road crossing.

With renewed eagerness I set out to follow the stream down to either the tramline or the road. The going was rough with heavy underbrush near the stream. Fearing that I might become more lost, I stuck by the stream and fought my way through the brush. I checked my pedometer as I started down the mountain so that I would know when the half-mile had passed.

After three fourths of a mile, I begin to realize that maybe this was a different stream. Since it flowed down the mountain it seemed logical that sooner or later it was bound to lead to the Pipestone, the Bow River, or the Trans Canadian Highway with the railroad beside it. These landmarks would be impossible to miss. With this logic I continued downward through a dense forest.

Soon, as the map had foretold, I came to a more or less level valley floor and with it a much larger stream. This must be the Pipestone River I reasoned. According to the map the highway to Jasper should be on this side of the river and I should hit it within the next mile downstream. The map also showed that the Pipestone River took a bend near where I thought I must be and the railroad should follow the river along the far side of the valley.

By the rumbling in my stomach, I knew it must be past my lunchtime. Since my watch appeared damaged by the fall (having stopped at 10:14) I could only guess at the time, but the sun foretold that it was mid-day. Stopping for lunch might calm me down I reasoned. The sandwich I had packed early that morning sure tasted mighty good.

After about a thirty-minute lunch break, I felt refreshed. I headed off with renewed vigor, fully expecting to hit the road within the next half hour. The going was again quite rough. The valley floor was engulfed in muskeg as well as larches.

Near the spot where I was expecting to find the road, I came out in a clearing.

I was quite shocked to gaze across a wide stretch of land that appeared to have been recently cleared of nearly every tree. Shock quickly turned to relief, for there some one hundred yards across the stream lay railroad tracks. At last, civilization I thought, letting out a sigh of relief.

Eagerly I searched for the road and bridge over the river. I was carefully comparing the topographic features with those on the map. An astonishing fact began to surface. All the natural features were where they showed on the map, the stream, the railroad, and the ridges tailing off into the valley. Everything seemed to be there except for the road and bridge. As odd as this was, I still had not comprehended my predicament.

In desperation I decided to try and find a shallow place in the river and wade across to the railroad tracks, the tracks being apparently my only tangible link to civilization. From the map I determined that the river would likely be the shallowest where it was the widest. Quickly I located just such a spot.

Before venturing into the water, I carefully stowed items in plastic bags to prevent water damage if I were to become swamped. I rolled up my pants legs, took off my boots and socks, and threw them over my shoulder. Ever so carefully I embarked on the crossing. As expected, the water was incredibly cold. Apparently though, I had chosen well as the river was only about two feet deep at the spot. The current, while strong, proved not a problem. After avoiding a slip near the opposite bank, I proudly waded out with a dry pack.

Quickly I tried to dry my shivering feet, re-booted, and scrambled up a small slope. At last I was standing on the tracks.

I felt like kneeling and kissing those iron ribbons which would lead back to reality. The panic of being hopelessly lost had now somewhat subsided. My eyes began to take in many oddities. The telephone poles had the old fashion glass insulators that I vaguely remembered seeing as a kid. It seemed as though the trees along the tracks had recently been cleared; another odd situation I thought, considering that logging was prohibited in the park.

According to the map, the Lake Louise Railroad Station should be one and one-half miles to the South. Hoping to find the station and resolve these mysteries, I headed south along the rails, stopping ever so often putting my ear to the rails to listen for a train just as I remember seeing in an old western movie. The walking was easier and I made good time. I guessed that it was about two thirty in the afternoon when I got my first sight of a little building off to the right side of the tracks some two hundred yards away. Even from a distance I was able to see the sign on the end of the station. It didn't say Lake Louise; no, it read "Siding #49—Laggan".

Drawing yet closer, the scene became more bizarre. There were no cars, or for that matter a paved road; instead there were several horses. The horses were tied to a rail fenced area next to what appeared to be a stable, set off some distance from the station.

As I approached, I noticed two men beside the platform on the side of the station. They were loading a horse drawn wagon. The dress of these men was different. Apparently, they had the same thoughts about my dress. "Hey mister where did you get those duds?" one of the men asked. Before I could answer the other man asked me, "Where you in from?"

Laggan Station

I was immediately irritated at their mocking comments and at the same time petrified with fear. Something was terribly wrong. Certainly, this must all be a dream and one whose end I now eagerly welcomed. I reasoned that it was a dream about another time and place.

My response to the men's questions was, "I came from the southern USA and this is how people there dress." I went on to ask these two where the road to Lake Louise was. "Why it's right over there, starts the other side of the bridge, up the ridge about two miles," the more vocal of the two responded as he pointed to a small bridge I had failed to notice, it having been hidden previously by the horse stable.

Having become extremely uncomfortable talking to these men I said "thanks" and quickly walked around to the front of the station toward the bridge. A number of signs quickly captured my attention. One read, "Carriage to Lake Louise .20." Certainly, twenty dollars was a bit steep for a nostalgic carriage ride I thought. I mean it had to be twenty dollars since twenty cents was ridiculous.

Curiosity got the better of me and I entered the tiny waiting room of the station. It was sparsely furnished with four benches and a half dozen straight chairs. The antiques such as the coal oil lanterns and the brass spittoon added a nice charm, I thought. My eyes quickly left the furnishings and became glued to the object hanging on the wall next to the station master's window. It was but a simple piece of paper with numbers. It was a simple piece of paper that soon would have an everlasting meaning. I thought to myself what a wonderful re-creation the park service had done. The station was perfect, even to the old calendar page for August 1894. And then I thought that those strange looking guys outside were a part of this reenactment for the tourists.

Eager to get to Lake Louise and back to a place I knew so well, I focused on the crude bridge over the river. As I crossed the bridge, I looked back in wonder at the little station, thinking what a nice museum, one I must come back and photograph later. I now realized that the two men I had spoken to had come around to the front of the station and they were staring at me. I became very uneasy again.

On the other side of the river I found a recently cut trail. Well, at least it was a trail, even though those men had called it a road. They were obviously kidding me since this path was only about eight feet wide. It was just dirt, no gravel or pavement. The trail wound around the slope to the West of the stream. The wagon wheel ruts and numerous horse droppings made it clear that the trail had been used recently by horse drawn wagons.

The trail meandered up and around the ridge. Finally, the mysterious station was out of sight. As I hiked along this trail, I wondered why the Park Service had not paved the trail or at least graveled it. The trail was in such a poor state that I was determined to complain to the park rangers about it. Certainly, they should have had a separate trail for hikers from the horse trail. It just wasn't right to have to hike amidst all those horse droppings.

Some distance up the slope, probably a mile or so, the trail met up with a stream cascading down the valley. The trail ran beside the stream through what was now again a heavily wooded mountainside. Squirrels startled by my presence offered their annoyed barking. These sounds were so natural as to be comforting. The stream might be the outfall from Lake Louise, I reasoned. However, that seemed unlikely since I knew that a paved road ran alongside that stream.

The trail took a sharp bend to the right and as I made my way around the bend, suddenly I could see a cleared area up ahead. Another hundred yards and I was standing on the edge of the clearing. That scene…that moment…became forever etched in my mind. Each tree, each rock, the sky and yes, the lake at that moment would be with me forever. There before me lay what could be none other than my beautiful Lake Louise. The afternoon sun glowed brightly over Victoria Glacier at the west end of the lake.

Although the lake and glacier seemed right, the general surroundings did not. A quick glance off to my right confirmed my worst fears. There was no Chateau. Instead in its place and slightly to the west stood what appeared to be a large wooden house. Scanning this building from a distance I could see what appeared to be a sign in front of the building. I could not quite make out what it said from that distance so I approached a few more steps. I then read, "The Chalet".

I closed my eyes, I slapped my face in hopes of ending what was becoming a nightmare, a nightmare I had grown quite tired of. Alas, the scene remained unchanged. If this was not a dream then…somehow, I must be in an earlier time. By this time there was no escaping, no rationalizing all the strange events of the day.

In the distance around the building I could see people. Suddenly I again felt terribly afraid. I felt as though I was soon to be attacked by human birds of prey, picking at my brightly colored attire. There was a dense grove of fir trees up-slope from my position; it was there that I sought refuge. I was breathing hard; my heart was pounding, and I felt quite faint. Finding a large rock, I took off my pack and collapsed behind the rock fortress.

The afternoon sun was now low in the sky. Slowly I was able to regain my composure. Realizing that the night would soon be upon me, I knew I had plans to make. It appeared I had little choice than to make contact with the people at the house with that sign The Chalet. Surely, I felt it not wise to reveal my story to them, at least not yet. I realized immediately that my colored attire seemed very out of place.

What date was it? Was it 1894 as that calendar had shown? I wondered if that could be possible. Did my coin foretell of this? I stowed my bright blue parka and my pack in two large plastic trash bags that I happened to have in my pack. I thought how fortunate it was that the weather was rather mild.

Leaving my parka behind left me sparely clad in a plaid shirt and a pair of blue jeans. My shirt seemed bright in comparison to the attire I had seen. Blue jeans apparently were not fashionable either. My dark green nylon and leather boots were a problem without a solution. Obviously, I couldn't go barefoot. I covered them with dust to make them more subdued.

After adjusting my attire, I summoned all of my courage and ventured off toward the Chalet. I knew that somehow; I must find out as much as I could and reveal as little as possible about myself. I needed to know simple things like the date. How could I ask that? Well I must think of a way. The stress had unraveled me totally and suddenly I found myself laughing. I was laughing at what my overloaded mind had dredged up. It was that profound movie line, "Toto, I have a feeling we're not in Kansas anymore."

The Chalet

3. Those First Days, "1894"

"Mister, do you know if there is a room available?" I nervously asked. "Why no I don't, sir, but you can speak to Mr. Ashley. He is the manager and I am sure he can tell you," the strange looking gentleman answered. "Where might Mr. Ashley be?" I inquired. "Why, in the parlor, I would imagine, there, the door to the left," he responded as he motioned toward the door.

Slowly I climbed the freshly painted wooden steps to the porch and made my way to the door that the gentleman had motioned to. As I approached the screen door, I could hear the sound of conversation. More inviting than the voices was the aroma of cooking that drifted from the little building. I then realized that I was hungry.

I stepped into what appeared to be a Victorian Parlor. The dark stained wood, the gas light, the hardwood floor. It all seemed quite natural, as did the wicker furniture and the elegant loveseats. The problem was that it was all from a different era than mine.

My perusal of the surroundings was quickly interrupted by the eyes of those in the room. Instantly I recognized those same stares that had so unnerved me at the train station. "May I help you, sir?" a stocky middle-aged gentleman asked.

"Are you, Mr. Ashley?" I inquired.

"I am indeed," he said as he flicked his long mustache.

"I am interested in taking a room for the night," I said, hoping he would not ask many tough questions.

"You are indeed a lucky man," Mr. Ashley said, "you see we have not had a room free for nearly two weeks until this morning when Mr. Jessup departed for the East. I must say we don't get many gentlemen arriving here without a reservation."

I nervously muttered, "Yes, I guess not."

"Sir, did you arrive on the 1:30 train today?" he inquired.

Without time to think of what to say I responded, "Yes." This seemed to satisfy his questions for the moment.

"I will have the chamber-maid prepare the room and have it ready shortly. The room and board will be four dollars a night. How long will you be staying? Sir, I apologize, I don't believe I got your name?" he asked in a curious tone.

I responded, "My name is Logan Bristol. I am not sure about my stay yet; may I let you know tomorrow?"

"Certainly, my good man. By the way, where do you hail from?" he asked. His words sure seemed strange, along with his thick English accent. Odder yet was his formal dress, bow tie, suspenders and all.

I responded to his question with, "The southern part of the United States…Georgia."

"Well, that explains your accent. You have come a long way. And pardon my saying so but they do dress rather differently there," he added.

I muttered, "Yes, I guess so," as I nervously tried to conceal my boots upon which he had fixed his stare. In an attempt to divert his mind to something other than my attire and the bundle of a few items of clothing I had for luggage, I asked how long he had been the manager at the Chalet.

He responded, "Sir, I have been here since The Chalet opened two years ago."

"Mr. Bristol, if you would like to sit here and have a spot of tea. I will see to your room," he said, as he quickly departed through the rear door. After he left, I poured myself a cup of tea from a steaming pot on the large table in the center of the room. Grasping the cup with two shaky hands, I made my way over to a small table with two chairs by the front window.

As I sat down by myself at the table, I looked around the room cautiously. I felt about six pairs of eyes piercing me. There were four gentlemen in the corner next to the large fireplace. Seated closer to me at another table by the window were two ladies. None of the inhabitants seemed overly friendly, which was both a relief as well as a source of discomfort.

I was seated in a large and surprisingly comfortable wicker chair. I sat there staring out onto that strangely familiar lake that I so loved. How had this happened? How was I ever going to be able to get back? Would I have to survive in these strange times? Could I survive? These thoughts consumed me, far exceeding the capacity of my meager mind. Surely this dream would end soon, I prayed.

In about ten minutes Mr. Ashley returned. It was right at six o'clock according to the wall clock which noisily chimed away on the back wall. Clouds had drifted over Victoria

Glacier, obscuring the rapidly setting sun. The room suddenly seemed even darker. Recognizing this, Mr. Ashley, proceeded to light a gas chandelier in the center of the room. Wow, I thought, no electricity. This was just all too strange.

Once he had completed the lamp lighting, he came over to my table. "Mr. Bristol, do you need assistance with your truck," he asked politely. I was speechless for an uncomfortable few seconds then I figured out by "truck" he was probably referring to my luggage. Finally, I was able to respond that I had but a few items. I then went on to lie, saying that my trunk was down at the station. He bade me to follow him to my room. I quickly obliged him as I was again becoming quite uneasy in the company of those strangers.

We proceeded up the stairs which were situated in a hall behind the main parlor. As we reached the door to my room, he again addressed me "Mr. Bristol there is just time for you to freshen up before dinner. Dinner will be served in the dining parlor at seven o'clock." This having been said, he left me alone in my room. Safely concealed behind the room's door, I became more relaxed.

The room was rather tiny, but nice. I surveyed it with great interest. The single window looked out at the mountains opposite the lake. The view closer at hand consisted of a small barn about fifty yards away and a corral with a half dozen horses. I gazed at the room's furnishings. They included a bright green metal bed, a large wicker chair, a small writing desk, and a washstand with a heavy china bowl and pitcher.

A narrow wardrobe cabinet stood next to the washstand. In one corner was a tiny coal stove with a stove pipe going into a small chimney. The rustic wood flooring was partially covered by a pretty red and blue woven rug. How very different this room seemed from the rooms of the Chateau that I remembered so well, and yet it was quite charming.

The stark absence of a bathroom in the room was a great cause for concern. Surely, they had indoor plumbing I thought as I again opened the door to my room and peered out. Sure enough, at the end of the hall I noticed the letters W.C. on a door. This discovery was quite timely as my nerves had created a severe need for such a facility.

The W.C. was indeed a real eye opener. The long narrow room contained a shiny enameled claw footed tub at one end, a large old-fashioned pedestal lavatory, and a water closet with one of those tanks high above operated by a pull chain. Making this whole setting even more eerie was the flickering of the two single gas lights that illuminated the room. I quickly availed myself of the facilities and made my way back to my room.

I was almost shaking with fear as I took a seat at the large communal dinner table that night. Sitting there with strangers from another era was going to be tough. My heart was pounding and I was sweating like a pig. "You must be the gent who arrived this afternoon?" Quickly I looked at the older man to my right who had just spoken to me. He was obviously of British descent, judging from his heavy accent.

Before I could answer his first question, he continued, "Fine weather we are having, don't you agree?"

"Yes sir, I did just arrive this afternoon, and most assuredly this is fine weather now," I added in a flawed attempt to imitate the language of the era. I wondered if my acting skills were up to playing this part. At least he hadn't asked about my past yet I thought in a sigh of relief. My relief was short lived.

"Sir, that is quite an accent you have. You must be from the South," he added.

"Yes, Georgia," I responded.

"Oh my, that far, what brings you up here?" the same gentleman asked.

"Oh, just looking for a little adventure," I answered, all the time thinking what a ridiculous understatement that was.

"Well, this is a great country for adventure," he added. 'Damn straight', I thought to myself as I bit my tongue.

By then my funny accent had piqued the curiosity of most of the guests. They would take turns speaking to me. The group that introduced themselves included a Mr. and Mrs. Green from Philadelphia; Colonel Thomas Darden from Montreal; Samuel Aaron and Grant Cord, college students from New York; and Miss Dawson and Miss Brown, two spinster ladies in their forties from Boston. The last two a Miss Dawson and Miss Brown were becoming uncomfortably friendly toward me. They were the two who had been at the other window table in the parlor when I arrived.

Dinner was quite good. My appetite, surprisingly, seemed unaffected by the traumatic events of the day. I had roast beef, mashed potatoes, creamed corn, and especially good lemon snow pudding for dessert. For just a moment my mind drifted to the freeze-dried food that I had planned for that evening's meal.

Apparently, it was the custom to take tea or coffee in the day parlor after dinner. Brandy, cigars, or pipes were the men's fare. I felt I could use a little shot of brandy but politely passed on the tobacco. It seemed the brandy was a favorite of Mr. Ashley. He soon became somewhat inebriated. Sitting there in all that smoke was rough. I amused myself thinking how these folks would react to the surgeon general's report on the perils of smoking. I wanted to broach the subject of the ills of smoking but, while tempting, I just didn't think the time was quite right for that.

The stress of the day, the brandy, and the caution with which I had to consider every word I spoke, quickly exhausted me. As the clock chimed nine o'clock, I bade the others good night and headed off to my room. I pondered what I had learned that evening as I climbed the stairs and readied myself for bed. What a pain it was, having to go down the hall to the toilet. I reasoned it could have been worse; they could have had an outhouse. The thought of giving up modern things boggled my mind.

Though I felt very out of place, I somehow seemed to blend in surprisingly well with these people. All in all, I was quite pleased with my evening's performance. The Chalet apparently attracted a wide variety of people, all somewhat odd. Well, maybe that's why I fit in so well, I thought.

Colonel Darden saw the area as one big gold mine and seemed eager to have the area commercialized. The spinster ladies…well they seemed to be looking for Indians, or more likely a handsome cowboy. The Greens were newlyweds seeking adventure in this romantic setting. Oh, to be young and in love in this time and place, how grand. They reminded me of the young couple, the Keys, who I had ridden with hours before. Last we had the two students. They were the hardest to relate to. They seemed to be spoiled snobs, acting so sophisticated, but they did seem to have a curious appreciation for these mountains. Time will tell about them.

Before I could make an attempt at sleeping, I had to formulate a plan for the next day. Maybe I would awaken from this dream and not need a plan, that was my first thought. That is what I prayed. I must concentrate my efforts on finding a way back. As the reality of all this was still sinking in, I kept telling myself, don't panic, just take things one little step at a time. Despite my anguish, I must confess my sense of curiosity was running rampant and I was eager to learn more of these strange times.

I had to face the prospect of adapting at least briefly to this lifestyle. Tomorrow I must do a better job of hiding my belongings, at least those that I could not explain in this era. As I thought about my clothes, another ominous thought came to me, I had no money. I didn't think my Amex gold card would buy much here. I might need to find a job to have the money for the necessities of life here. Then again, I probably wouldn't be here that long. I did need clothes that would let me fit in. That would be one of my first necessities. Mercifully those bothersome thoughts were finally given up to delightful sleep. My dreams were of a lifetime away.

The unmistakable sound of dishes being stacked was the first thing that I heard that next morning. Quickly the grogginess of sleep turned to panic as I began to look around the room and remember the previous day, realizing it had not been just a dream. The sun was barely peeking through the window. A slight breeze ruffled the curtains at my open window. I looked out to see the pink tint of a beautiful sunrise. There was the smell of wood smoke and coal oil in the air. A most pleasant awakening it would surely have been, were it not for the past I remembered and so missed.

Upon arising from bed, my body wasted little time telling me how stiff and sore I was. Maybe I was aging more rapidly. A quick glance at the mirror failed to reveal any change. Not being able to deal with rapid aging right then I rationalized that my aches and pains were from the fall from the gondola or sleeping on a bed (a feather bed, I think) much softer than those I was used to.

I had packed a few toilet items and some of the blandest looking clothing I owned in an olive colored canvas bag that usually contained my sleeping bag. I rummaged through this bag and produced my toothbrush and a change of clothing. I opened my door and was relieved to find the W.C. appearing to be vacant. I quickly left my room and made my way there. While freshening up I debated about using my electric razor. Surely, I would not be able to recharge it here and the noise it would make was also a concern. In the end I attempted to use a straight razor someone had left on the lavatory and soap for shaving cream. This was not a very pleasant shave, leaving me with several nicks and a very red neck.

As it turned out, I was the first one down to breakfast. The door to the kitchen was open so I cautiously peeked in. "Why sir, you are up early indeed, have a big adventure planned for the day?" The person speaking to me was apparently the cook. She introduced herself to me and me to her. It seemed her name was Maggie, though she said everyone called her "Cookie". She was a matronly type who, from her significant proportions, appeared to enjoy her own cooking. As I continued my conversation with her, I realized that she was extremely friendly and that she could be helpful to me in trying to sort out my predicament.

"You know, Cookie, I just love it out here and I may not be able to bring myself to leave," I said. "Where do you think I might find a job?" I inquired.

She laughed, "Why, Sir, we don't get many Southerners who can stand the harsh winters here."

I joked, saying, "Oh, you mean it really gets cold here in winter." She again laughed at my flippant comment.

"Sir, that lake out there freezes so solid it takes till June for it to thaw. You better really like the cold and snow if you choose to winter here. As for a job, Mr. Bristol, certainly you must know that just about everybody in these parts works for the good old C.P.R. (Canadian Pacific Railroad, I correctly surmised). They own The Chalet of course, and just about everything else," she added. The importance of the C.P.R. was rapidly becoming apparent. The dinner conversation of the past evening had largely centered on the good and bad of the rail service to the area. The consensus being that the trains never ran on time. They had a saying, "instead of Mountain Standard Time it should be CPR Time."

"What type of work do you do, Mr. Bristol?" she asked.

"Oh, please call me Logan," I responded and then answered by saying I built things. I had already given some thought as to how to answer that question without drawing suspicion. Realizing that I needed to expand on my response I went on to say, "I have built buildings and houses. I am sure I could build trails, lodges, or do surveying or mapping."

"Well Logan, there is most likely a job awaiting you here. There are few trails, not enough lodgings, and not many maps either, I'd venture to say. I think you will do well," she added.

When I asked who she thought I might talk to about a job, her response was to start with Mr. Ashley. Her suggestion seemed quite logical. She did however; recommend waiting till later in the morning to discuss this with him. I concluded that was to give him time to recover from his inebriated state of last evening. And so, I planned to meet with Mr. Ashley later that morning.

"Sounds like you are a man of many talents," Mr. Ashley said. "You probably should go to Banff and talk to Mack Palmer at the C.P.R. Office. He could maybe put you on helping with the construction of one of the new buildings they seem to always be putting up. By grabs, every time I go down there some confounded new building is going up. If you want to stay here at Lake Louise, I would be willing to let you have a go at building the new trail that the C.P.R. wants built up to the Saddleback," Mr. Ashley offered.

"Those impatient bureaucrats want the trail done before the start of the next tourist season. You know that only gives me two months before the snow will stop work, maybe less. It will be a tough bit o' work. I already told them I didn't have anyone to put on it this year. It would be a feather in my hat though if I could get it done this year. Do you think you might be up to it?" Mr. Ashley asked.

Having no other immediate source of income to pay for my lodging and tantalized with the excitement of blazing a new trail, I decided to accept the challenge.

With that agreement began the start of my work for the C.P.R. The job would pay thirty dollars a week, with food and lodging being provided. Lodging was to be in one of the employee tent-cabins behind the Chalet. "Craig, thirty dollars a week didn't seem like much but considering I had only the face value of your gold coins to spend, it seemed a blessing."

"Can you start tomorrow, Logan?" Mr. Ashley asked. "On second thought, let's wait till Monday since today is Thursday, besides its bad luck to start a new project on Friday. That should give you a day or two to get settled and it will give me time to round up a couple of the stable hands to help you," Mr. Ashley added.

It all sounded pretty good to me. That schedule would also give me time to go back and search for the tram line. I was still fairly confident I could find it and a way back. I thought that probably I wouldn't be around long enough to start a job anyway. At worst case I could go to Banff and get some clothes before Monday. It seemed as though I had a plan and that perked me up considerably.

After thanking Mr. Ashley, who by this time had insisted I call him "Roy", I walked down to the lake. Near the shore I found a large stump to sit upon and contemplate all that had just transpired. My eyes riveted themselves on the mountain on my left which I knew to be Saddleback. Could I really build a trail up this wilderness of a mountainside, I wondered?

That afternoon I carefully studied my map in preparation for retracing my journey back to the tramline. Perhaps I had missed some sign of it. Perhaps if I were back there the same time tomorrow, I might be whisked back. Upon thinking that last thought, I determined to leave before daylight the next morning on what I figured should be about a six-mile hike back to the spot. Too bad I didn't have my GPS, but then I realized satellites were probably but a glimmer in a few science fiction writers' minds.

I told Cookie that I was planning to go on an early hike the next morning and she was good enough to prepare me a bag of biscuits, ham, and a small jar of jelly. With these picnic supplies, a crude rump sack, and an old pocket watch I borrowed from Mr. Ashley, I headed out by foot in the darkness at 5:30 am Friday morning. I wanted to arrive back at the spot where I fell in plenty of time. I guessed the time of the flash of lightning to be around 10:14 a.m. since that was when my watch had stopped.

I made good speed and was back at the stream crossing by 7:00 a.m., just as the sun rose over the mountains. Using my compass, I set my course up the mountain. Again, I safely negotiated the stream and having dried my freezing feet I put my boots back on and picked my way up the mountain, retracing my steps of two days previous. I was thankful that I had had the forethought to leave a few blazes on trees. With these crude marks to follow, it was fairly easy to retrace my steps.

So far, the only animals I had seen were an abundance of noisy jays and, of course, ground squirrels. That changed abruptly as I stepped out from a clump of large trees; there only about a hundred feet away was a rather huge black bear. We saw each other at about the same time and fortunately both acted in somewhat the same manner, that being terrified of each other. Quickly the bear turned tail and lumbered off to my right. Not wishing a repeat of this scary experience, I became even more vigilant of my surroundings.

After a bit of searching, I arrived back at what I felt was the spot where I had awakened on the ground the previous day.

The watch showed it to be 9:35. I spent the next several minutes searching the area carefully for any evidence of the tram. It also dawned on me that that 1894 gold coin which was now missing might hold some importance. I diligently searched the ground for the coin.

As 10:14 approached, I lay down where I had been when I awakened the day before. I began watching the pocket watch carefully and praying. As the ten o'clock hour came and went, the sky remained sunny overhead. I closed my eyes in prayer. No changes occurred. With the passing of minutes, so too passed my hope for any quick return to a life I now so missed.

Finally, I got up. After a couple more hours of searching the area in vain for the coin or a portal to my lost life and after wiping the tears from my cheeks, I resigned myself to head back to the Chalet. A sad trek back it was, all the way I was thinking I might never be able to return. Oh, how much I had lost, my dear little boy and his wonderful mother. . .

Somehow, I started thinking about what lay ahead. I thought it was fortunate that I had my topographic maps. I must study them well. Maybe it would be easy to just pick the route up Saddleback. The maps showed the future trail up to the pass. Maybe it would be easy to plot its location. I was soon to learn that nothing about the assignment would be easy.

Upon arriving back at Lake Louise that afternoon, I turned my attention to the painful task of sorting through my belongings to see what of the twenty first century gadgets I could use in these primitive times. Before drifting off to sleep the night before, I had worried about what would happen if my real past was discovered. In a way I felt a desperate need to tell someone. My inner voice cried out to tell my incredible tale, yet something also told me I could never do that.

In a matter of minutes, I reached the spot where I had stashed the two trash bags the evening before. I spotted a patch of green plastic through the brush cover. With a sigh of relief, I uncovered them, all safe and sound. Shouldering my pack, I headed into the forest. My plan was to circumnavigate the lake, staying out of sight of people at The Chalet. Memory told me that there were some likely hiding places on the side of Mt. St. Piran, some two miles from The Chalet. "Craig, you obviously now know of one of my hiding places."

The scenery was far from what I remembered, a major difference being the massive deforestation near the lake. My heart grew happy again when some three hundred feet above the lake I once again entered the sanctuary of a virgin forest. Even though the trails that I had previously known did not exist, there were animal paths which I used to my advantage. I relished picking my way through the natural forest as opposed to the ugly stump infested lower reaches.

The thick smell of smoke hung in the air on the mountainside. In a way it smelled good and natural, although I suspected the smoke was more from the clearing and burning rather than from heating and cooking. I soon learned that the CPR locomotives were the main fire starters. Those monsters gorged themselves on trees from the forests and gave back sparks and embers to further decimate the remaining forests.

Yet another astonishing sensation was the complete absence of the sounds of mankind. I realized that everything I heard was nature. Gone were the usual ever-present distant sounds of planes, helicopters, or cars. I panicked at the thought that I might never hear those sounds again. The sounds I used to find such a nuisance, I now longed for. Only the sounds of the gentle breeze through the tree-tops interrupted the sounds of birds, squirrels, and waterfalls. It was to be a long time before I would get used to the loss of the sounds of modern technology.

Finding the perfect hiding spot was not very difficult. There was a cave like rock outcropping just below the ridge connecting Mt. St. Piran and Goat Pass. The spot seemed ideal. The topography shielded the spot enough so that it would be safe from avalanches. It also appeared the entrance would be easy to conceal with the various sized rocks available.

The task of sorting my belongings was indeed a very sad one. I dumped out the contents of my pack onto one of the plastic trash-bags. Certainly, I would have no use for the tiny Sony 2" color TV. Likewise, my miniature Panasonic Camcorder and tapes seemed useless. I couldn't resist the temptation to play one of the tapes I had. A few minutes of this was all I could endure. Tears rolled down my cheeks as a picture of you, Craig, came on the screen. Our home, you, your mother; it was all there and so much more that I couldn't face the loss. I quickly turned off the camcorder and continued going through my treasures. Gingerly I placed the precious objects in the plastic bag.

Each previously mundane object was now like a child I had to leave behind…maybe forever. The Gaz stove, the binoculars, the pedometer, the Gortex parka all seemed luxuries without present value. Of particular regret was my parka. I feared I would be in for many a cold wet day without it; but alas the bright colored wonder fabric was just too much to explain.

There was one bright spot however among my belongings; the topographic maps. I had already thought that these could prove of great value. Obviously, I could not show them to anybody, but I was already thinking of copying them. Without the date and other suspicious information, I could pass myself off as a great surveyor and map maker. Why with these I could find routes and blaze new trails, trails that would endure through time.

Another stroke of good luck was that little film container with the two remaining gold coins in it. "Craig, as you undoubtedly know by now, I had planned the crazy habit of hiding gold coins for you every year. This year I still had the twenty-dollar gold pieces that I had not hidden yet. I thought of these coins as my immediate salvation from complete destitution. I rubbed them gingerly between my fingers. These would provide me a source of funds for two or three weeks should I need them. Certainly $40.00 in gold wouldn't last long when room and board was $4.00 per night. Oh, if only these coins were now worth the $1,000.00, I had paid for three of them."

My excitement further waned when upon closely examining one I saw that one of the two bore a date of 1905. Since it was only 1894, that presented a real problem. The obvious solution quickly came to me, that being of course to merely rub off the date. I again amused myself with the idea of handing Mr. Ashley my American Express Gold Card for payment. Oh, for that good old plastic, how was I to survive without it. Alas my gold card went into storage along with everything else.

Hiking back down toward Lake Louise, my thoughts became focused on my immediate needs for material goods such as clothes. I decided that first thing the next morning I would take the train to Banff and do a bit of shopping. I had money enough for a few of the most basic of essentials.

I found out that the Greens were also going to make a trip to Banff the next day and so I took a carriage with them back to the station at Lagan. The Greens had told me that there was a store in Banff called 'Dave White's'. It seemed that they carried a wide variety of goods that I might need. This sounded like the place I needed to visit. As I entered the station to buy my ticket, my eyes again became transfixed on that eerie calendar hanging on the wall in the station. So, it had been right all along. How incredible, I thought.

As the train whistle announced our arrival into Banff, I was anxious to see how my favorite little town looked a century earlier. Oh, how different it was. There was almost nothing that looked familiar. Even the landscape around the town was different. It too, like Lake Louise, had suffered the scourge of man's disregard for the forest. The station sat by itself some one hundred yards or so from another small group of buildings situated along the river. The station was essentially a long log cabin.

From the station I made my way down a dirt and gravel road to the little cluster of buildings that I took to be the center of town. The town consisted of only about two dozen commercial buildings, largely one- and two-story wooden structures. There were in addition to the commercial establishments, a number of quaint little log cottages set along the bank of the Bow River. These appeared to be the homes of the local inhabitants.

As I approached the river, I saw a small crude bridge with a large hotel like structure directly opposite. The building was still in the final stages of construction. I soon learned that it was Dr. Brett's Sanitarium and Hotel. Then my eyes caught a view of the predecessor of the famed Banff Springs Hotel. The top of the hotel could be seen clearly from across the river, even though it was located some distance away. I determined to go and explore this wondrous structure as soon as I completed my shopping.

I had already seen the sign on one of the larger two-story buildings identifying it as Dave White's Mercantile. I made my way to the entrance, stepping back in time into a genuine old country store. As I gazed about at the store's curious contents, the clerk at a long counter became similarly curious about me. She offered her assistance. "Sir, can I help you with some goods?" she inquired.

"Why yes, mam, I am looking for some clothes and boots," I explained.

"Certainly, sir, I am sure we will have clothes and boots to your liking."

After a bit of time I managed to find three pairs of pants, shirts, a coat, some dreadful long underwear, and even a pair of halfway fitting boots. Most of the pants were made for use with suspenders, but I finally found a couple of pair that didn't require the horrible suspenders. Apparently short sleeve shirts were also not in style. The total bill was twenty-four dollars. I was amazed at the cheap price, though having only two twenty-dollar gold pieces, I had just spent about half of my net worth on a few items of clothing. That was a bit frightening to me. The shopkeeper wrapped my purchases up in a neat bundle of brown paper tied up with sisal string. No plastic bags here I thought. She offered to hold my package so that I could pick it up on my way back to the station.

I walked about the town for a couple of hours and ate a picnic lunch down by the river at a spot I knew one day would be my favorite picnic ground. After eating, I walked across the bridge to explore the Banff Springs Hotel. Though it was quite different, it was still a grand structure. This early rendition of the famed hotel was an all wooden building that stood five stories high, contained over one hundred fifty rooms, and had grand parlors and the same marvelous view of the Bow Falls. The otherwise grand view was diminished though by all the stumps where beautiful pines and spruce had once stood.

Finally, it was time to pick up the package and hike back to the station, thinking the four o'clock train might just be on time. As I had been warned, it was late, though by only an hour. That didn't seem too bad based on the dinner table conversation of two nights earlier. Seated alone on the ride back to Laggan, I contemplated how much growing up my town of Banff had to do and wondered if I was to help it grow. I found all the thoughts to be very exhausting and I was nearly asleep as the train pulled into Laggan later that evening.

4. The First Trail

The heavy frost and the crisp morning air signaled that an early winter might be soon at hand. Other than it being a bit chilly, the weather seemed fine that Monday morning in September. Though I might not have to worry about the weather that day, I was very nervous about meeting my helpers and with the undertaking that lay ahead.

Just as promised, Mr. Ashley had rounded up a couple of guys to help with the trail work. When I first met the two guys, I was not overly impressed. My crew consisted of a seventeen-year-old stable boy named David Tipper and a derelict looking man named Bill Roand. I took Bill to be in his late-thirties. Both David and Bill seemed to be physically fit and David at least seemed quite eager.

I quickly struck up a friendship with David. He was a tremendous help by quickly educating me in the art of horsemanship. In this day and time, it seemed as though everyone was an expert with horses. Everyone, that is except me. David showed me how to pack, ride, and about feeding and care, all the while never ribbing me too much about my lack of horse knowledge.

As it turned out, David and I would develop a rather strange father/son relationship which was to last for some time.

Bill, well, he was a different story. Apparently, he had worked as a fireman stoking wood into the boilers of locomotives. He had been fired by the CPR. Mr. Ashley for some reason had felt sorry for him and had taken him on to do odd jobs around The Chalet. Though Bill may have been of sound body, I regret to say that he appeared not to be of too sound of mind. Had drugs been common in this era, I would have quickly dubbed him a 'crack head.'

Bill made me nervous. There was just something about him. I was eager to find out why he had been fired by the CPR. That was a minor detail that Mr. Ashley had overlooked telling me. I started to come right out and ask Bill about his firing but stopped short of that, sensing such a question could send him into a rage. For the time being I was determined to focus him on the work at hand and try not to worry too much about him.

As we packed the tools on the horses that first morning, I kept thinking about the time when I was in Boy Scouts and volunteered to do some trail maintenance. I thought to myself, I bet this bit of work would sure have qualified me for a merit badge. Up to this point I had never really thought much about what was involved in creating a new trail. Sure, I had hiked a lot of trails. I guess I felt creating one just involved marking a few trees with blazes and moving a few downed trees.

I decided the first step in our work would consist of establishing the best possible line for the trail and blazing trees along the selected route. I did this considering the topography and abundant natural features. I took into consideration obstacles such as large boulders and areas of dense trees. On the lower reaches, the trees were in much disarray due to indiscriminate logging and the apparent frequent forest fires. I spent the first couple of days picking the route and blazing trees along the way. While I was doing this, I set my two helpers about the task of gathering a few good logs and preparing them for a small bridge we would need to place over a stream that carried snow melt down from the north face of Mount Fairview.

With a rough trail outlined with blazes, the real work started. We cut brush and trees. We pulled the dead trees and bothersome rocks out of our path. For the first bit there weren't too many trees in the way that had to be cut so we made fairly good progress. Using the horses, we moved large rocks aside. We used the horses to pull a plow like device or drag scoop that David had brought up from the stables. With this device it helped create a more level tread-way. We would wind the trail around most of the rocks that were too large for the horses to budge. For the smaller ones, we then employed big iron bars to pry them loose. Bill kept wanting to get some black powder and just blast hell out of all the rocks, an idea I quickly nixed.

On the more level terrain, our progress was swift, covering maybe four hundred yards a day. As we hit the steeper slopes where the dense forest remained, the pace diminished. Once we broke out of the forest and onto the steep rocky slope we were slowed even further. We started using switchbacks that were needed to gain elevation in a more acceptable manner. The work was backbreaking and dirty. We were really filthy at the end of each day's work. All the dirt we stirred up caked to our sweaty bodies.

For the first several days we returned to Lake Louise every

night. This was great because even though there were no hot showers, at least one could make an attempt at getting clean in one of those horrible old cast iron tubs, usually with only a little warm water. The warm water came from a primitive version of a solar hot water system. It consisted of a metal tank on the back roof of the Chalet. It had been placed there to catch the sunshine. As you can imagine, on cloudy days we were out of luck. In addition to being able to get sort of clean at the Chalet, we had cots to sleep on rather than on the ground. Another special reward at the Chalet was Cookie's great meals.

Once the trail reached a distance of some one and a half miles, we set up a camp and returned to that camp at night. Both David and Bill allowed as how they weren't much at cooking. That job fell to me. My trail cooking up to this point had largely consisted of low impact camp cooking with a tiny gas stove and freeze-dried food. Cooking over an open fire for the crew was another learning experience for me.

After camping for three days, our supplies were running low. I decided that one of us would have to take two horses and go back to the Chalet for supplies. Reluctantly, I sent Bill on the re-supply detail. He had begged to go, which concerned me, as I fully expected him to desert us. I was surprised when Bill returned promptly. I was beginning to feel guilty about having misgivings about him.

My new found level of comfort with Bill though was short lived. That evening after dinner I realized he was nowhere to be found. It was getting dark. I became worried and enlisted David to help me search the surrounding area. It wasn't long before we found the rascal at the base of a large pine about a hundred yards from camp.

It immediately became clear that Bill's re-supply mission had included more than food. Over Bill's vigorous objections, I dashed his new found spirits against the rocks. This action involved some risk, considering that Bill was bigger than I. Certainly this man was unsettled enough without adding alcohol. Fortunately, he calmed down overnight and seemed fine, though a bit hung over, the next day.

After working our way upward for two weeks, our trail came to the talus slope about a mile from the pass. It was now a real challenge creating the best route through this talus slope of loose rocks. Once I figured the best path for the series of switchbacks, we built small rock piles called 'cairns' to act as sign posts for the trail. Building the small rock piles was something David and I sort of enjoyed. Bill made fun of us, calling it child's play.

As happens so frequently in these mountains, the beautiful weather we had been having suddenly changed. Snowflakes started to drift down upon us. The stone cairns that we had built to mark the trail across the talus were collecting snow and quickly they looked like miniature snowmen. The sight of all those snow-covered cairns led David to suggest that we name this trail the "Snowman Trail," a name that stayed with the trail for several years.

The snow storm turned out to be a brief one and by the next day the sun came out, turning the three inches of snow to mush. We continued on up the now rather steep slope trying to create a foot path. The going was rough and back breaking. The more rocks we moved, the more seemed to appear in our path. We were challenged in creating some semblance of a trail amidst the huge boulders which lay on the slope, most too large to move.

One comfort to me were the ever-present marmots. They would run about standing upon their hind legs and letting out their shriek shrills. These critters, as well as the ever-present jays, kept us amused.

Pain and fatigue increased with every foot we made toward the saddleback. Finally, on September 29th, a little over three weeks from when we started, our trail was finished. We had reached the pass between Saddle Mountain and Mount Fairview. From there we encountered a truly spectacular view. We could see for miles. Below us to the East lay the awesome Bow Valley. On the back side of the pass was a beautiful valley that I remembered was called Paradise Valley. I yearned to continue on down to that valley. That would have to wait for another time though.

We set about building the last cairn at the pass. A grand one it was indeed, standing nearly six feet in height. We each placed a note with our names on them in a tin and buried it deep within our cairn. My note described the snowstorm and how we came to name this the Snowman Trail. I gave David credit for the name, and I dedicated the trail to you, Craig. I wondered at the possibility of you finding that note someday. It was then and there that I first got the idea of writing and leaving this diary for you, Craig.

We had completed the last cairn by midafternoon. No sooner did we finish and sit down to rest than the clouds that had been building in the West began to produce snowflakes. The unsettled weather of the last few days had definitely changed for the worse. A cold North wind blasted us as we made it back to our camp. We hastened our efforts to break camp, pack our gear, and retreat from the mountainside.

The snow was falling hard as we started our journey back to the Chalet.

We were fortunate to get down through the talus slope before the trail became really treacherous. As we arrived back at the tree line, we paused just long enough to once again marvel at the strange sight of the little row of tiny snowman like figures we had created up the mountain. It was there where we rested that we had the only accident of three weeks' worth of work. Bill, for some unknown reason, decided to climb a large snow covered bolder. He slipped, landing flat on his butt or hinders, as David called his posterior. David and I laughed quite hard once we realized he was not seriously injured.

It was almost dark by the time we got back to the Chalet that night. We had made it down the mountain without further incident. Looking back on it, Bill turned out to be ok. If you could keep him sober, he was a pretty good worker. The time spent with the pair had really helped acclimate me to this place in these times. The work too had helped, at least a little bit, in freeing my mind from thoughts of back home.

That night after a wonderful hot meal, we congregated around a blazing fire in the parlor fireplace. We pretty much had the place to ourselves since most of the guests had departed. Mr. Ashley joined us. Cookie kept hot buttered rum flowing until the spirits had claimed the lot of us. Bill wasted little time in making up for his lack of consumption. With some great effort I helped him back to his tent shelter that evening.

As tough as the job had been, it had also been fun. We had really created something that others would enjoy. With mixed emotions I thought how great it might be to show off my new trail to next season's flock of tourists. I knew that the

Snowman Trail to Saddle Pass would be a hit. Mr. Ashley was already thrilled with our accomplishment. He bestowed handsome bonuses on each of us. David and Bill each got an extra twenty dollars and I got forty. Not bad for the 1890s, I thought.

"Logan, while you were away, I had the opportunity to speak to Joe Tanner, the Section Manager with the CPR. I told him about you and the good work you were doing here. Joe allowed as to how he could really use someone like you on his snow removal crew this winter up at Rogers Pass. He said the work would be tough, especially if we had a lot of snow, but the pay would be pretty good and all the food you could eat, and good lodging would be provided," Roy said.

"Well, that sounds like a fair job for one who likes snow as this southerner does," I responded, promising to go down to Banff and meet with Joe the next week. With the remainder of my salary and the forty-dollar bonus, I would have enough money to last me until my winter job with Joe started next month. I decided to hang on to my one remaining twenty-dollar gold piece for a reserve if things turned bad.

The main reason for the mid October deadline that we had for the completion of the trail was that the Chalet closed down for the season then. The little village of Laggan also pretty much was abandoned till spring. The handful of folks who remained in Laggan for the winter were there mainly to keep the railroad open. There were no winter tourists at this time. When I asked about skiing, I got a blank stare. Apparently, that was a sport whose time had yet to arrive.

In the two weeks following my return from the trail, I helped Mr. Ashley with the tasks of closing down the Chalet.

The water tank up on the hill had to be drained as well as the warm water tank up on the tin roof. In addition, all the pipes and fixtures had to be drained. Linens were packed away and the windows shuttered. The livestock was moved down to Laggan and the horses were taken to a sheltered valley some thirty miles away for winter pasture. Putting away the porch rocking chairs was one of the last tasks before heading down valley to winter.

At the station, Roy Ashley and I said our good byes. He was catching the west bound over to visit relatives in Vancouver for the winter and I, well I was off to Banff to do a bit more shopping before the winter work started. Mr. Ashley had suggested that I take up quarters in the employees building at the Banff Springs since it would be remaining open for another few weeks until the serious snows started. After that I would be off to the crew's quarters up at the pass.

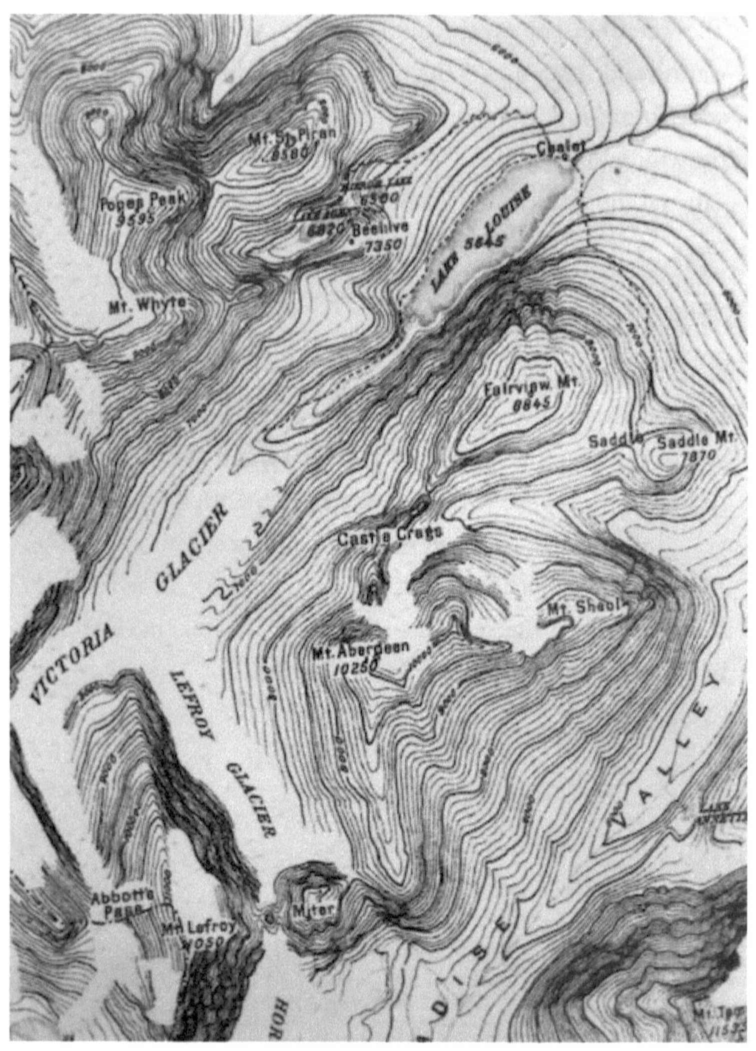

Topo Map of Lake Louise

5. A Winters Work — Snow

The original deal was bunkhouse accommodations, food, and a meager salary of sixty dollars per month (not too good compared to my trail building for Ashley). The job was to last from mid-November until about March. The salary was for standby (that meant sitting around waiting for snow and avalanches, then working like hell). On top of the salary, we were paid five dollars extra for every day we actually worked clearing snow from the tracks. Considering the very real risk that an avalanche could bury a crew at any time, it made the pay seem even less adequate.

As it turned out, my friendship with Mr. Ashley paid off quickly. I received special treatment from Joe. Instead of the bunkhouse where the rest of the crew was housed, I was given a modest cabin for lodging. Fortunately, my special treatment didn't cause too much resentment amongst the other men. I guess this was due in part because some of the crew considered me an 'odd bird.' Since most were younger than me, perhaps my age equated to seniority in their minds. In any event, I soon established a pretty good friendship with the majority of the men.

By mid-November, not much had happened. I had settled quite comfortably into my little cabin in Laggan. My main task was to make sure I had enough firewood for my little wood stove. From what Joe and some of the other guys on the crew told me, by that time most years, there was usually enough snow to keep the crew laboring long hard hours.

Not so this year. Maybe the good Lord was looking after me and this would be easy money. Perhaps I could just hang out in Laggan for the winter. A few times I would avail myself of the dog team and sled that was to be used to ferry supplies to the snow crew. By doing this I honed my skills at dog mushing.

Things changed on the day I knew as Thanksgiving Day back in the States. Snow had arrived. The first snow was what the men called "easy snow." Apparently, it was called that since most of it could be removed from the tracks be a giant rotary snow plow affair that was attached on the front of the lead locomotive. This machine worked fine in snow of up to a foot as the locomotives pushed forward at about ten miles per hour. The scene was really very spectacular to witness. The billowing clouds of smoke from the engines in the crisp air mixed with surf of white powder being thrown up by the giant plow.

If all went well, the locomotives could do all the work themselves. Unfortunately, as December advanced that became less the case. The snows increased and the avalanches began. Our crew would ride as far as the locomotives could push the plow and then twenty or so of us would attack the back-breaking task of clearing what the plow couldn't.

The equipment we had mainly consisted of an assortment of shovels and picks. Gloves were essential. If only they had waterproof boots, but alas no. It was quite a feat to find space by the potbellies for drying our gloves and boots.

The avalanches were by far the worst challenge that we had to deal with. Frequently we were up against a mangled conglomeration of trees, rock, ice, and snow that obscured any sign of the tracks. That mass might be ten feet deep and solid as concrete. Some avalanches took days to clear. In a few cases, the entire track bed had to be replaced. We had the help of black powder to blast some of the avalanche debris out of the way.

Each time we let loose a blast I thought about old Bill, too bad he had decided to go back East for the winter. Lucky bloke was probably curled up by some warm fire with a bottle. I was a bit envious. He sure had been one character.

When we went out on a clearing assignment, our work train usually consisted of two wood burning locomotives, a bunk car, a rolling kitchen car, a dining car, and a car that carried our tools. The bunkhouse car and the dining car had the potbellied stoves. These iron stoves were gathering places for the crew when not out fighting the snow. One would think that sleeping at night would be easy after a hard day's work out in the cold; however, the distant and sometimes not too distant sounds of avalanches made sleep a difficult proposition at best. The chorus of snoring in such close quarters didn't help much either.

This landscape, in deep winter, was something to behold. It was now common to see moose, elk, and wolves lumbering about in the snowy setting. Occasionally one of the men would shoot a moose or elk in order to have fresh meat.

Horse drawn sleighs or dog sleds were used to carry men and supplies where the train didn't go. Fuel and food were the key to survival in the long and hostile winter months. Survival, while always a challenge in these rugged surroundings, was even more an issue on the minds of everyone during winter.

To say the work was hard was an understatement. Had it not been for the recent conditioning from trail building and the fact it was a rather mild winter by Canadian Rockies standards, I am quite sure I would not have survived the ordeal. I am also sure that I shall never again enjoy snow quite as much.

Our crew was fortunate though, for none of us were lost to avalanches. From what I learned; this hazardous work had claimed quite a number of men over the past few years. Most were lost due to sudden avalanches. There were no avalanche preventative measures used at the time. Explosive charges were not yet used to try and dislodge unstable cornices and slopes. The railroad was just starting to build snow sheds over the most avalanche prone sections.

During the work we had a number of minor injuries, mainly from frostbite. We did lose one of our crew though. The poor old fellow was one of the older workers who had no business being on the crew. Jim Louis was his name. He caught pneumonia. It all happened so very quickly. We had noticed he had a bad cough for a few days. A couple of the guys who knew him the best tried to get him to return to Laggan for a week or so.

One day he said he felt bad enough that he thought he better stay in while the crew went out. The next afternoon it was obvious he was in a bad way and a doctor was summoned. He died that night before the doctor arrived. I had not known him very well. It was all quite sad. He had no family that anyone knew about. We made him a coffin and took him to the cemetery in Banff for burial. At his funeral I thought to myself this could soon very well be me, being laid in the ground without any family present.

The death of a co-worker didn't help my already depressed state. When the exhausting work wasn't enough to shut down my mind, I would spend the long cold winter nights lying awake trying to formulate some plan to get back home and fighting a bad case of melancholy. Surely this could not be my destiny I thought. Just as I was at my lowest, something happened to draw my attention in another direction.

I guess as is often the case in life, when all hope seems gone and the pain becomes too great, some divine spirit seems to always step in to offer up some relief. One night back in my cabin in Laggan while I laid in bed contemplating my fate, I started to think about the maps I had folded up in a newspaper in my bag. I pulled out the maps and began gazing at them.

In 1895, about the only maps that existed were those made while surveying the railroad right-of-way a decade earlier. Maps such as my 1971, Canadian Geological Survey Maps showed everything in the finest detail, far better than the crude maps of this era. I started thinking that with the influx of people venturing into the wilderness, good maps would be much in demand. I realized that I could sell hand drawn copies of my maps. I could also use them to guide tourists. This idea seemed like something I might enjoy and be good at.

It was now well into February and a lull in snow clearing work provided me with a bit of free time. After successfully rounding up a bit of paper at the train depot, I took the opportunity to begin making copies of my maps. I would work on them at night in my cabin by lantern light. A few evenings into this endeavor, February 19, 1895, to be exact, I was copying a map of the area North East of Laggan, not far from where the tramline was supposed to be.

The Pipestone River was the major feature in this quadrant. I had nearly finished the tracing when I lifted the paper to check an elevation. It was at that moment that I noticed a faint crossed picks symbol near the river about ten miles up from Laggan.

6. Prospecting For Gold

As I thought about that crossed picks symbol on the map for a moment or two it suddenly hit me what that was the symbol for. Why…that was the symbol for mining. I quickly reasoned mining was not permitted in a national park and the area was definitely within the park. But…was it in the park in 1895? I wondered. My reasoning told me that this mining must have been from an early period, like now! And mining for what? Copper, silver or better yet…gold! I wondered?

Eagerly the next morning I sought out Bill Parsons. He was one of the most widely traveled pioneers of the area and he was wintering in Laggan. I asked if anyone had ever found gold or silver hereabouts. He responded in his usual gruff fashion, "Hell man, there's gold out there, just no one's found it yet. But you just wait, I'll hit her soon. Just you wait and see." He went on to admit that nothing other than a few nuggets had ever been found in those parts.

Now silver and copper, those were different stories he said. While on the train to Banff, I had already seen the signs of a little silver mining near Castle Mountain. Bill confirmed that there was a lot of interest in silver near there and said he had heard of some luck with copper in the nearby mountains. He allowed as how these weren't worth his time. He was all about finding gold. I thought to myself, he sure is a single-minded old guy. I thanked Bill and told him I might want him to show me a thing or two about gold prospecting sometime. He said he would be glad to.

I was suddenly consumed with gold fever. There was no way of knowing if that particular crossed picks symbol meant gold, but that didn't matter, I just had a feeling about it. There wasn't much I could do to confirm my suspicions at the time since the valley was still engulfed in its beautiful winter wonderland coat. Snow would keep the Pipestone Valley inaccessible until early April.

Joe had wanted me to remain on the snow crew until the end of April, just in case of a late season snow, but I could wait no longer to start my adventure. Panning for gold was something I knew absolutely nothing about. Bill Parsons had told me about swirling the water and soil mixture around in the pan. It didn't sound too hard. I knew that if I were willing to wait a bit longer, Bill would probably take me out and show me the ropes, but I just couldn't wait. I decided that I must have the best gold pan I could find, so I set about planning a trip to Dave White's in Banff to get a pan and supplies for my adventure.

Miss Patrick, the store keeper laughed when I asked if they carried gold pans. "Sure, mister, I think there's one or two behind those kegs of nails," she said smiling. "We don't get many calls for them; sell maybe half a dozen a year. You know if I sell you one you got to bring me a coal scuttle full of gold when you strike," she added. I laughed and thought to myself that I might just surprise her with a bit of the gold. Somehow, I just knew I was going to find some.

While planning and acquiring equipment, I generally made an effort to conceal my plans for prospecting. What I told Joe and the others was that I was off to do some mapping. I thought that if I did find gold, it must be kept a secret. I was pretty sure there was never a gold rush in the area. I was also a bit embarrassed about prospecting and didn't particularly want to be called a fool prospector as I had heard Bill Parsons referred to. I had decided to devote a month to my prospecting efforts, reasoning that should be sufficient time to prove out the map's accuracy.

Joe had rewarded my winters work by putting in a good word for me with his boss. Based on Joe and Mr. Ashley's kind words, the CPR had offered me the prestigious job of guide for the upcoming season. This seemed to me like a good endeavor. I was to be stationed at the Chalet at Lake Louise and would start when the Chalet opened on May 15th.

My thinking was that, if nothing else, the prospecting adventure in to this new part of the country would help me as a guide. I had a little less than one month to find my fortune. It was April 14th, the day I started out on my hunt for gold. With great excitement I set off up the Pipestone River that brisk April morning. Crossing the bridge at Laggan, I thought back at how bewildered I had been at that same bridge only a few short months ago. Already that seemed a lifetime ago.

I struggled through the muskeg and downed trees as I made my way up the river valley. All the time I kept thinking that if precious metals existed in the area, others would have already discovered them. But what about the map, I wondered? Time would tell, I thought, as I picked up the pace.

Since no trail existed, the going was anything but easy. This particular location was far enough from the rail line so that it was still heavily timbered. The numerous patches of snow lurking beneath the trees crunched under foot, still frozen from the previous night's cold. The pair of badly worn snowshoes I had bought for a dollar from Bill Parsons came in pretty handy on the soft snow where the sun had done its work. Occasionally I would see elk and mule deer foraging for the emerging new growth.

The warm sun over my shoulder confirmed what my stomach's growls were already suggesting, lunch time had arrived. Eager to reach my destination, I made it a quick lunch of beef jerky and a biscuit. The spot I had chosen for lunch was a nice flat rock by the river. While sitting there, several good-sized trout taunted me as if begging me to catch them. On most occasions I would have welcomed the overture with a skillfully placed hook.

After my lunch break, the terrain became much more difficult. It soon became apparent that with the heavy undergrowth I would likely not reach my destination before nightfall. I was becoming a bit worried about going so far into such a remote and dangerous spot. Yet, at the same time I was thinking just maybe no other white man had ever walked this way before. Surely, I was blazing another new trail, my own private trail.

I set up my canvas tarp lean-to on a little patch of ground near the river where the trees were a bit thinner. There the sun had penetrated the vegetation and melted the lingering snow. I estimated the location was about three miles from my destination and the great adventure I just knew awaited me there. Excitement delayed my sleep that night but after the fire had died down and the night sounds became more acceptable, sleep finally claimed me. Later that night, I was abruptly awakened by a most inconsiderate owl that had taken up residence on a large tree by my tent.

Despite the owl, I woke refreshed and primed for adventure. I quickly packed up, forgoing breakfast. Another couple of miles upstream and I knew I must be approaching the spot on the map. I now started eagerly searching the shallows along the stream for any specs of yellow, or "color" as I remembered the gold seekers referring to it. By noon, after several hours of searching and swishing grit around in my pan, my hopes of quick wealth began to dim slightly. The river took a bend and there was a gravel bar jutting out from the bank opposite the bend. It was on this gravel bar that I decided to rest and consult my map again.

I seated myself on a large tree that had been uprooted and washed downstream by a stream much mightier than the placid one that now flowed at my feet. I studied the map carefully, but I was having great difficulty finding the exact spot where the mining symbol had been shown. One problem was there were few notable landmarks in the topography close to the spot where the mining symbol showed on the map. I pondered the bend in the river and tried to match it to the river on the map. As I sat there trying to decide whether to continue on northward, my eye focused on an eddy pool some twenty feet away.

The water was so clear that I could see every stone quite clearly. The water looked so refreshing that I thought it would be a good spot to fill the small canteen that I had with me. I bent down and was letting the frigid water quickly fill the canteen. After taking a big drink, I bent down again to top off the canteen. There, not three feet away, was something that glittered. Reaching down I quickly grabbed the object. Incredibly it appeared to be a pea sized gold nugget. It glittered in the sun. I let out a yell that probably sent an avalanche down Mt. Temple some twenty miles away. I was one dancing screaming fool.

The wondrous little rock appeared to be almost solid gold. Remembering something I had seen in an old movie; I gently bit the nugget to see if it were soft like I understood real gold to be. To my pleasant surprise I left a nice tooth mark. Fortunately, a tooth was not broken doing this fool test.

Holding that single nugget, my heart raced. I just knew it was the pot at the end of the rainbow. Quickly I set about a furious search of the stream bed. To my complete amazement, after about an hour's search I found another slightly smaller nugget nearby. It was laying wedged next to a large bolder. Again, I was shouting and dancing as though I had won a lottery.

It was about dusk and I was still floating on cloud nine. So far, I had found both nuggets without using my pan. Hell, I didn't hardly need a pan, I thought to myself. Anyway, I decided to give that a try in the waning light. Panning turned out to be a bit more difficult and a lot less fun than just picking up nuggets. I clumsily swirled the water out of the pan and just as I was ready to give up for the day, I was rewarded by finding a few flakes of gold at the bottom of the pan.

I set up camp only when it became too dark to see the gold. My appetite that night seemed to be only for gold. I was so caught up in the frenzy that I attempted to continue my search by candle light, soon realizing the frugality of that. Try as I might, sleep was darn near impossible. I lay awake for hours. Throughout the night I kept looking at my pocket watch in the moonlight to see how long till daylight. Finally, I slept for a few hours.

When I awoke, the sun was just beginning to light the tree tops. Normally I would have built a fire and made coffee and cooked up a bit of bacon, but no, not this morning. The excitement of gold fever was far too great to waste time on such mundane things. My search was to be hampered by a cloudy sky. The gold that had glittered so well in the sunlight the day before was now quite elusive. Even so, I could hardly complain.

During the next couple of days, I worked up and down the riverbank. It quickly became clear that the concentration of the deposit was near where I found the first nugget. I set up my base camp in a thicket of aspens about two hundred yards from the river. The site was pretty well concealed. I felt it unlikely anyone wandering up the river would venture into the woods that far. Knowing that I would be coming back to this camp, I carefully tried to plot its location on my map. I marked the location with the $ symbol.

As I searched, I wondered if the nuggets came from a vein that might lie nearby. Eager to locate a vein, I undertook some digging. For mining equipment, I had an old climber's ice ax and a small shovel. With these crude tools I set about digging into the stream bank at various locations. Each location I explored I took great care to cover up signs of my digging. Shovel by shovel I washed the dirt and rocks with water from the stream. Occasionally one of those wonderful little chips of glitter would appear.

After several days of such probing, I came upon an especially rich location. Frequently now, my pan yielded color, albeit only a few grains. My excitement was now again running rampant. It would have to wait however. I was hungry. It had now been a week since I left on my trip and my provisions were running very low. If I didn't obtain some game soon, I would have to return to Laggan. Earlier that week I had taken a rabbit while looking for a camp site. I needed a more substantial bit of game, like a deer. I figured I could bury the meat in the snow and it should last me some time.

There appeared to be an abundance of deer in the valley. I had a general reluctance to kill wild game. Another concern I had was the possibility that the carcass might attract a grizzly to my camp. The scent of the fresh kill would certainly be appealing to those great beasts. I understood grizzlies were quite abundant in the valley and by now they should be emerging from their dens and hungry after the winter. With the rifle I had borrowed from Joe, I set off into a lightly wooded area west of my camp.

Near dusk I got my chance, taking down the deer with a single shot. I decided that the site of my kill was far enough away from my camp so I butchered the deer there. I lugged the hind quarters back nearer to camp and carefully buried all but my immediate needs in a large patch of last winter's snow.

As I was digging into the snow bank to bury the meat, I realized that the fine weather I had enjoyed appeared to be changing. It was the afternoon of April 26th. Clouds were building up in the west. A cold wind was now blowing down the valley. Quickly I set about gathering extra firewood and securing my camp. Hardly had I finished my dinner of deer roast than it began to snow. Soon it was really snowing hard.

That night winter again reclaimed the valley, covering all with its frosty white beauty. My tent walls were sagging quite noticeably from the snow. Flurries lasted till noon the next day, keeping me confined to the tent most of the day. Fortunately, this early spring snow was short lived. By afternoon the following day the sun had come out and four or so inches of snow were rapidly melting.

While waiting for the storm to break, I had kept myself busy daydreaming about the gold. I tried to estimate how much the gold I had might be worth at its present market value, a value I did not know. By the end of the first week I figured my take to be about a pound. Let's see at $20.00 an ounce that would be over three hundred dollars. This sum seemed huge to me, considering that I had just recently been working for $30.00 a week. At that rate, a week of prospecting would last several months.

I focused my attention to amassing as much as possible. There was no telling when someone else might stumble upon this. As I continued over the next few days, the nuggets proved more elusive. Offsetting this, my skills at panning had increased and I turned up a fair quantity of dust. Time passed quickly now and soon I was nearly completely out of supplies.

A poor diet, a lot of work, and an abundance of excitement had led me to lose quite a bit of weight. I now had to turn my attention to getting back to Laggan. It was then May 5th, the pre-determined date I had set to head back in order to get ready to start my new job. As I set about striking camp, I considered not starting the job, what with my new found wealth and all.

I tried the best I could to hide all signs of my activities in the area. I had already dubbed the spot on my map "lucky bend." As I headed out of camp, I was already planning for my next trip to my "digs," my own little bank, a bank I could rob without penalty whenever I felt the need or urge. It was comforting to me that with all the challenges this era presented, at least now money wouldn't be one of them.

During my prospecting I had decided to sell the gold in Calgary in small amounts so as not to draw too much attention. If asked where I found it, I decided to reply simply that it came from the mountains around Canmore. Since Canmore was some fifty miles to the South, that should throw the prospectors off course should they get word of it.

On my trip back, shortly after lunch, I had my second encounter with a grizzly in the wilds. I had just stepped out of a dense patch of trees onto a more open brushy area when I spotted the large bear. Fortunately for me he had a young elk to feast upon. I gave him plenty of room for his dining and he only gave me an annoyed look. Shucks, I couldn't be bear food before I spent some of the gold burning a hole in my pocket, or so I thought.

I got back to my cabin in Laggan near dusk. After a good stove cooked meal and a hot bath, I proceeded to again measure and package the gold. I used a couple of tobacco tins I had picked up to measure and store the gold. The dust half-filled one tobacco tin while the dozen and a half nuggets pretty much filled another. It was astonishing to me to have amassed so much gold in so short a time.

I measured out a bit less than half to take to Calgary for assay and sale. Before leaving for Calgary, I had to find a secure hiding place for the rest of my newly found wealth. I decided on a spot up near Lake Louise. The spot was one still heavily wooded, approximately three hundred yards behind the Chalet, well off the road and any trail. I was careful to avoid leaving telltale footprints on my way to and from the place. By now I was quite paranoid about being found out. Under a large ledge of rock beneath a leaning aspen tree I dug a small hole sufficient to hold a large jar into which I placed the tins. Carefully I covered it with stones.

Was I ever excited, as I hopped aboard the train for Calgary the next evening. I couldn't wait to sell the gold and have real money in my pocket again. It was nine that night when the train pulled into Calgary Station. Wanting to conserve cash, I opted to stay in a hotel near the station. Better digs later, I thought.

The next morning, I found the government Assay and Mining Office, which turned out to be only a short walk. I looked rather disheveled as I imagined an old prospector might look upon venturing into the mining office. Fortunately, when I handed dust and nuggets to the crusty old man behind the counter, he didn't ask many questions. His disinterest was quite a surprise.

In a few minutes he gave me the results. "Let's see, mister, the nuggets assay out at 90%, pretty good …well let's see, the dust will fetch a hundred ninety and the nuggets another hundred fifty-eight," he said in a calm voice. I was anything but calm, exercising extreme control, I think I managed to say, "That's good."

The wheels in my head were turning as the clerk counted out my money, why at that rate the balance I had stashed might be worth nearly a thousand dollars. That should carry me for quite some time. On the trip back to Laggan, I decided to minimize my spending and go ahead with the job I had waiting. I did afford myself some luxury though by spending about fifty dollars in Calgary for more period clothes and another pair of boots. It was an odd feeling having wealth, a good feeling.

In the days that followed back in Laggan, I got the idea of minting some of my own coins from some of the gold. There was a blacksmith, or smithy as he was called, there in Laggan. I cozied up to the smithy and asked to use his forge one evening after he shut down. I had carefully made some molds from clay. I also had borrowed some small old news type from the newspaper in Banff. I used these to create my own coins. Craig, you should have found one of my coins in the jar with this diary. The name inscribed on the coins was one I chose from this wild place "Timberstone." I hope you like it.

7. Molly Arrives

Having now attained some degree of wealth from my winters work and prospecting, I thought about playing tourist for the summer. This idea was certainly a bit tempting. The more I thought about it, I realized that I had to keep busy to relieve the melancholy of my lost past. Too, I was excited about building trails and showing others the wonders of this place. These things were my reality now.

I followed through on the job that Joe and Ashley had arranged for me with the CPR. The job of guide was becoming more important and prestigious. Most of the tourists at this time relied on the services of guides or packers to lead them through the wilderness. This was something different for me and I wondered if I would be any good at it.

Perhaps I would lack the patience to deal with a bunch of stuck up greenhorns. I was also a bit concerned with how well my southern accent would be received by the Boston crowd or the English set. Concerning, too, was my lack of horsemanship. I had been working on my packing and horse skills recently however.

Upon arriving back at the Chalet, my first assignment before the tourists began arriving was helping get the Chalet ready to open. There was a lot of work to do. I helped build a new corral for the livestock and removed downed timber from the trails around the lake. I even got to test my skills as a plumber. Over the winter a tree had fallen across the wooden water pipe that carried water from the spring fed water tank down to the Chalet. It became my task to repair the waterline. Cutting and splicing a pipe made of tightly bound pieces of wood certainly was more difficult than soldering copper, but after a spell I completed a satisfactory patch job.

Ashley had told me of all the letters requesting accommodations for the year. It sounded like a busy summer. Based on some of the letters that Ashley showed me, it looked as though we would have quite a wide assortment of humanity coming to our little Chalet. The requests came from some obvious rich snobs, more college kids, and even some artists. The facilities had been put in shape and we would be ready to handle them.

Though the lodging business appeared to be good, there were, however, storm clouds on the horizon. Apparently, unbeknownst to me, the CPR home office had received a number of complaints that had come from some upper crust guests at the Chalet over the past season. I think these complaints came from guests earlier in the season, before I arrived. The complaints centered on poor service and the rough mannered workers.

Many of the early employees in the lodging establishments were ex-railroad workers, such as Bill, a rather unpolished bunch by nature. Having worked in construction, I guess I was somewhat desensitized to their ways. Unfortunately, their temperament did not mix too well with the particular demands of the society guests. The isolation of the Chalet and the rustic manner of the establishment created the perfect climate for a poorly disciplined work force. Ultimately, it was these complaints that brought Molly to Lake Louise.

From what Cookie later told me, it really hit the fan the previous June. Apparently, several of the staff, including Ashley, were holding regular drinking parties in the evenings and were frequently too intoxicated to tend to the guests. Ashley must have gotten a hint of the concern since the situation didn't seem that bad to me the end of the last season.

Back in Montreal, over the winter, the decision had been made to replace Roy Ashley. I was somewhat saddened to learn about Ashley. He had certainly been good to me and I knew I would miss him. Actually though, the old fellow took the news quite well, seeming to be almost relieved. He said he was ready for a change. I guess he must have seen it coming since he had already made plans to buy a little spot up at Lake Minnewanka (it seemed Spirit Lake was to have a new name as well). He was going to run a fish camp there. This surely was an endeavor he would be well suited for. I told him that if the CPR kept me on, I would try and steer some business his way.

Mr. Bill Wilson, the major domo of lodging, decided that a firm manager was needed for the Chalet. He also felt it highly desirable to have someone with a gentile nature that would be pleasing to the guests. Finding someone with those qualities would surely be difficult, I thought. As luck would have it, the CPR didn't have to look far to fill the bill; they already had just such a person in their employ at the Banff Springs Hotel.

Her name was Molly Kimmons. Ms. Kimmons was the head housekeeper at Banff Springs. She had been there for three years and in that brief time her friendliness and hard work had caught the attention of the CPR executives.

Assigning her command of such a remote outpost as the Chalet was quite a bold move. Old man Wilson was really ahead of the times by putting a woman in such a management position. There were plenty of skeptics to his decision. Molly was a tender twenty-three years of age. This frisky Irish lass was soon to become quite a hit at the Chalet. But, let me back up a moment and tell you of how I first met Molly that day in June.

It took a great deal of concentration for me to pilot the horse drawn carriage down the road between the ruts and stumps. Most assuredly, the road from the Chalet down to Laggan was a disgrace. Despite a little bit of patch work we did on it the month before, it was still bad. The road had never been constructed to drain properly. Recent heavy rains had carved deep ruts and left large rocks exposed. Cinders and gravel were also too sparsely used.

Roy Ashley, while carrying out the company mandate to build trails, had failed miserably in obtaining the funds for a proper all-weather road to the Chalet. There had even been an accident last August, before I arrived. A carriage had turned over, injuring two guests and severely injuring the driver. One would have thought the CPR folks would have jumped to get it properly repaired and avoid further such accidents.

As I drove down this excuse for a road, I thought about whether the new manager might have enough clout to get a real road built. I chuckled to myself; imagine sending a woman, and a very young one at that, to run a remote facility like the Chalet. When Bill Wilson sent me, a telegram requesting that I pick up Miss Kimmons at the train and escort her to the Chalet, I felt somewhat surprised and honored. I was quite amazed that someone in his position even knew who I was. I guess Ashley had done quite a job promoting me, despite his own difficulties.

The picture I had painted of her was that of an overweight matronly type who would be very domineering and demanding to work for. I expected her to be a woman whose head was almost as large as one of those hideous bonnets that women of this era wore. I sure was glad I wouldn't be a regular employee of hers. I did understand that technically my guiding duties were to be under the direction of the hotel manager. Thankfully, my trail building was to be under the direction of the CPR. So, I felt that if the new Ms. Molly and I didn't hit it off, I could still build trails for the CPR.

I couldn't decide if it was hunger or just the jarring of the road that gave my stomach that feeling. Certainly, the washboard road could upset one's insides. Assuming the 1:15 was on time, which was rare, I should beat it by a good thirty minutes, I thought. There should be plenty of time to eat those extra biscuits with ham Cookie had given me that morning. Cookie was bound and determined to fatten me up.

A full belly and the warm sun did the trick. As I lay there spread out on the carriage seat, I quickly dozed off. The horses jerking on the wagon awakened me just enough to hear the familiar wail of the train whistle from down the valley. Pulling out my newly acquired pocket watch, I found it to be 1:40. Pretty good I thought, only a half hour late. From the sound of the whistle, I estimated the train would pull into the station in about ten minutes. Better check the horses and get down to the platform, I reckoned, better check the horses and get down to the platform

I watched the various colorful human forms disembark, clueless of what was about to happen. I had turned away for just a moment to look toward where the carriage was tied. As I looked back, a beautiful young woman stepped down from the second passenger car. I was captivated by her. My eyes became fixed upon her. I became mesmerized and oblivious to my assignment.

After an impolite period of staring at her, it finally dawned on me that this angelic young lady might just be the one, the one, I was sent to pick up. "Hello…are you Miss Kimmons?" I managed to get out.

"Why yes sir, and you must be Logan," she said.

"At your service mam," I replied. I was a bit surprised at her calling me by my first name, something not as common in these times.

Craig, certainly my humble words cannot begin to describe Molly, but I must try to tell you of her enchanting beauty. Her long flowing red hair was topped by a simple hat. She had a slightly pug nose and beautiful brown eyes that could melt the coldest heart. She was I would estimate to be five foot five, quite ideal for her slender build. Beyond her outstanding beauty, her sparkling outgoing demeanor was like a delighted child. Though having just met her, I was drawn to embrace her.

"Mr. Wilson tells me you are quite a talented fellow. He

says you are a guide, accomplished trail builder, and great handy man," Molly commented.

"Certainly, ma'am, you overstate my talents. I am astonished that he even knows who I am, and I am flattered that he chose me to transport you to Lake Louise." I added all the time thinking to myself how outgoing and easy to talk to she seemed.

Molly then announced, "I am anxious to see the Chalet, I have never laid eyes upon it, or Lake Louise either for that matter. I hear it burned a couple of years ago and that it has been rebuilt in great form."

"Well, Ms. Kimmons, I certainly hope you like the Chalet and as for Lake Louise, if you have not seen it you have a real treat coming up. It offers the best of what these mountains have to offer. Miss Kimmons, I am afraid you may find the Chalet a bit rustic after the Springs. I hope you can put things in order to your liking," I said.

"Please call me Molly, Logan," she begged.

"I am very excited about this new job," Molly stated.

"Excuse me for saying so, but you aren't at all like the person I expected to be sent to manage the Chalet," I commented.

"Why is that, Logan?" she asked.

"Well it's just that, shall we say the staff has a few rough edges," I added.

"Well hopefully things there are not so bad. Anyway, I have dealt with some pretty tough cookies in Banff over the last year or so and I believe I am up to the task," she proclaimed.

"Most certainly you will be a pleasant change," I responded.

As I hoisted her trunks onto the back of the carriage, I

couldn't help but comment on their weight. "My for such a wisp of a lass, you certainly pack a mighty wardrobe," I joked.

She blushed slightly and shot back with, "Logan, my clothes are not what give the trunks their weight; you see I like to read and I have a few books."

"A few," I laughed. So, she likes to read, I thought to myself. Maybe she would like to read my diary. Who knows, maybe I would let her read it some day? I was quite impressed with Molly's confidence.

I was totally smitten by this young lady. Not knowing when I would ever get to spend time alone with this angel again, I asked all the questions I could think of. "You are Irish, aren't you?" I asked.

"Guess my voice or the red hair gave that away? Yes, I am Irish. I came to Montreal from Dublin with my parents when I was ten." After hesitating a moment, she continued. "My sister and I were orphaned shortly after we arrived. My parents died in a fire," she added.

"That's terrible," I said.

"Yes, it was a bad time, but we made it past that ok," she added.

"Logan, where are you from? That accent doesn't sound very Canadian. You seem quite different from most of the men here," she commented.

I laughed and said, "I will take that last as a complement, yes?"

With that she also laughed. Somehow, I suddenly had a warm feeling that something wonderful was happening between this young lady and me. All the time a little voice inside of me kept saying "You dirty old man, you are much too old for this sweet girl."

Eager to learn more about her and to express my interest in her, I said, "Before I tell you my unimportant life story, I must know how you ended up in the Canadian Rockies."

She said, "after my parents died, my sister and I went to live with my aunt and uncle. My uncle worked for the railroad. He had traveled here when the line was being built. He would tell stories of his trips out here, he glowed with excitement as he described the scenery and great opportunities. He said he believed the Rockies would be a tourist resort equal to the greatest in the world. He used to say these mountains were prettier than an Irish lass in the heather. When I was eighteen, my sister and I decided to come and see the mountains for ourselves," she paused.

"And…?" I asked.

"Well Logan, my uncle didn't even begin to describe the beauty of this wild wonderful country. I just loved it," she said.

Hearing her say that almost brought tears to my eyes. I had found another kindred soul who loved this land as much as I.

"Logan, the rest you probably know," she went on to say, "my sister Jean and I went to work as housekeepers for the Banff Springs Hotel. Now she is manager at Bow River Hotel in Calgary and it looks like I am to manage the Chalet."

"Enough about me now, where in the world does that accent of yours come from?" she asked, more determined now than ever for an answer.

All the time a bit of my brain had been trying to prepare a response for her questions about my background. I obviously couldn't tell her the truth, at least not right then. She would think me completely crazy. Before I could answer, she commented, "You sure don't seem like the typical mountain man."

"I am afraid my life is not all that exciting right now (this was undoubtedly the biggest lie I had ever told). Like you, I work for the one and only CPR. I build trails, draw maps, build things, and think I will be a pretty fair guide. My favorite duty by far, however, is giving pretty hotel managers carriage rides at every opportunity," I quipped.

Again, her smile grabbed my heart. "But Logan, you still haven't said where you are from and how you ended up here," she pressed.

"Persistent aren't you," I responded. "Well," I began reluctantly, "Molly, I am from the state of Georgia in the southern USA. I came out here to see this beautiful country, just like you. I arrived here last August and couldn't bring myself to leave (I was proud of how close to the truth I came with this).

"I managed to stay busy doing the variety of jobs I just mentioned. This current assignment I am finding to be by far the most fun."

She laughed her infectious laugh at my foolishness. "Logan, the way you try to flatter me makes me think you are quite a lady's man," she joked.

"Who…me?" I said joining her in laughter.

She then added a comment I shall never forget: "Logan, I think we are going to get along just fine."

"Logan, do you have any family?" she asked.

I responded in a much more serious tone, "Not any more. I lost my wife and son in a storm about a year ago."

"Oh, I am so sorry, Logan. No wonder you didn't want to talk about your past," she said in a genuine sympathetic voice.

Quickly I changed the subject. "Molly, I didn't realize that Jean was your sister. I met her this spring. I spent a couple of nights at the Bow River Hotel while in Calgary. She was very friendly and made me feel right at home. I can see a resemblance, but I must tell you I find you the prettiest," I added.

She again laughed. "Surely you are a devilish lady's man," she quipped.

Suddenly I hit a particularly rough spot in the road. This quickly drew my attention back to the problems at hand. Before I could speak, Molly commented, "Logan, this road is terrible."

"You know, Miss Kimmons, oh I mean Molly," I grinned, "I was going to talk to you about that very thing. Maybe with your clout we can convince the CPR big wigs to spring for a real road," I commented.

"Well I certainly hope so," she agreed.

As the carriage rounded the last big bend, I knew that I was running out of time with Molly and there was still one big question I was burning to ask. "Molly, how come such a beautiful young lass as you is not married?" I asked.

She laughed, "why do all men ask that same question? Logan, it's really very simple, I have never found a man who dreams the dreams I dream."

Wow! what an answer, I thought, smiling and wondering at the possibilities.

"Well there it is, Molly, your castle or Chateau as it will likely someday be called," I said while pointing to the little brown Chalet.

"I am sure it is nicer than the one that burned, but it is hardly a Chateau," she commented.

"Just you wait. This place is destined for many wonders. Some well-traveled people, myself included, think this is the most beautiful place on earth," I added as the carriage came within full view of the magnificent lake with the vast mountains and glacier reflected in its mirrored waters.

Molly gasped at the view. "Ever since arriving in Banff, I had heard of this place and how beautiful it was, but I never imagined it to be so grand," she said.

"Grand it is," I added.

PRESENT DAY

As Craig read of the growing relationship between his father and 'this woman', a girl really, who was not much older than he was, he found himself feeling jealous of this stranger he didn't even know. Could she become his stepmother in this bazaar dream? He wondered. How could his father have fallen for another woman? What about his mother, had he forgotten her so soon? Craig thought.

The emotion contained in his father's words, gradually dispelled any negative feelings he had about his father's relationship with this woman. This is time travel here, Craig kept saying to himself. His father was in another world with different people. With the flip of the page, he was back in time with Logan and Molly.

1895

That summer after Molly arrived was by far the happiest time I had spent since arriving the previous year. Even finding the gold was not as wonderful as Molly. Molly was to fill the huge gap left by losing you and your mother, Craig. For so long I had fought to find a way back, now at last I realized I would not be going back, and that a wonderful life awaited me here.

As I was soon to learn, this sweet young lady was one spunky woman. She had a head for business and wasted little time in cleaning up problems at the Chalet. Within a week of her arrival, she had dismissed all but four of the staff. I encouraged her to keep Cookie and David and even Bill. In a brilliant move, she requested that the CPR office supply her, as replacements, some of the Cantonese porters they had working on the trains. The Cantonese temperament and pleasant nature made them immediately popular with the guests. They had picked up enough English to pass muster.

I was grateful that Molly had kept Cookie. She also kept David, as I had suggested, and Tom, the wrangler. She was however afraid to gamble on Bill. I wasn't too surprised at that, especially considering he had been one of the main drinking partners of Ashley.

Molly's dismissal of the workers and her seemingly stern ways did not sit too well with some of the locals down at Laggan. Most were not accustomed to a woman with power. Others were disgruntled that their drinking buddies had been fired. Criticism proved to be short lived. It wasn't long before she had won over everyone. I really admired her "go with me or get out of my way" attitude. She quickly instilled the staff with her vision. She wanted to give every guest such a grand experience so as to guarantee their return. This was certainly a great marketing tactic in this day before mass advertising where word of mouth was the best source of business.

As far as competing with suitors for the young Molly, it quickly became apparent that even though many were captured by her charm, most were turned off by her strong-willed demeanor. Perhaps it was my awareness of male / female equality in the twentieth century that led Molly to find me different and to be attracted to me. I don't know, but I did keep thinking that I was old enough to be her father, for God's sake. I also knew only too well that May / December romances were usually doomed.

With reckless abandon and in spite of the age thing, I wasted little time in courting Molly. After she settled in, I lied and told her that June 30 was my birthday and asked if she would do me the honor of accompanying me on a picnic up to Lake Agnes? She said she would be delighted.

It was to be the first time I took her to visit what was to become our special place. The trail, I was ashamed to call it a trail, was pretty poor. I had at least cleared most of the winter's downfall off the previous month, but it still needed a lot of work before it would be a proper trail. Even so, we managed to guide the horses up the mountain pretty well.

We found a perfectly placed log on the shore of Lake Agnes, right above the falls. From there we could just make out the little Chalet below. On this spot we spread out our oil cloth. The lunch hamper was full of delights that Molly and Cookie had fixed; complete with my own little birthday cake. I opened a bottle of wine Joe had given me for my birthday. The weather was good, the food delightful, the view spectacular, and of course Molly, well…I couldn't have been happier.

It was on that picnic that beautiful cool day in June that Molly tried to pry from me some more details of my past. I came very close to telling her everything. I really wanted to so badly. Two things stopped me. First, I feared she would not believe me, rather thinking me quite insane thus ending our relationship. Of equal concern was my overpowering fear of doing something to change history, thereby creating a paradox. Craig, I feared possibly changing things such that you would never be born. That was too great a risk to take.

"You know Logan I don't even know how old you are. Cookie and I decided that you were probably older than the candles we could fit on the cake," she mused.

I laughed, "Why dear girl, how foolish, surely you two could have just made a larger cake."

"You old goat, just how old are you anyway?" she asked with a big smile on her face.

I laughed, "Well, you two were right about candles on the cake. Let's leave it at that," I added.

With great reluctance and after a bit more of her arm twisting, accompanied by some wine, I admitted to being forty-six years old. "Well let's see, that means you were born in 1852, then," she said. I avoided looking into her eyes as I gave an untruthful nod. "My you are old," she laughed, "you really are old enough to be my father."

Not to be overly insulted by her remark and being by now well within the spirits, I shot back with, "Not too old to be a damn good lover."

Fortunately, she laughed at that forward response. "Maybe we'll just have to see about that sometime now, won't we," she teased.

During that picnic, the subject of children came up. "Logan don't you want to have more children?" she asked.

I said that I was afraid of losing another child. "How about you, Molly, don't you want children?" I asked.

"Yes, I would, though I am not sure I can have children. Besides I have never met the man I wanted to wait on hand and foot the rest of my life," she said.

I was somewhat surprised by her children remark. I decided to pry further. "Do you not find children fun to be around?" I asked.

"Logan, it's not so much that I don't enjoy or want children," she said almost tearfully, "it's just one of those, you know, womanly things. A doctor a few years ago told me I probably could never have children."

"Well, Molly, children are great and fill a special place in one's life, but as for me, all I really need is the love of a special woman, and of course these wonderful mountains," I said, hoping to comfort her.

With tears in her eyes, Molly said that was very sweet. I think at that moment we both realized that we had found that special person we each had been looking for. It happened just that fast. We then embraced in an unforgettable first kiss. Suddenly this tender moment was rudely interrupted by the roar of an avalanche behind us up on Victoria Glacier.

"Boy, that was some kiss. It moved the mountains," she quipped. Her wit had both of us rolling on the ground with laughter.

Molly told me of her childhood in Ireland. I sensed she missed Ireland a little. She had lived in a modest cottage in a beautiful little village in Northern Ireland. Their cottage was on a farm and her father had been the village's apothecary. In addition to her sister, she had one older brother who had remained in Ireland when her parents had moved to Canada.

We sat there talking until the sun grew low in the sky. "What a wonderful birthday this has been, I am only sorry it has to end," I lamented to her.

"We must do this for my birthday too," she added.

"And when might that be?"

"Oh, not that far away, the 2nd of August. Yep, I will be a ripe old 24-year-old spinster," she said with a wicked smile.

"Well, my dear, I hardly see you as that. Do you see me as a lecherous old man trying to rob a cradle?" I asked, laughing.

"You bet your hinder I do, you old goat," she responded.

As we were preparing to leave and taking a final look down at Lake Louise far below, I couldn't resist toying a bit with the future. "You know, Molly, wouldn't it be grand to have a little Teahouse up here, a place where people could rest and enjoy the view while taking afternoon tea," I suggested. "What a wonderful idea, Logan, I think that would be magnificent. You must bring that idea up to Bill Wilson. Logan, I will certainly support the idea," she said.

Molly serenaded me with some of her Irish favorites as we made our way back toward the Chalet. She had the most marvelous voice. About halfway back, we encountered some of the abundant porcupines (porkpies as they were called) crossing the trail. I could only wonder if these were the ancestors of the ones, I remembered in this same spot in the 1970s.

PRESENT DAY

Craig shivered as he read the last passage. How could things have changed so little? It was as if his father was there with him right then. His mind raced beyond the porcupines as he turned the next page of the diary.

8. Life At The Chalet "1896"

The first snowflakes of the season are falling outside, as I sit here this evening writing this. I have decided to catch up on these scribbles about my adventure. Hopefully I can update this again in the future. Writing this diary for you, Craig, helps me deal with all the loneliness. It is my medicine. I am especially lonely now with Molly being away.

So much has happened since my wonderful birthday at Lake Agnes. What wondrous times I have had. At the present I am alone, wintering here in one of the employee cabins at the Banff Springs. I am to be here for the next several months helping with this winter's work on the Banff Springs Hotel.

Molly, much to my disappointment, is wintering in Calgary with her sister, Jean. Her sister is getting married next month and then going back to Ireland for several weeks on her honeymoon. Molly had volunteered to look after the Bow River Hotel while she was away. Already, I sure do miss her. I suspect I may be a regular on the Banff to Calgary train this winter.

I guess I should back up a little and tell you a bit more about this past summer at the lake. Molly hadn't hardly been on the job a week and she had put together this "wish list" of things she needed to make the Chalet better for the guests and employees. I did have a bit of input in the list. Being the wise manager, Molly realized that employee satisfaction could lead to guest satisfaction. One of the items she had at the top of her list to tackle was the desperate need for employee housing.

Our staff at the Chalet this season consisted of Cookie; David, my young trail builder helper from last season; Tom, the senior wrangler; a Cantonese housekeeper, Yen Knipp, a chambermaid, Sarah Benton; Lei Cuton, a Cantonese porter/coachman; Molly and yours truly. All in all, the staff did a pretty good job of keeping our usually full house of nineteen guests happy while expanding our little lake settlement.

Once the staff changes had been made, the next task to be undertaken by Molly, or (number one), a nickname I had taken to calling her sometimes. As manager, Molly got Mr. Ashley's cabin, one of the two small cabins that sat on the slope behind the chalet. Cookie, being that she had been there since the Chalet opened two years earlier, was given the other cabin. I had one of the rather crude tent cabins. On the rare occasion there was a vacant room in the Chalet, I would take that. Craig, I expect you had been wondering if Molly and I were shacking up, well, no…not yet, but this old dog is sure thinking that would be pretty nice.

Like me, Tom and the others were put up in tent accommodations. These were very crude shelters, similar to those I remember from scout camp, consisting of large hip roofed canvas tents erected on wooden platforms about ten feet square. The tents were meant only to be temporary shelters.

Making our housing situation even worse, the brilliant person who located these shelters must certainly have lacked a sense of smell, as they were situated only about a hundred feet from the corrals and barn. Molly enjoyed ribbing me about the situation. Every time I referred to her as "number one" she quickly reminded me that I was "number two," therefore I must live in an appropriate location to the barn. I would tell her to watch her step or else she might find a polecat in her cabin.

As I have mentioned, Molly wasted precious little time correcting anything she felt needed fixing. She and I made one hell of a "fix it up" couple. She found employee housing easy to remedy. Yep, now that she had her own personal builder under her spell and the good old CPR to bankroll her, new employee quarters were no longer a problem. And so, my first building project that I was to undertake would be to construct proper employee housing. The new cabins were to be located behind the chalet near Molly's cabin and thankfully further from the horses.

The two new cabins were to be larger than Molly's and Cookie's. Each was to have two bedrooms with twin beds and each had its own WC. Since the staff all ate at the Chalet, there were no kitchens in the cabins. I quickly drew up a list of materials and just as quickly Molly obtained them from the CPR. I was just beginning to learn that this young lady could accomplish great things. Bill Wilson must have sensed this as well.

To put the cabins up in short order, I needed some seasoned carpenters. Once again this was seemingly no problem for Molly. She reported that she had struck a deal with her old boss, Roger Cane, the manager at the Banff Springs. He would round up several of the old carpenters he knew who had worked on the building of the Banff Springs ten years earlier. I drafted David from my past seasons trail building.

As exciting as all this construction was, there was still a hotel to run and guests that were arriving that had to be attended to. Soon after Molly arrived, I had my first guiding assignment. Boy was it a dilly. A middle-aged couple from Boston had arrived. They informed Molly that they had been assured, through a friend who knew the president of the CPR, that a fine guide would be put at their disposal upon their arrival. "Logan, guess you are my fine guide," was Molly's comment as she told me of the assignment.

"Fine guide I may be my dear, but if this pair is half as bad as you make them out to be it will take more than money from you to square with me," I teased her.

"Ha, if they are that troublesome, you won't have the energy anyway, old man," was her smug reply. Well, nothing like a challenge I thought.

Their names were Roger and Catherine Barge. They were true Boston aristocrats. As incredible as it seemed to me, neither had ever ridden a horse before. The first order of business therefore was to give them some instruction in riding. I looked to Tom for help with this, considering he and David had done so well with me the year before.

I certainly was not looking forward to having to put up with their high and mighty airs for two weeks. Molly took great pleasure in teasing me saying, "Be sure to tip your hat to them." I told her that she would be lucky I didn't tip a chamber-pot on them and maybe on her too. Fortunately, they quickly mellowed quite nicely.

After that first day in the wilds, they began to realize that they were dependent on yours truly for their survival. Once they realized that, they began to treat me better and with more respect. I figure they thought they must keep themselves in my good graces so that I might see them through this some-times-scary adventure they had chosen.

The five-mile ride to Saddleback was enough for the first day and we camped that night upon Saddleback Pass. I don't think they took too well to my comment about what an easy trail it was since I could tell they were not too happy about getting back in the saddle each time we stopped along the way. After a night of camping, they wanted to go back to the Chalet for a day of rest. My but they were softies. I was determined to toughen up their hinders.

For our next excursion, I decided to take them on a three-day adventure into the Moraine Lake valley, a twelve-mile ride over a rough trail. I figured that would make or break them. I was right, that's just what it did. They espoused to having a great time in spite of the ruggedness. None the less, when we returned to the Chalet, they allowed as how they had decided to just day hike for the rest of their stay, returning to the feath-er beds at the Chalet rather than pine boughs on the ground.

This suited me fine and so I led them on some of my fa-vorite hikes. We went up to Lake Agnes and to the summit of Mount Saint Piran. By the end their two weeks, I felt rather proud of myself. As Tom and I were talking about it later, we agreed they had arrived like wild mustangs and I had broken them to be quite pleasant agreeable folks. They must have been rather satisfied with my service as they gave me a generous tip as well as the gift of a fine alpenstock, they had brought with them.

By the time the Barge couple had departed, my crew and materials were ready to begin the cabins. I pointed out to Molly that it would be difficult to be both a builder and a guide at the same time. Somehow this problem was lost with this fast-paced lass. I was to learn later that she had worked out another deal with Roger Cane to supply her with one of the Banff Springs guides whenever she might need one. It was sometime later that I learned that my services were also part of that deal. It seemed she had promised my service to Roger for the winter's work on the Banff Springs. That was my Molly, always the deal maker, doing whatever it took.

The cabins went up very quickly, what with some long hours from my crew and with Molly expediting materials. Molly, being a bit sneaky, once she had gained approval for the materials told the CPR folks that the road was not adequate to get the materials up to the Chalet. She told them that they really must widen and improve the road. To my surprise, a railroad track crew was dispatched within a week of her request to re-grade and cinder a fine new road.

Once the new cabins were completed in late August, there were good accommodations for the seven of us who lived at the lake. We even had a couple of extra beds for additional staff if the need arose. The new Cantonese employees, Yen and Lei, were given a small cabin down the hill in Laggan and rode horses up daily. I think by the seasons end they were becoming more comfortable with the rest of us and I wouldn't be surprised to see them staying up at the Chalet next year.

It was this summer that another lasting symbol of this place took root, literally. I quickly learned that Molly adored flowers. One day she commented that she missed the flowers of her home in Ireland. I pointed out that in the summer the upper meadows in the mountains were teaming with flowers. She lamented that she wished to have some of them there by the lake.

I agreed that the Chalet could use a bit of color around it. She asked me what sort of flowers might be able to survive the climate there. We discussed several possibilities. This was an amusing game for me since I knew quite well what flowers the Chateau would later become famous for.

"Well you know, Molly, we could always transplant some of the alpine wildflowers down here, but what might be even better…," before I could get out the words, as if she read my mind, she said, "How about Iceland Poppies? I bet they would survive". I excitedly agreed, all the time think-ing…Yep, they will survive, that is, at least for a hundred years or so.

Like everything else, Molly requested the CPR promptly send two dozen containers of the poppies and so by summers end another lasting symbol of this grand place took root.

In the weeks that followed my wonderful birthday at Lake Agnes, Molly and I would often take walks by the lake. It was so relaxing there in the evenings after most of the day's chores were done. On these walks we shared our thoughts, our dreams, and the joys of living in this marvelous place. I shared with her some of my adventures in the wilds. On occasion, when feeling mischievous, I would tell her of my dreams for the future. She just thought I had such a vivid imagination. For her part, Molly told some pretty funny stories of her days as a housekeeper at the Banff Springs.

I think one of her funniest stories was one that happened two years earlier, just prior to a visit from a member of the royal family. It seemed there was a housekeeper working at the Banff Springs who was secretly having an affair with one of the tallyho drivers who worked there. Frequently after delivering guests to the hotel from the afternoon train, the two would rendezvous in a vacant room that she was supposed to be cleaning. On this occasion, what with all the royalty that would be visiting, Bill Wilson of the head office, decided to make a surprise inspection a week in advance to make sure all was in order.

Wanting to show off the grandest of the hotel's accommodations to her lover and believing the royal suite to be vacant prior to the prince's arrival, the housekeeper chose just that room for an afternoon rendezvous. What the pair was soon to learn was that Wilson's special train arrived about an hour after the regular train and he was met and transported to the hotel by Roger Cane, the hotel manager.

Desiring to check out the accommodations for the prince, Wilson chose to stay in that very room where the prince would stay. Mr. Cane proudly accompanied him to the royal suite. Molly also went along to the suite so she could address any deficiency that might be discovered. You can only imagine the scene that must have played out when the manager opened the door to that room for his boss. Molly described it as hilarious.

It seemed that the young horseman, complete with riding crop in hand, was caught with the young lady in a most embarrassing position and in a state of full undress, except for that riding crop. Molly said she thought old man Wilson might have a coronary right there. The next day the two, then former employees, departed town and have not been heard from since.

I had learned that in addition to her books, Molly was quite fond of music. It just so happened that a well-known pianist and soprano were giving a performance in Banff on her birthday. I arranged to surprise Molly by taking her to Banff for the performance. It was a wonderful evening, complete with a good steak dinner at the Banff Springs dining room. Later we even did a bit of dancing to the music of a small orchestra performing in the bandstand, which at that time was down near the Bow Falls. We had a grand time, but still it wasn't quite as special as my birthday up at Lake Agnes.

It was a day or two after Molly's birthday, while on one of our evening strolls by the lake, that I commented on how nice it would be to have an ice cream cone right then. "What in the world is an ice cream cone?" Molly asked.

I stumbled with, "Well, Molly, it is putting a dab of ice cream in a bit of hard pastry that you then can pick-up with your hands." I then began to realize that this delicacy might be ahead of its time, but too late, the cat was out of the bag. Trying to further explain an ice cream cone, I told her it was a southern delicacy that apparently had not made it this far North.

"Wow, I only have had ice cream a few times, but I really enjoyed it and I bet it is especially good that way," Molly added.

That conversation got me to thinking, a dangerous thing for me to do sometimes. The past week or so the weather had turned unusually warm. This warm weather was a concern for food storage. Molly and Cookie were worried as to how to provide refrigeration for the rest of the season, mainly for food and milk. Since the lake ice had long since melted, we were forced to rely on occasional wagon loads of ice hauled down from the glacier. Getting the glacier ice was a tough and somewhat risky endeavor.

I thought what we need is a really good ice house and so I suggested that we build one. What I had in the back of my mind was far more than such a utilitarian structure. I envisioned an ice house carved into the bank at lake's edge near the lake outfall. In addition, a first-class boathouse could be built in front of it.

There were a couple of canoes tied up in front of the hotel for guests to use, but I thought we needed a proper dock and a facility to store canoes and paddles during the winter. Once I sprang the idea of combining the two structures, everyone thought it to be a great plan. I proudly set about sketching up my CBH (cool boat house) the nickname I gave to the affair.

By mid -August, as the construction of the staff housing had wound up, the timing was right. I was eager for another project. I excitedly started construction of the CBH. Originally, I thought it could be built in four weeks, that was assuming I was left alone with only that task. As it happened, the arrival of some young adventuresome mountain climbers got in the way of my schedule.

August 15th the Allen party arrived. They were determined to climb some of the lesser peaks. At the same time, the Banff Springs was running at capacity. They could not spare a guide so I was drafted back into the guide business. My group consisted of Daniel Allen, David Case, Dr. Grissom, Sam Wheeler, and two brothers, Bill and Jonathan Nelson. The entire group was from the States. All but the Nelson brothers were from Philadelphia and they were from New York. Apparently, they had met at school or were family acquaintances. They were all eager to conquer mountains and hunt grizzly bears. Quite a foolish bunch, I thought.

Though I had done a bit of climbing in past years I was none too keen on climbing with this wild bunch of youths. I did however feel some degree of responsibility for my charges. After a couple of day climbs of the peaks surrounding the Chalet, the group wanted to explore other peaks. With some reservation I led the group southward into the valley of ten peaks where they climbed Mt Babel, a simple climb.

Before departing, I researched the route from my trusty map. The main challenge we faced with this route was the constant danger of the advancing climbers showering those below with rocks. Since we had no helmets, this was a real concern. I kept telling myself their hard heads would protect them, not to worry. Guess my head is probably pretty tough as well.

Allen was by far the more congenial one of the lot. I was quite impressed with his taking so well to these mountains. Unlike most of his associates, he had both a spirit for adventure and, more importantly, a healthy respect for nature and his surroundings. Just the little signs of his consideration impressed me, little things like his wanting me to ensure the pack horses were not overloaded and to avoid cutting green trees for our camps.

Following a successful climb of Mt Babel, we camped for a couple of days at Moraine Lake. It was while camped there that they decided on an attempt to climb Mt Temple. I knew only too well that Temple would be a difficult climb. I knew this as a result of the difficulties I had encountered in my past, even with the benefit of modern gear. Trying to dissuade the group was of no use. They were bound and determined to be the first to conquer this 13,000-foot giant.

Since we had the pack horses and a lot of gear, I thought it better that we backtrack and make the approach to Temple over Saddleback Pass and then up through Paradise Valley. We had just finished setting up our base camp in Paradise Valley on August 23d when our fine weather changed. I took the onset of sleet and snow flakes as certainly a bad omen. With the help of this weather delay, I was able to convince them to abandon the pursuit of Mt Temple.

The group had planned to climb for two weeks then hunt goat and bear for two weeks. They had signed up with a hunting guide from Banff for the second two weeks, so I led them back to the Chalet on August 25th. I must not have been too bad of a guide since as we parted Daniel Allen vowed to return for a longer period the next year. He allowed as how he would conquer Mt. Temple on his return, with me as guide.

Resuming my construction work was a welcome change. Before I left, we had framed the icehouse and boathouse structure. What now remained was the roofing and wall siding. As I applied the siding on the Icehouse portion, I longed for a good insulating material. Alas, there was no such thing as fiberglass insulation, in fact, as I was to learn, no one knew much about the benefits of insulation. The best I could do was to use two layers of siding and utilize the air cavity for insulation. As for the roof, it was wooden shingles. I did put in a low ceiling to help contain the cold.

The icehouse would work like this: large blocks of lake ice would be harvested in the winter and stacked on the board floor that had slots for drainage. The ice would be covered with layers of sawdust. The little structure had been recessed into the lake bank near water level. In theory, ice should keep most of the summer, especially since the temperature seldom got above 60 degrees in the day time and was near freezing at night.

The boathouse, being in the forefront and the more prominent part of the structure, was more ornate. It had a first-rate dock where the six canoes could be properly moored. Inside, a series of pulleys were rigged from the rafters where the canoes could be hoisted up in winter. All in all, these two little buildings should service well for some years. I knew electric refrigeration was just a few years away. I thought to myself the ice house could serve well for beer storage or for chilling champagne.

The big day had arrived to christen Lake Louise' two newest buildings. The morning was another glorious one in this mountain paradise. Though it was now September 20th and cooler weather should be upon us, that day was unusually warm. It was a great day for boating on the lake. All our tourists from the Chalet had gone and most of them had departed from the Banff Springs as well. This gave some of the Banff Springs employee's a chance to come up to visit. They caught the train up for our boathouse christening.

In all we probably had about 30 crazy souls. Leave it to youth to find a way to add excitement to anything. While some of us, such as this old man, were content to calmly paddle the lake, David and Rocky, an 18-year-old houseman from the Banff Springs, decided to attempt to harness the moderate breeze blowing across the lake.

The two enterprising youths rigged a sail on one of the canoes and were going to sail the lake. They obviously had no concept of how a sailboat worked and how important a keel was. Boy did they get one quick lesson. They had lashed two row boat oars together then attached a bed sheet for a sail. At first all was well. They took off at a pretty good clip across the lake, however, when one of the two attempted to steer the craft to avoid being blown ashore a disaster occurred.

The craft capsized in a grand fashion, tossing the lads into the icy water. Having fully expected this result, I was nearby with a rescue row boat. Molly, Cookie, and about a dozen others were on the shore dying of laughter. I dragged the two nearly drowned rats from the icy waters. I thanked them for providing the day's entertainment.

After everyone had partaken of the water sports, we served cakes, tea, and yes, champagne dockside. As part of the fun, we had a drawing of names for our little fleet of the eight canoes and two rowboats. Everyone whose name was drawn got to name one of the craft. I lovingly stenciled the names on the canoes and row boats. Soon we were all well within the spirits. The last name drawn in the boat naming contest was yours truly. Guess what I named my boat ….? "Lost Time." "Logan, what a crazy name for a canoe," Molly admonished me. "What does it mean, Logan?" she asked. Several others also listened for my answer.

"Oh, just thought that here it is easy to lose time," was my response.

That night, while still under the effects of the days drinking, as I kissed Molly good-night, again I came pretty close to telling her everything. I sure wanted to. Even as relaxed as I felt at that very moment, somehow, I held back my secret. I guess I somehow knew the time was not yet right. I was sure dreading parting with her for the winter.

Too soon the time came to close the Chalet for the season. That meant Molly would be leaving to go to Calgary for the winter. I could have gone and wintered with Molly. I was certainly tempted to do this. Unfortunately, she had made the deal with Roger for my services that winter to work on the expansion of the Banff Springs Hotel.

Molly

9. A Warm Cave

It was sure one long lonely winter without Molly. With each snow, I became more melancholy. I kept thinking about how much she loved snow and longing to be a kid with her playing in the white stuff. I did make a trip over to Calgary a couple of times to see her and of course we sent letters to each other. I wondered if she missed me as much as I missed her. The outpouring of her affection when I visited kept me thinking she just might.

Banff was still an active little community that winter. Of course, there weren't many tourists but still there were quite a few locals. I was becoming aquatinted with a good number of them. My work there on the expansion of the Bow Falls Pavilion part of the hotel kept me pretty well occupied. Occasionally I would join some of the older fellows at the Lynx Pub for a brew after work. The Pub got its name when a few years back a crazed local released a Lynx in there. Frequently though, my mind would wonder back to the great times the past summer and yearn for more of the same.

By April, Molly had wrapped up her winter job in Calgary.

Jean was back and had taken over again running the Bow River Hotel. The Banff Springs work had gone well over the winter due in no small part to a relatively mild winter. I had been marking off the days on my calendar and finally spring had arrived. On May 2nd , with great delight, I met Molly's train. I presented her with a new hat I had bought for her at Dave Whites. She looked so radiant I could hardly stop kissing her.

It would be a couple of weeks before we would head north to open the Chalet. In the meantime, she set about ordering supplies for the summer season. I was determined that Molly and I should make up for lost time. I desperately wanted us to spend some time together, just the two of us, before we got busy with all the summers work. Apparently, Molly had similar thoughts. It was a few days after she arrived in Banff that she pulled a grand surprise. I must say for once she sure got the better of me with her plans. I was usually the schemer of the two of us, but not this time. What she had cooked up was to be about the most wonderful experience of my life.

During this period, the Upper Hot Springs and the Cave and Basin were enormously popular. Of course, were it not for these hot springs, these amazing geological features, probably Banff would not have ever come into being. The discovery of these wonders the previous decade had started it all. Their discovery had destined the area to become Canada's equivalent of the United States Yellowstone Park. Undoubtedly my fate would also have been quite different but for these amazing geothermal features.

The old and infirm were coming from all over to bathe in the miraculous sulfur waters. Entrepreneurs such as Dr. Brett had taken full advantage of the situation. He was even selling bottled water from the springs. A few called the doctor a snake oil salesman; however, I quickly came to respect him as a fine doctor, considering the primitive medicine of the time. Although I respected him as a doctor, I didn't buy any of his bottled "miracle" water.

Dr. Brett had constructed a place he called The Grand Sanitarium. To me it seemed more of a hotel. It was a somewhat lavish structure, though it certainly wasn't on par with the Banff Springs Hotel. If you had ailments, it was supposed to be the place to stay and as they said to "take the waters." The Sanitarium site was where the park headquarters building would later stand.

After crossing the narrow and shaky bridge, the road from the Banff town site forked with the left leading to the Banff Springs Hotel, straight ahead going to the Sanitarium, and to the right about a half a mile lay the Cave and Basin. Continuing up past the Sanitarium, there was a wagon road that led to the source of the hot spring on Sulfur Mountain. It was from that spring that hot water was piped to pools at the Sanitarium and also to the Banff Springs Hotel.

At this time, the CPR and its Banff Springs Hotel still maintained control over and managed the Upper Hot Springs and the Cave and Basin. A few years after the discovery of the Cave, a tunnel had been blasted into the lower side of the cave for easier access. This tunnel entrance to the cave and hot spring was kept padlocked at night and at times when it was not open to the public or hotel guests. Being early in the season, the Cave was only open on certain days of the week, and never at night.

While in Banff the previous year, I had bathed at the upper

hot springs. It was quite nice. It was smaller and more rustic than the large pool and bathhouse I had remembered from the twentieth century. I had however, only visited and never bathed at the Cave and Basin.

I had heard some stories of wild parties held at the Cave involving some of the CPR's visiting executives and various lady friends. Molly probably had heard these stories as well, though I feel it unlikely she had heard some of the raunchy versions told over brandy and cigars by those so-called gentlemen. Certainly, it never crossed my mind that she would have been involved in such scandalous doings. All the same, I was more than a bit surprised at what she served up at dinner that night.

Brewster's had just opened a new Dining Room and on Friday May 6th, Molly and I had gone there for an early dinner. Midway through dinner she produced a closed fist and with an impish twinkle in her eye blurted out "guess what I have?" Having not the foggiest idea and the dinner wine having made me somewhat more foolish than usual, I piped up with, "Why my dear, you probably have your pet rock."

She laughed though likely not as hard as she would have had she known about the brief pet rock craze. "No, you fool," she said "I have this," and she proceeded to open her hand, revealing a large brass key.

I again said something stupid, like, "Oh the key to my heart."

"Even better," she said, "it's the key to the gate at the Cave." She went on to tell me how she had borrowed it from Roger Cane at the Banff Springs Hotel.

Again, with that impish twinkle in her eye she said, "I

thought we might go for a swim after dinner." The very thought of something so clandestine and sinful as our own hot spring for the night immediately rekindled excitement such as I had not known since my youth. No, not since the days of a vacation home with the hot tub had I had such steamy thoughts.

"Are you sure it will be ok?" I asked.

She said, "Yes, don't worry."

Somewhat nervously I asked, "Will anyone else be there?"

Again, she answered reassuringly, "There isn't supposed to be. What's the matter? Afraid to be alone with me?" she teased.

"But we don't have swimming suits," I piped up.

"Well, you may not, but I was born with mine," my spunky gal shot back. Needless to say, we passed on Brewster's usually irresistible desserts that night.

As I now eagerly envisioned the evening that lay ahead, I realized there was an ingredient that was needed to make it perfect. Even though I knew that Molly was not one to indulge in spirits very much, I felt we must have champagne, it being by far the most appropriate drink for such a special occasion. She had surprised me now so I must do my part. After dinner I suggested that we stop by the Banff Springs to pick up some more towels so that we would be assured of having plenty.

I told Molly to wait in the carriage while I ran in the employee's entry. I quickly proceeded to the kitchen. Luckily, my friend Andy, the Assistant Chef was still there. I asked him to sell me a bottle of his finest champagne. He insisted on knowing the occasion. I sheepishly and yet proudly told him of our evening plans, but only after eliciting an oath of silence from him. I felt very much like a wolf about to dispatch a lamb.

Andy said he would be delighted to supply me with the champagne. He insisted that it be complementary from Uncle CPR. As Andy packed the bottle in a bucket of ice, he said, "You best take care that you and mermaid Molly don't come out like cooked lobsters." At that moment, I couldn't have been redder if I had been one of those crustaceans. I wrapped up two champagne glasses in a napkin, thanked Andy, and headed out. Fortunately, it dawned on me then to go down the hall to the maid's pantry to get some towels, after all, that's what Molly was expecting me to bring back.

Molly, already somewhat suspicious from the length of my absence, soon recognized that I was carrying more than a mountain of towels. She quickly ferreted out my stash. We both broke into laughter as she said, "Why you wicked old man, planning to ply me with spirits, then what? As if I don't know." Like a couple of love-stricken kids, we sent the horse to galloping down the bumpy road all the way to the Cave.

Playing the part of the dutiful innkeeper, Molly produced a bag of candles and a lantern as we arrived at the entrance. I quickly mated the key with the lock and the gate swung open. After fumbling for the matches, I succeeded in lighting the lantern. The lantern flickered as we walked through the damp tunnel. The smell of brimstone made us feel as though they were on the threshold of hell and the dancing shadows created a setting like something out of a horror movie. I fully expected bats to come flying out at any moment.

I had been to the Cave a couple of times before but not in these present times and never at night. I must say the atmosphere was totally different from what I had expected. The pool in the Cave glowed with an eerie yellowish appearance.

The steam rising from the waters created ghost like shadows against the damp cave walls. The whole scene bordered on just plain scary.

When I turned out the lantern briefly, we gazed at the moonlight streaming through the hole in the cave's roof. We quickly decided the best mood lighting would be a series of candles placed around the pool. I promptly set them up. Our senses could not have been more alert. The moist sulfur smell which had initially been so unpleasant was now hardly noticeable as our visual senses took in the enchanting surroundings.

Having left the champagne in the carriage, I hurried back to retrieve it and make sure the horse was properly tied. Upon my return, I found Molly already immersed in the glowing waters. Oh, how beautiful she looked. It was a picture my mind will never lose. With great finesse, I opened the champagne, letting the cork pop with a sound of a cannon reverberating in the small cave. I served us both generous portions of the lively brew.

Nervously and very modestly, I turned away from Molly as I quickly disrobed and jumped into the steaming pool. All that was missing from the perfect romantic scene was soft music in the background. Quickly I assured Molly that I would bring music for our next such outing. "My old goat (this had become her affectionate term for me), I really don't believe we need a band right now, do you?" she asked in a mocking voice.

"I guess not, now that you mention it," I said while making myself a mental note to obtain a music box for her birthday present that year.

There by the light of our four candles and with just a dash of moonlight from the hole in the caves roof, we proceeded to slip into another world. Our bodies became one for the first time there in those incredible waters. Without a doubt it was the most sensuous experience I had ever had. We were like the kids we were at heart. Age and cares drifted away with the steam, we sat on the rocks that ringed the pool, kicking our feet in the delicious water, returning to immerse ourselves when a chill overcame us. The combination of the water, the champagne and our enjoyment of each other's bodies had us quite relaxed. Why we didn't drown while in this state of ecstasy, I do not know.

We spent two wonderful hours there sipping the spirits and indulged in the greatest pleasure of life. We vowed to repeat this experience again and as often as possible. We were both so weak upon emerging from the waters that it took every bit of combined strength to get dressed and back to the carriage. Fortunately, we had a smart horse and the word hotel was enough to set him in auto pilot. Somehow, we managed to get to our separate rooms in the employee quarters for the balance of the night.

Unfortunately, I fear our escapades of that night were rather obvious the next day. We were both extremely red all over from the long exposure to the heated water. Andy's comment about lobsters was about right. I don't know if it was Andy failing to keep his mouth shut or if for the excess exuberance Molly and I showed each other after our adventure, what I do know was that we were to take a lot of kidding from our friends for a long time to come.

For any other young unmarried lady of the town, such an adventure would certainly have condemned her reputation for all time. Not so for Molly. She was so natural and so well liked that few batted an eye at this situation. Her infectious personality and bubbly spirit transcended all. As any good gentleman would, I, of course, denied everything. Most people probably couldn't believe there could be anything going on with an old goat like me and a beautiful young woman anyway.

There will likely be other memorable experiences at the Cave and Upper Hot Springs during the years to follow, but I doubt any will ever to be quite as wonderful as that first night when my Molly and I went caving.

10. The Teahouse

This past fall, before saying goodbye to the Chalet for the season, Molly and I made one last trip up to Lake Agnes. We again marveled at how great it was to look down on our little domain of Lake Louise from that lofty site. We talked about how great it would be to be able to live up there in the clouds. Getting a little bit more realistic, we both agreed that creating a first rate trail up there should be a priority for the next season. I had little doubt that this spot would be a hit with our visitors.

Soon after getting the Chalet ready for opening in May, I rounded up my faithful trail crew of David and Tom and we tore into upgrading the Lake Agnes trail. We seriously considered trying to create a wagon road, but there were only a few spots where a carriage could turn around or pass. I finally decided that a horse trail would be much more practical. Still, where we could, we made the trail wide enough to take a wagon. In the end, we made the trail wide enough for wagons all the way to Mirror Lake.

As we started the trail, it quickly became apparent that I

had overlooked one major obstacle in planning the work. I had failed to consider that the trail was going up a northern facing slope and was largely shielded from the sun. This orientation meant that the winter snows lingered longer there. To make matters worse, certain portions of the trail caught numerous avalanches in the winter.

We encountered masses of downed trees and we were trudging through mud and snow. Despite these difficulties, in two weeks we carved out a very nice trail all the way to Lake Agnes. Well almost. Whenever I had previously visited Lake Agnes, I always had to leave the horses some seventy-five feet below the lake since those last seventy-five feet were particularly treacherous. There was a cliff face there that continued to challenge us. In the end, the best we could do was to create a small corral for the horses there at the base of the cliff below the lake. We then built some steps along with a hand rope to facilitate getting the rest of the way up to the lake.

As we worked on the trail, I had other plans simmering in the back of my mind. No longer could I resist the desire to put a Teahouse on the shore of Lake Agnes. It would be a place where people could rest from the hike up and where they could gaze out upon the wonders of the lakes in the clouds. Selfishly, I wanted a place Molly and I could get away to sometimes. I had been thinking about this ever since that first trip up to Lake Agnes with Molly. I knew a marvelous little cabin was to grace the Lake Agnes shore someday. I knew that it was to be one of the great highlights to millions of visitors to this grand place over the years.

I wondered when the Teahouse would be built. How well I remembered sitting on that little porch looking out on the beautiful little jewel, Lake Agnes a few feet below the porch. I also remembered that the lake was trimmed in ice nearly year-round. The Teahouse I remembered was home to countless jays and ground squirrels that would amuse the throngs of tourists to this Mecca in the sky. It was a grand view looking out over the Lake Agnes waterfall down some thousand feet below and some two miles distance was the jewel of Lake Louise.

My daydreaming took me to one especially fun experience…in August I think, when the Teahouse was bustling with tourists. All but one of the few rustic log tables on the porch was taken. I took the remaining table at the rear that had the best view of Lake Agnes. Regretfully, my favorite table that had the best view of Lake Louise was occupied. Since space on the tiny porch was limited, I had laid my pack down next to me on the steps leading up to the porch.

I had noticed upon my arrival that there seemed to be an abundance of the friendly ground squirrels. Having been fed all summer, they had become pretty tame. I tried to keep a sharp eye on my pack as the little rodents appeared to be sizing it up for an attack.

Seated next to me at a table on the corner of the porch was a family who, from their accent, I took to be British. Since they were obviously tourists, new to the area, they perked my curiosity. My eye caught one of the pesky ground squirrels climbing up the log chair where the older gentleman was seated. In a flash, as this gentleman went to pick up his sandwich to take a bite, there, much to his amazement firmly attached to his sandwich was a ground squirrel. The little creature showed little sign of relinquishing his claim, despite the shrill screams of his daughter and wife. Surely this little pest must be deaf, I thought.

Shock, amazement, and laughter broke out from all who witnessed the event. I laughed till my side hurt. I fumbled to get my camera out of its case and snap a picture. This incident diverted my attention long enough so that when I glanced again at my pack, I saw one of the furry creatures diving into it. Quickly I went to secure my pack from the little beast.

Thinking of this funny experience made me yearn for those fun times there again. I kept trying to remember what year the first Teahouse had been built. It seemed that I remembered an old picture of a Teahouse with a caption saying built in the late 1890s. Maybe I wouldn't have to wait too long for it to reappear, I thought to myself. The notion that I might be the one to craft this little piece of history was so tempting, still messing with history might be risky. Then I realized that I had already mentioned the idea to Molly so, as they say, the cat was out of the bag. Since Molly had the CPR in her pocket, I felt confident we could get their backing for the project. I was ready to push the idea.

Bill Wilson's new assistant, a mister Bart Howard, was due to arrive at the Chalet for a quick one-night visit on May 30th. Molly was anxious to meet him. She invited me to join them for dinner. Bart asked me about the new trails that we had built the past season. I responded that they would open up some of the most scenic and rugged areas to safe travel for tourists. "Come see for yourself," I implored him.

"I shall at my earliest convenience," Bart promised.

It was obvious that Bart subscribed to the CPR philosophy that it was essential for guests to receive the proper pampered

Rockies experience. I had come to understand that the Victorian lust for adventure was second only to their love of cushy luxuries. Anything to pamper the guests was viewed as a grand idea. Their saying was that a pampered guest will be a returning guest.

I told Bart that I felt it would be a great experience for those guests at the Chalet to be able to take tea and rest at a facility with a grand view overlooking Lake Louise. This idea was not totally original with me. Others had talked of a series of rest huts along the trails. Now with the completion of several trails, it seemed as though it was an idea whose time had arrived. To my glee, Bart grabbed hold of the idea with tremendous enthusiasm. "Logan, do you know of a good site for such a structure?" he asked.

"Funny you should ask," I responded "Lake Agnes would be perfect."

Unfortunately, Bart had not been to Lake Agnes and so he could not appreciate fully the grand scenery to be experienced there. However, this lack of first-hand experience did not keep him from some degree of excitement. "Terrific idea, Logan, let's do it. From what Molly has told me, you are a builder of buildings as well as trails, think you could handle the construction?" he asked.

"Sure," I responded.

"Why don't you sketch up a plan and send it along to me with the materials you will need and I will meet with Mr. Wilson as soon as I return to the CPR office," he added. Out of that meeting began my exciting project for the summer of 1897.

Molly loved the idea. She was almost as excited as I was.

She was probably the real reason I decided to suggest the project. Form our picnics of last summer, I knew how much she enjoyed the spot. We would have our own Teahouse, a Teahouse we would share with our guests, except when we were using it in private.

My design for the little building began immediately. I sketched it the way I remembered it. It was to have only two rooms, those being the main guest dining area and the kitchen. The dining area would have two doors, the center front entry and a rear door into the kitchen. There would be windows on the front and both sides of the dining room. The dining room would have a nice little pot-bellied stove to take the chill off those cool early and late season days. The kitchen would be located to the rear, would have a little pantry and a rear entry. It would be equipped with a wood cook stove, a large counter, a sink with running water, an ice box, and cupboards.

The most prominent feature would be the front porch, the feature I remembered best. It would extend from the dining room to near the edge of the waterfall. The porch would wrap around two sides of the dining room and its rustic railings would encompass space for eight little tables. The prime table would be the one closest to the beautiful waterfall where the snow melt from Lake Agnes and Victoria Glacier cascaded down some two hundred feet to the tiny Mirror Lake below. From this table, one would have a great view of the Chalet and Lake Louise.

Though the staff lodgings and boathouse of last year had been rewarding accomplishments, this was to be a special challenge. Unlike the boathouse/ice house, this would be a building I knew was to last and be the most remembered place for the average visitor to Lake Louise. With the trail upgrade work almost complete, I started thinking about help for the Teahouse construction.

As much as I would have liked to have both David and Tom full time for the endeavor, I knew that just wasn't realistic considering the number of guests due to arrive soon. It just so happened that about this same time Bill Roand had reappeared looking for work. With a bit of coaxing, I got Molly to go along with rehiring the fellow. Lei, our Cantonese porter, had a brother who had just arrived. He claimed him to be a carpenter. His name was Malu. Unfortunately, he spoke little English. What a crew. I had a part time drunk, a guy who couldn't speak English, and two good but part time helpers. As I always said, I loved challenges.

I was like a little boy with his first set of tinker toys when we started up the mountain with the first load of materials. We had been able to create a trail wide enough and not too steep for a wagon up to a point near Mirror Lake. This was just a half mile from our building site. Our plan was to stockpile the supplies there and then they would have to be carried the last half mile up a steep trail by horseback or man power. I knew full well that this would be slow backbreaking work for man and beast.

The site of the Teahouse was our first hurdle. It was to reside on the north shore of Lake Agnes on the brow of the cliff where the waterfall cascaded over the edge. This location was out of the path of avalanches and such that a grand view of Lake Louise and the Bow valley could be obtained. While my crew worked at hauling up supplies that first day, I drove the first corner stake for the little building. I thought, "Logan, you have just staked out a bit of history for yourself. If I am to leave something behind, what could be grander than this."

The men and I set up camp in a lovely spot by the lake about a hundred feet from our site. I started laying the stone foundation for our little edifice on June 10th. For most of the first week, my crew of Tom, David, Bill, and Malu hauled supplies up. Establishing a sound stone and mortar foundation was difficult. I knew quite well how important it was to do this step correctly. All the cement, sand, and lime had to be packed up. Stone was not much of a problem, being quite abundant around the lake. But what I wouldn't have given for some really good wheelbarrows. The foundation took me a week.

The wood framing went slower than I expected. First, we had to transport all the lumber to the site a few pieces at a time from our stockpile at Mirror Lake. Then there was the task of sawing boards by hand, which was a real pain. It was hard for me to decide what I missed most: a cell phone to order supplies, a helicopter for the remote deliveries, or just a good old skill saw.

Molly and I had already worked out a schedule for once things got going with the season down at the Chalet. Tom and David would rotate, taking turns, helping out on the Teahouse. I wanted one of them at the construction site whenever I had to be away. I trusted both of them and felt OK about leaving briefly as long as at least one of them was there. That plan worked fine until about ten days after we had started construction.

I came down to the Chalet for dinner the night of June 18th. Molly told me she had a VIP scheduled to arrive the next day. Naturally she wanted me to be their guide for a couple of days. It just so happened that at the same time both David and Tom both had gone to Banff to pick up a string of horses for a large group expected the next week.

In a complete lapse of judgment, I had decided to leave Bill and Malu alone at the site for those couple of days. Before I left the pair, I lined out specific work they could do while I was away. What I assigned them was to gather rocks of a specific size for the fireplace and to complete hauling up the remaining materials. If they still had time, they could start prefabricating the walls the way I had showed them.

Leave it to Bill to want to do things differently and as always in a crazy way. I certainly should have known better. They did gather a few rocks and carry up most of the remaining materials, just as I had asked, but then Bill went astray. He decided on his own that since we had built a porch on two sides, we should indeed have a porch on the third side as well. That seemed logical to him, especially since there was a grand view on that side. He completely ignored the fact that the third side where he wanted to add the porch was over the edge of the cliff face and above an eighty-foot shear drop-off.

While I was gone, Bill undertook the construction of a porch projecting out some ten feet over the cliff face. He wanted to surprise me with the porch addition. For supports, he had employed two small diagonal timbers, one at each end of the porch and braced them on the cliff face. Malu, I am sure, tried to convince Bill not to do this. I laugh to myself now when I think of all the hand gestures, he must have used in his efforts to communicate with Bill and dissuade him of this folly.

Bill's misadventure almost proved fatal. I was coming up the mountain late in the afternoon two days after leaving the pair. The sounds of hammering were growing louder as I approached. Sounds good, at least they are working, I thought to myself while wondering what hammering had to do with gathering rock. I was just arriving at our storage area at Mirror Lake when suddenly the hammering was replaced by the sound of snapping timbers and yelling. The next sound was that of an avalanche of material coming down the mountain at the far end of Mirror Lake.

My heart was pounding. Whatever had happened? Surely a disaster I feared. I abandoned the pack animals and ran up the steep slope toward the site. A few anxious moments later I arrived. To my relief and surprise, both Bill and Malu were standing there seemingly unhurt though in somewhat of a daze. It seemed as Bill's supports for his porch, being quite inadequate, had failed. All the porch structure he had attempted to add was now strewn down the mountainside.

Angry over the near loss of the two and the waste of materials, I chastised Bill in language not used since my earlier construction years. Later I apologized for losing my temper so badly. After calming down, I realized that Bill had meant well, he just didn't know any better. I thought about the porch addition a bit more. I was convinced that I could structurally accomplish what Bill had wanted and it would have been quite a nice touch. There still remained a problem though. You see, the structure I remembered did not have such a porch. In the end I lied and told Bill it just couldn't be done.

The pace of the work picked up. Soon the walls were all raised and a day later the roof was framed. We built the chimney and in a matter of another week we were finishing the wood shingles on the roof. When a wagon brought up the cook stove a couple of days later, Molly and Cookie accompanied it. They had great praises for our work.

Since the next day was my birthday, she begged me to take the day off and spend it with her down at the Chalet. After the last incident when I left the work unsupervised, I decided this time to give my whole crew the day off. The weather was terrific, far too good to just stay inside eating, so we decided to spend it on the lake.

I rigged up a rather foolish looking contraption of two canoes lashed together in sort of a catamaran affair with a couple of lawn chairs and umbrellas and we floated about the lake, drawing stares from the shore folks. These "water chairs" as they were dubbed, were a hit, and soon others were begging us for rides.

What a birthday dinner she gave me. Molly and Cookie, convinced that I must miss southern cooking, came up with every southern dish they could find. I bet that was the first time anyone in that part of the county had grits. I didn't have the heart to tell them that grits was one southern dish I was not too fond of. The black-eyed peas and fried chicken they made were mighty tasty though.

Back at the building site, soon we were putting on the siding, trimming out and installing the sink and water lines. A small sparkling clear stream cascaded down the mountain behind the Teahouse. This stream would serve as a source of running water for the kitchen. We constructed a wooden pipeline from the stream to the kitchen, a distance of about sixty feet. Using a bit of ingenuity and some iron piping I managed to connect the water lines to the kitchen sink and provide a valve to control the flow. The task would have been easier had

I chosen to use lead piping which was then common, however, knowing what I did about the dangers of lead, I couldn't bring myself to use it. The hot water would still have to come from the water tank of the cook stove since hot water heaters, especially something small enough to get up the mountain, were not to be had.

I carefully selected a location for an outhouse. It was to be below and away from the stream and hidden from view by the trees behind the Teahouse. As we were building the outhouse, I kidded Bill, asking if he didn't want to put a deck on it as well. He sheepishly allowed as how he didn't expect people would want to linger there very long. I laughed and said, "Bill, I spec you are right about that."

By July 1st, Lake Agnes had about given up its winter ice cover. Our work was now finished. Proudly our rustic little Teahouse stood guard at the head of the lake. The inside smelled delightful. The fresh cut pine and spruce gave the aroma of the wilds of nature that mixed with the aroma of the morning fire from the stove all just perfect. We had contracted with one of the carpenters in Banff to make some rustic Adirondack furniture. This furniture went well with our little building. It was some sight watching those chairs strapped to the back of the pack horses coming up the trail. I could just picture Bill riding up in one.

Molly had hired a new cook named Kate to prepare meals at the Teahouse. The position of hostess was filled by Sarah. She was one of last year's maids and had agreed to come up and serve as hostess / waitress for the Teahouse. The two would ride their horses up in the morning and down again at night. This really proved to be quite an exciting assignment for the pair.

Their stories of fending off the critters, desirous of home-steading, always left everyone laughing. Porcupines were especially taken with the structure and proved to be frequent guests. Tom, David, and I took turns filling the third employee position for the Teahouse, that being the job of packer. We took turns packing up supplies every couple of days.

The grand opening was a gala affair. It was held on July 14, 1897. The tourist season was in full swing and the Chalet was full. All eighteen guests, along with most of the staff, joined the fun at the Teahouse that afternoon. The weather couldn't have been grander, with a clear blue sky, a light breeze, and temperature of seventy degrees. Bart and several other CPR folks came up. He was most complementary of our accomplishment. He kept going on about how it was the perfect spot. I had to agree with him on that.

After a bit of coaxing, I had been successful in convincing Molly to serve champagne for the occasion, in addition to the proper British tea. Fortunately, the bubbly spirits did not lead anyone to plunge over the falls or even to take a swim in the lake as Molly had suggested might happen. Cookie helped Kate prepare some extremely tasty delicacies. We all ate, drank, and took in the wonderful scenery that afternoon until the shadow from the Little Beehive Mountain told us dusk was approaching.

That was sure one fine day here in the Canadian Rockies. Playing host at that wonderful little spot had been a tremendous treat. The little Teahouse fit perfectly into the charms of this wonderful Victorian era. I was quite proud of my little contribution to history.

Molly decided to have the Teahouse open from 10:00 am to

5:00 pm. In those days, unlike later years, the Teahouse served food at lunch, as well as afternoon tea. The regular lunch menu included Roast Sirloin of Beef, Corn Pudding, Mashed Potatoes, Biscuits and Honey, Lemon Pudding, and of course, Tea or Coffee. The thinking was that to have such a meal available would really impress the guests after the long trek up there. I expect it did just that from all the comments I heard.

The Teahouse was so popular that first year that I was concerned that we had not built it large enough. As a result of the popularity of the Lake Agnes Teahouse, the CPR set about planning other such establishments which were to be built over the next few seasons. I knew that others would be built in places like Saddleback and the Plain of Six Glaciers, but I also knew few would survive, and that none would surpass the one at Lake Agnes.

One thing about the Teahouse continued to haunt me; that being having my name connected with its building. My relief for this concern though, was remembering having read that the original Teahouse was damaged in a fire years after it was built. Perhaps the builder of the original would be lost with time, as I was. I hoped so, as I still considered my anonymity vital. For Molly and me, it was to be our special place, a place to go and to escape the problems of life. It was like a special vacation home where we chose to entertain friends and guests. It was truly our little corner of the world.

11. The Tallest Peak

In early September 1897, the last large party departed from the Chalet. The Gibson brothers were still there, but they were leaving in a couple of days to meet up with their guide in Banff for a hunting trip. With the guest's departure, the Chalet began to take on a strange, silent sound. After a non-stop summer, Molly and I at last had some time to ourselves. The crisp fall air had ignited our spirit for adventure. We decided that we would spend a few days exploring the wilderness south of Lake Louise.

I suggested a trip to the upper end of Paradise Valley. This lovely, wild valley had just been explored for the first time a couple of seasons ago. A year ago, I had taken the Allen party over the new Saddleback trail and down into the valley. We had to cut a crude trail from the pass down to the upper end of the valley, some five miles from the pass.

The Allen party had camped several nights in the valley. They were primarily interested in climbing and they climbed some of the surrounding peaks. Actually, the spot we camped then was in the same location as a campground where I overnighted in 1976. My trusty map had helped greatly on that expedition into the area. It had shown the best routes to the passes and summits of the then unclimbed peaks.

Molly had yet to experience the wonders of this valley and I was quite eager to show it to her. Our camping gear was both cumbersome and heavy. It consisted of a large canvas tent, two blankets, a skillet, a cooking pot, and an assortment of dried and fresh food. Climbing was not in our plans for our leisurely outing; even so in my usual manner of trying to be prepared for anything, I carried a length of rope and two alpenstocks.

Normally for such a trip we would each ride and then take along a pack pony or two for the gear. Horses were used in large part for most camping trips due to the heavy cooking gear and tent. At Molly's suggestion, we only took a couple of pack ponies for the gear, choosing ourselves to walk. This slower pace gave us time to fully take in all the scenery. Even though I knew we could have entered the valley from the new trail to Moraine Lake, I chose the Saddleback Pass route. I still enjoyed showing off my first trail with all the little cairns. My trail had the added benefit of affording a spectacular view of the valley from the pass at 7,400 feet.

I remembered this area quite well from my future life, having crossed this pass one June day in waist deep snow. It had been miserable. Such experiences with lingering snow on the trails through the passes had caused me to postpone my annual vacation trips to the mountains until August. Hopefully there would not be any snow this trip. I knew quite well that it could snow at any time of the year here. The weather for the past week though had been great, Indian summer weather with mild sunny days and cool nights.

Cookie had gotten up early that morning to fix breakfast. She had made us a batch of her delicious biscuits with ham. Molly and I often wondered what we would do without our dependable and wonderful Cookie. In addition to ham to go with the biscuits, we also carried some honey. We got off to a proper mountain start before sunrise, having packed our gear the night before.

The crisp fall air and my lively companion made me feel young and spry. Our timing was just right. As we broke the tree-line, we were greeted by one of the most beautiful sunrises. Molly commented on how nice the trail was up to the pass. She said she was sure it would be a popular hike for the guests. I thanked her for the compliment. We both agreed that the trail was easy enough for the average tenderfoot. Certainly, any hiker would be rewarded with a splendid view. To the East lay the vast Bow River Valley and to the West the beautiful Paradise Valley, presided over by the mighty Mt. Temple.

"Logan are you sure you know where you are going?" Molly asked as we headed down the rugged East slope of Saddle Mountain.

"Sure," I said with a fair degree of confidence. "I found this shortcut when I brought the Allen bunch in," I responded. "Guess I could have done a bit better job of blazing the trail though," I added, commenting about the crude trail that our group had carved out through the scrubby balsam. Travel through this scrub was difficult. The freshly cut branches gave the mountain air an exciting wild aroma. By 9:30 we had made our way down into Paradise Valley and were standing beside Paradise Creek.

I knew that the stream started some five miles up the valley at Horseshoe Glacier. My plan was to journey up to the head of the valley and camp there. The most scenic part of the valley was at the upper end. The campsite I had planned was near an unusual waterfall which was yet to be discovered. It would be called "The Giant Steps." I wanted Molly to be the first to see the remarkable falls. When I took the Allen bunch in, I had deliberately held off showing it to them, preferring to reserve that experience for Molly.

Our trek along the North side of the stream was becoming very difficult. Avalanche plumes from the south face of Mt. Fairview had left masses of gnarled trees and boulders. These proved tough to navigate for us and our horses. I led the horses and was scouting out a trail about fifty feet ahead of Molly.

We were preparing to ford the stream in an attempt to find easier walking on the far side when suddenly I heard Molly gasp. My eyes quickly picked up the source of her panic. There off to our right side some fifty feet away stood an immense grizzly bear. Apparently, the bear had been relaxing behind one of the numerous large boulders and had been startled by our approach.

I knew only too well how dangerous a startled grizzly could be. Panic now on our part could prove fatal. I immediately realized that somehow, I must keep Molly from running as well as the horses from panic. "Molly," I half whispered, "stay calm, don't run, stay calm, please don't run". In as near a normal voice as I could muster, I started talking to the giant beast (later Molly would kid me for saying "nice bear"). I began slowly moving closer to Molly. As I continued to talk, I reached out and took Molly's hand. Slowly we backed away from the threatening beast. The bear moved only slightly, apparently still trying to size us up.

Crossing the stream, as we had previously planned, still seemed the best way to quickly distance ourselves from the bear. Fortunately, the bear merely watched as we stepped into the stream. Ordinarily the icy water would have made us shiver but since we were already shaking with fear, the cold water went almost unnoticed. Apparently, our destiny was not to be that of a dinner for this mighty bruin.

From that point onward, we followed the advice of books I had read about bears. The books, as I remembered, strongly advised making plenty of noise while traveling in bear country to let the beasts know of your presence. I joked with Molly, "I guess that gives them time to get out of our way."

She laughed saying, "By all means let's go slow and make a big noise." I thought of the jingle bells that would later be sold as bear bells for that very purpose.

As soon as we felt secure that the bear was not following us, we stopped for lunch and to dry our socks. I built a small fire by the stream in a fairly open area where we could spot approaching danger. With the bear still fresh in our memory, we found ourselves frequently looking over our shoulders to insure there were no bears nearby. After our nerves calmed, we had a most pleasant lunch. The marmot's shrill whistles and the calls of the magpies provided musical accompaniment for the sound of the cascading stream.

By mid-afternoon, we reached the spot I had planned for us to camp that night. The site was about fifty yards from where I had set up camp for the Allen party. It was a beautiful spot, located in a clump of larches and aspens on the edge of a meadow.

The slightly elevated meadow was near the head of the valley. The confluence of the stream dubbed Paradise Creek was some seventy-five yards away at the tip of the Horseshoe Glacier. We were surrounded on three sides by the majestic mountains with the stream and lovely valley forest on the fourth.

Molly had become a real pro at setting up camp and she set about that task while I tended to the horses feed and water. We worked at cutting and clearing underbrush, removing troublesome rocks, and stringing a rope between two larches to support our tent. We then cut larch boughs to soften our pallets. Our housing needs having been met, we turned our attention toward building a fire circle and gathering firewood. Soon we had a cozy fire blazing away, piercing the virgin blue sky with wisps of delicious smoke.

"Logan where is the surprise you promised?" Molly again asked, as she had frequently while we had been setting up camp. I had promised to show her something special when we arrived at our camp site.

"Come, I'll show you," I said with pride. Making sure the fire was properly contained, we set off toward the place I knew as the Giant Steps. Without the benefit of a trail, we picked our way through some pretty thick underbrush and deadfall. It took about forty minutes to cover the half mile distance from our campsite to the spot.

"It's beautiful, what an unusual waterfall. I have never seen anything like it," were Molly's words upon viewing the huge blocks of stone with water cascading over them. "It looks like giant steps, doesn't it, Logan?" I couldn't help but laugh, knowing that name would stick. "I am sure that this place will be named the Giant Steps," I said, "perhaps Molly's Giant Steps," I mused.

Dusk was upon us as we rushed to retrace our way back to our campsite. A chilly wind was blowing up the valley, promising a brisk night. In spite of the noise we were making in our retreat, we caught sight of a wolf at the edge of the meadow. "Perhaps he will serenade us to sleep tonight," I laughed. Molly was not quite as amused. She said she already had her fill of threatening wildlife for the day.

As we sat beside the dancing campfire that night, polishing off the last of Molly's delicious dried venison stew, we talked about the peaks that surrounded us. These peaks until only recently had been nameless, some still remaining so. They appeared as awesome giants from our lowly vantage point. By far the most impressive silhouette against the moonlight southern sky was that of the mighty Mt. Temple.

Temple, as we called it, lay just across the valley, due south of our present position. "Do you think anyone will climb it soon, Logan?" Molly asked. "I mean it hasn't been climbed yet, has it?" she asked.

"No, Molly, it hasn't been climbed yet, and yes, I expect it will surely be climbed next season, if not by Allen, then by some other crazed adventurer. Allen's bunch had wanted to climb it last year but bad weather prevented it. They vowed to try again next year," I added.

"What about you, Logan, don't you want to be the first to climb Mt. Temple?" Molly asked.

Oh, how I wanted to boast and tell Molly that I had scaled it alone in 1976. "Sure, I would like to be the first, but maybe I will climb it someday," I added.

"Logan let's do it now, together!" she blurted out.

"You are kidding…aren't you?" were the first words out of

my mouth. Craig, this may give you some idea just how impetuous and wild this young woman was. Keeping up with her kept me young and provided for never a dull moment.

By now I should have been accustomed to Molly's impetuous nature, but still, I wasn't prepared for such a crazy suggestion. "Are you serious? We are talking about a nearly thirteen-thousand-foot peak that expert mountain climbers have not yet climbed. Do you really think you, a mere child, and this old man can do such a thing?" I responded.

"You bet yah, old man," she shot right back in her chipper voice. What spunk this gal has, I thought.

"Oh, the wonders of youth."

By now Molly had started the wheels turning. After all, I had climbed the mountain before and knew the easiest route. Shucks, I even had a map that had the route marked on it. The weather was great, not a cloud in the sky. Why not, I thought. "Let's go for it, my Irish lass. You will be the death of this old man," I jested as I excitedly agreed to undertake the challenge.

And so, at daybreak we were to begin the great Mt. Temple climb of 1897.

By now the fire had died down and the darkness of the wild country was upon us. Gazing up at the stars we realized that we had a strange treat that night as the Northern Lights were putting on a spectacular early season show for us. Knowing that we would need all our strength for the day ahead, we retreated to our tent early to get a good night's sleep. It was to be a wonderfully peaceful sleep. We later commented that there was probably no place we had ever been that was such a natural resting place.

The steam from the coffee pot gently rose toward the

ever-brightening sky. Above us to the southwest lay Sentinel Pass. The mountains framing the pass looked as though it was a golden crown in the sunrise. From all appearances, we were in for another grand day, a great day for adventure. I was confident enough that the horses would not wander off, so I let them pasture in the meadow. Hopefully the wild beasts wouldn't bother them.

For the climb we decided to dispense with many of the contents of our heavy rump sacks since we planned to return to our campsite by nightfall. Most of the food and all the cooking pots we placed in Molly's rump sack which we hoisted up on the limb of a large fir near the campsite. I carried the other pack with a minimum of emergency essentials and a bit of food for our lunch. One thing I did pack was our blankets and a tarp, just in case the weather did suddenly change, forcing us to bivouac on the mountain. Molly insisted on doing her part. She said she would carry the rope, not wanting to overload "the old man."

As we headed off to our destiny, I had no trouble picturing the trail in my head. It was as though my previous climb had just been yesterday. Actually, I was rather startled at how well I remembered the terrain, now devoid of a trail, other than that made by goats and sheep. Even more surprising was how easy it was to pick our way through the talus slope going up to Sentinel Pass.

My mind wandered back to my last trip up this slope. Then there was a well-worn path set off by a string of little rock cairns zigzagging up the slope in a connect the dots fashion. Now without the cairns, we just proceeded upward in a more direct, though somewhat steeper, path.

Moving upward through the talus, I pointed out to Molly the distinguished rock outcropping that led me to name the pass we were approaching. Tall rock formations which looked like chimneys stood above us. Others had thought this rock looked like a stone sentinel standing guard, hence the name Sentinel Pass. We marveled at how such precarious looking pieces of stone could maintain their stature. They looked to be at least seventy odd feet tall.

Suddenly off to our left, and not too distant, came the frightening hollow sound of cascading stones, at first just a few and then an increasing shower. These served to remind us of the ever-present danger of rock slides on such slopes. Fortunately, there had not been any recent snow to add to the threat of avalanches.

We set foot upon Sentinel Pass right at 10:00 am Though a bit strenuous, the hike up the slope had been rather pleasant. The scramble up to the pass had warmed us up and we had shed our heavy coats. Now upon the pass we found a much more foreboding environment. The wind was much stronger and it seemed quite a bit cooler, though it was not as bad as I remembered from my last trip.

It had been about the same time of year when I made that trip. Back then I had a thermometer with me and I remembered it registered twenty degrees. The wind had been blowing about the same velocity as the temperature and it had been spitting snow. Of course, then I had modern clothing. Well at least it wasn't that bad now, I thought.

Looking around the pass I immediately noticed the absence of signs that anyone had preceded us to that spot. Gone were the stone circles which had encircled the tents of those foolish souls who chose to camp in this most inhospitable spot. Gone too were the candy wrappers and bits of foil that always seemed so out of place. There was an absence of the well traveled trail I remembered seeing winding up the side of Mt. Temple to my left. Only the awesome assemblage of rocks remained as they continued their battle with the elements. We wondered at the great age of these mighty boulders.

My eye picked out one large rock in the center of the pass. Craig, it was under this rock, on a previous trip, that I had planned to leave you another gold coin. Unfortunately, on that trip when I had found the place to hide it, I discovered that the film container I had brought up there was not the one I had put the coin in. Instead of the coin, the container did indeed contain film. I later left that coin in a much easier place to get to, more on that later.

As we looked South from the pass, we had a great view of what was then called Desolation Valley. I remembered a most pleasant meadow through which a trail wound down to Moraine Lake and that it was another of my favorite picnic spots. Molly and I commented on what a poor choice of a name Desolation Valley was for what appeared as a lovely valley. I told her I was sure the name would probably be changed to a more descriptive name, like Larch Valley.

Following the map ingrained in my mind, I led Molly upward along the south slope of Mt. Temple. After some effort, we gained the col which rose up from Moraine Lake. We could now see the lake. It was like a beautiful jewel at our feet. The real challenge began there with the traverse of the South ridge up to the false summit.

We were no longer scrambling over boulders but were in

a much more serious concentrated climbing mode, rope and all. I was so thankful I had brought along an extra rope. What I wouldn't have given for my Merrill boots with those great Vibram soles. Alas, we had to make do with what we had; hobnailed boots, a length of rope, and an alpenstock each. Surely the hobnailed boots were a poor substitute for those Merrill's.

Unbeknown to Molly, I tied myself very loosely to the rope when I was climbing, while I tied her to me very securely when she was climbing. If I fell, I wanted the rope to pull free rather than take her down with me. Had Molly realized I was doing this; she undoubtedly would have been furious with me. I knew that whatever I did, I couldn't risk her life any more than necessary.

We were climbing one at a time. With each step upward, I carefully picked the route and then even more carefully belayed her as she climbed. Slowly we inched our way upward. As we approached the southern most summit, the false summit, the snow and ice became a serious problem. Up to that point, the snow and ice had been just patches, but now it was pretty much everywhere.

Several times our feet suddenly broke through the seemingly sound surface of the snow and we would bury ourselves to our knees. Soon we were on the glacier, the upper part of which we had to cross to gain the actual summit. With the final goal in site, a new surge of energy enabled us to kick steps in the crusty snow for footings. Molly was a real trooper. She never once complained or offered to turn back, despite the tremendous physical fatigue or the severe cold we were experiencing.

Fifty feet from the summit, I stood aside and invited her to take the lead to the top. "Molly, you, a mere woman, shall be the first on the head of this mighty beast," I joked. My watch showed it to be 1:22 PM as she claimed the mountain as hers. Imagine being the first to climb the highest summit yet climbed in the whole territory, what a great thing it was.

During the rush for the top, we had postponed lunch. We were now getting quite hungry. I quickly unpacked a blanket and the tarp. We wrapped ourselves in the blanket and huddled close together on the tarp. Our lunch consisted of some nearly frozen biscuits and bacon which was mighty tasty. Had it been warmer without the ferocious wind, this would have been a wonderful spot for a picnic.

A fire would also have been quite nice. The wind and the lack of firewood made this impossible. We were fortunate that the water in the canteen was not totally frozen. "My how good some hot tea would be, Logan," Molly lamented.

"Well yes, my dear, that would be nice, but of course what we really should have for such a special occasion is …."

Before I could finish, Molly chirped, "Champagne. Logan, is that all you ever want to drink?"

"Well no, just on special occasions. It seems I have quite a few of those occasions when I am with you," I added. I think at that comment she probably blushed a bit, but since our faces were already wind burned, I couldn't be sure.

"Logan, can you just imagine getting down from this mountain with spirits in us, why we would surely become spirits ourselves on the trip down. But you know … a sip or two of bubbly would be sort of tasty." We laughed at the thought of getting inebriated up there. I think the excitement and thin air already had us a bit light headed.

I must tell you that the view was beyond belief, even better than I remembered. You couldn't see Lake Louise since Mt. Fairview blocked the view, but there was little else that couldn't be seen from our lofty mountain. The beautiful wide Bow Valley lay off to our East. We could just faintly pick out the shiny CPR rails in the valley alongside the glistening ribbon of the Bow River. The sun light hit Castle Mountain just perfectly to show it off in all its majesty, some fifteen miles distant.

Smoke from fires in the valley sent wisps of smoke mingling with the low clouds accumulating over the valley. Moraine Lake was like a dark emerald, occasionally shining as rays of sunlight pierced the clouds. The mighty mountains forming the Valley of Ten Peaks off to the south seemed somehow diminished in size when viewed from our lofty perch. The prettiest view though of all, we agreed, was at our feet to the north, that being the aptly named Paradise Valley. From our vantage point, some four thousand feet above this valley the stream which ran the length of the valley was but a hair on this fine valley's head. Try as we might, we were not able to quite make out our tent.

With great excitement we undertook the task of constructing the first cairn on the peak. Gathering and stacking stones in the rarefied frigid air left us breathless. We knew it was the custom to leave something on or in the cairn at the top of a mountain. When we had planned our trip, we had not considered conquering any mountains so a flag or other such mementos were not brought. Finally, Molly suggested that we leave the linen napkin our lunch had been wrapped in. The white linen napkin had the CPR logo on it. We penciled the initials MJ & LB 1897 on it and placed it in the cairn.

We stood briefly admiring our little monument; Molly

mentioned how she wished a photographer were there to capture a film of the occasion, fearing no one would believe we had accomplished such a feat. We speculated at who would find our napkin and at the astonishment it was surely to cause.

Since the icy wind was now cutting through us, we quickly said goodbye to our edifice and started the treacherous descent. Again, I had Molly securely roped and had her lead the descent while firmly belaying her. The descent proved much more nerve racking than our accent. We descended just past the false summit through the worst of the snow and ice. After having passed this area, we moved with greater ease. We had regained our confidence, which we were soon to learn was a mistake.

As I was descending over one of the last patches of ice, I heard the sound of falling rocks below me. My first thought was that Molly might have slipped and I quickly jerked around to see. Just as I turned my left foot slipped on the patch of loose rock upon which I had been standing. Before I knew it, I was sliding down the slope.

The miraculous placement of one large boulder was all that prevented a surely fatal fall for me and perhaps Molly. She was still lightly tied to the rope. Also fortunate was the amount of slack in the rope. It had prevented Molly from being pulled with me. Regaining my senses, I found that much to my amazement, other than a few scrapes and bruises I seemed fine. The only loss appeared to be my alpenstock, which now lay far below. I left it there and said a prayer of thanks that I was not laying there beside it.

Molly appeared more shaken by the fall than I. After promising to be more careful and pointing out that the worst was surely behind us, I was able to coax her into resuming the decent. We reached Sentinel Pass without further incident. Our feet were now hurting from the rocky terrain. The decent of the steep talus slope down to the valley still lay ahead of us. Eager to end what was now becoming an ordeal, we quickly pressed on with the descent to the valley floor.

Quite fully exhausted, we finally arrived back at camp. My watch showed it to be six o'clock. We had made it to the top of the world and back in twelve hours, pretty good, hell, pretty incredible I thought to myself. As we collapsed we were almost too tired to think about eating … almost but not quite.

Before we had started our trip from Lake Louise, I had decided to use this trip as an occasion to play one of my pranks on Molly. I had decided to surprise her with a little magic conjured up with some of my left over modern technology. I still had three freeze dried meals left in my stash. Recently I had tried one and found it to still be quite tasty, despite all the plus or minus of the years. The idea of slipping one of these to Molly, unexpectedly, seemed like a fun thing to do.

The timing for my pratical joke couldn't have been better. I knew she was tired and probably would not want to cook. "Molly, I will do dinner tonight…maybe some TV dinners, ok?" I offered up.

"What was that about dinner?" she asked.

"Oh, I just said I would do dinner," I commented, this time leaving out the other part. "Molly, you go into the tent and lie down a moment and I will call you when I get it ready," I offered. She took me up on my offer without much resistance.

It didn't take very long to boil a pot of water, so in about fifteen minutes I was ready to dish up dinners of beef stroganoff and chicken and rice. After carefully hiding the wrappers, I took a large cooking spoon and banged it on a skillet to anounce dinner. I heard a yell from the tent, "Logan, is there a bear?"

"No, my dear, just dinner is served," I said.

"Quit joking Logan," was her response.

I responded with, "Come quick before it gets cold,"

"Quit joking and call me when its ready," was her reply.

"Its ready now, no kidding," I shot back.

As Molly popped her head out of the tent I began serving up the delicious smelling dinners. "My what smells so good?" Molly commented as she looked at the food. "Logan, what is this?" she asked, obviously quite puzzled.

"Well let's see, a couple of my favorite things…here we have beef stroganoff and then here we have chicken and rice," I said, proudly pointing at my instant meals.

"But…. but, how? This isn't possible. No, Logan, really what is this? Where are all the pots?" She asked while gazing at the lone steaming pot of water on the fire; that being the only evidence of cooking left in sight.

"Eat it before it gets cold," I implored her. With some degree of hesitancy, she sampled both dishes. "How is it?" I asked.

"Wonderful," she commented. Well I knew that was not entirely true since no freeze-dried food I had ever eaten was as good as fresh. Immediately her amazement was reconfirmed with another round of questions. My response, "Well, Molly, see I can cook given the right circumstances, but don't expect me to do this again, no, not in a hundred years," I laughed.

"Bon apatite, Molly. Seriously, someday I will show you how to cook this," I said, having fully enjoyed my mischief.

The excitement of the day and physical toll it had taken led us straight to bed right after dinner. We lay together, warm in each others arms. Sleep reached for us as the wind sang through the trees above. The wind and the sound of the distant waterfall were the finishing touches to a wonderful day and another night of delightful sleep there in Paradise Valley.

Sometime in the early hours of morning, the ruffling of the tent flaps told me that the wind had picked up. Sunrise confirmed what I had suspected. The weather that had been so fine the past few days had changed. Pellets of sleet greeted us as we emerged from our tent. The white pellets were rather unusual. They were not sleet but not quite snow either. To me they seemed like beads of white Styrofoam.

Concern that this might be the start of a more severe storm, led us to forgo breakfast and to rapidly strike camp. This beautiful valley could turn treacherous if we became stranded without food. Oddly, when I camped here in 1976, I left under similar weather conditions. Then as now, packing up a tent in the wind and snow was not an easy task. The large tent being partially frozen seemed considerably heavier and more cumbersome. At least I had Molly to help me this time, I thought. We rounded up our two trusty horses. After quickly packing the gear on them we set out.

As we neared Saddleback Pass, the ground was covered with the funny looking snow. Then, just as it started to snow even harder, we saw a break in the clouds to the North. Soon the sun peaked out and only snow flurries remained. With the appearance of the sun and the mid-day warming, the trail became quite soggy. Our feet were soaked and cold. We debated building a fire to dry out but elected to push on. We couldn't wait to get to the Chalet and some hot tea.

We were two tired, damp, and hungry folks as we arrived back at the Chalet by late afternoon during tea time. Cookie greeted us with hot tea and cakes. These we much appreciated, but I couldn't resist asking if she had any beef stroganoff. Molly busted out laughing at my silliness. She proceeded to tell Cookie that she had found a replacement for her if ever she decided to quit. I only laughed, saying "In your dreams, Cookie, I think the altitude has left Molly a might touched in the head."

"Tell me about your trip," Cookie begged. We had vowed to keep our conquest to ourselves, deciding rather to await the response from Samuel Allen next season when he found our cairn at the top of what he thought was to be his mountain. And so, we responded by telling her about the bear and that otherwise it had been a pleasant relaxing trip, nothing too exciting, ha-ha. Molly did tell Cookie to get me to show her how I made beef stroganoff. I commented, "I only do that for special people on special occasions."

12. Changes With The Century — A New Chalet

It all started with a big meeting. Any time the CPR calls a meeting with its managers, they know something big is up. In these days, meetings seem to be reserved only for big deals. It was just such a big deal meeting that Molly was summoned to. In September of last year, 1898, Molly was requested to travel to Ottawa for a meeting with Bill Wilson and others. She was a bit nervous about it all, having never been summoned to CPR headquarters before. I tried to assure her, telling her there was nothing to be worried about. They just probably wanted to reward her efforts.

I met Molly's train on her return. From the Cheshire Cat smile she greeted me with, it was obvious something great was afoot. She poured forth her exciting news. With the coming new century and the prosperous tourist business, the CPR had decided to celebrate in a grand way. They planned to add a whole string of new hotels.

The part of these plans of particular interest to Molly was

the plan for a completely new Chalet at Lake Louise. Though it was not to be the grand Chateau of the future, it would be its parent. In a way it is a bit sad, I will miss our little building, but as they say, time marches on. Molly went on to report that the plans also called for a great addition to the Banff Springs and a new hotel over at Field.

The plan given was to have all the new hotels open and ready for guests in the summer of 1900. Everyone, myself included, agreed it would be one huge challenge to pull it off in such a compressed time frame. In more modern times, such an endeavor would have taken years of planning, but no, not in these times. Molly had volunteered my help in overseeing work there on the Chalet. Bill Wilson apparently thought that to be a great idea. I was again flattered to be included in such an exciting project.

The CPR had already selected architects for the projects and had put them to work. The architect chosen for the Lake Louise Chalet was Bruce Dillon. He was from back east, Philadelphia, and well known at the time for his outstanding Victorian buildings. His most noted building to date was the Grand Hotel in New York.

Mr. Dillon faced a major challenge with the Chalet commission. There was a stipulation in his contract that he had to design the new facility so that it could be completed before the existing Chalet was demolished. It just wouldn't do to lose the summer business in 1899. I thought that was a good idea as well. We could keep our little homelike accommodations for another year.

It had been two weeks since that meeting in Ottawa and Molly is like an expectant mother, a mother expecting triplets, no less. Ever since she came back from her meeting, all she has talked about is how grand the new hotel will be. "Logan, Bill Wilson has said to plan on one hundred guest rooms, can you imagine that, why that is more than five times what we have now. I shall have to hire at least six new chamber maids and more kitchen help as well; I am sure" she added.

I told her that obviously it would take a larger staff and assured her that she was most capable of handling the new operation. My big concern was to make sure that new staff accommodations had been properly addressed in the new plans.

Molly had recommended that I work with Mr. Dillon and the builder to ensure the CPR's expectations are met. What she really was about, I suspect, was making sure she got what she wanted. It had been one thing to do modest buildings with this fiery lass. I fear such a major project will be a whole new kettle of fish; still I am looking forward to the new Chalet.

October 22nd rolled around and it appeared as though Molly and I would be spending a bit of the winter in Ottawa working with Bruce Dillon. That should make for an interesting winter, especially since it would be the farthest, I had been since going back in time. While having some reservations over traveling that far, I did look forward to sharing the experience with Molly and in planning such an exciting project.

We arrived in Ottawa on November 10th. The weather was clear but quite cold, perhaps 20 degrees or so. Our second night in town, Bill Wilson took us to a fine restaurant called La'Que. We had a grand meal. For accommodations, we were staying in one of the CPR's hotels, which was a spectacular establishment. Despite all this grandeur, I would still rather be back in my little cabin in the mountains.

Molly and I are just back from our second meeting with Bruce. I dare say he was ill prepared to be working for such a pert young woman as my Molly. She had to set him straight on a couple of important points right away. I think he now has little doubt where the main Dining Room should be positioned. She also set him straight on how the Grand Sitting Room (or lounge) should be laid out. One of the grand features of the new building is the marvelous long colonnade porch extending all across the front of the hotel where people could sit under shelter and take in the view.

All things considered; our meeting went well. It seems as though construction should get underway in April. The schedule is quite ambitious. If we are very, very lucky, the construction should complete by years end. I stressed that the only way to achieve such an aggressive schedule would be to have a large number of well-trained construction workers and no delays getting materials. I was ensured by Bill Wilson that the CPR understood our needs and would supply a contractor and materials to make this happen. Even so, November and December will be tough winter months. I have my doubts if the schedule can be kept, but we shall see.

It's now January and we are back in Banff for the rest of the winter. On the way back, we stopped off in Calgary for a few days visit with Molly's sister and her family. That young son of theirs, Ben is really a pistol. It made me a bit sad that Molly and I didn't have a little tyke. The stop-over gave us our first opportunity to meet with the builder.

The builder, a Mr. Dickens, is from Calgary and he seems like a decent sort. His selection is oddly typical. Even though he had never done a project of this size he was selected, undoubtedly, because he is the cousin of one of the big CPR muckety mucks from Montreal. Like I always say, the right connections never hurt. Hopefully his CPR connections will not present too much of a problem for Molly getting what she wants. My biggest worry right now is whether Dickens will be able to get enough qualified help. With all the new hotel work underway at that same time in Field and at the Banff Springs will require bringing in workers from other areas.

Due in no small part to my persistence, we broke ground on March 28, 1899. Dickens had wanted to begin on Monday, April 1st but I nixed that. Somehow starting such a grand project on April fool's day just didn't seem prudent. Dickens allowed as how he was superstitious about starting a project on a Friday so we settled on Thursday, March 28th.

For ground breaking we invited all the folks from Laggan and a few from Banff. Taking a queue from my old pal Bill, we did a grand explosion for a ground breaking. This sort of seemed natural. A large tree stump was in the center of the new building site so we decided to dynamite it for our ground breaking.

It is now early June. If Bruce Dillon thought Molly was a hand-full, I can only imagine what builder Dickens thinks of her. I suspect he is pulling out what little hair he has left. He sure got a good taste of fire from my red-haired Irish lass today. It seems he had failed to order enough windows so he was going to put only one window in some of the fancier rooms, wow, when Molly got finished with him, he sure regretted having such a foolish notion. I dare say Dickens will not make a mistake like that again. The rumor has it that he complained to his connection at the CPR head office and was politely told

Molly was the boss. I don't expect we shall have any more such problems with Mr. Dickens.

August has arrived and to say things are hectic is an understatement. As Molly put it today, "How do they expect me to take care of guests with all this construction mess? Those *** construction workers should have been made to do this work in the winter, I am just fed up with the mess and noise," she exploded and then added, "besides, I understand that the new addition at the Banff Springs is going to be built over the winter, so why not here?"

In one of my more stupid moves I attempted to explain. I was feeling a bit sorry for Dickens and so I said, "Well, Molly dear, in the first place as bad as winter is in Banff, it is much worse here, and besides you should look at this as a challenge."

"Challenge! I'll give you challenge. If that blankety blank—Dickens doesn't repair my road by weeks end, I will have his head. You can challenge him with that," she expounded.

Having been a builder I was somewhat sympathetic to what poor Dickens had to endure and as delicately as possible I tried to keep the peace between these two strong willed persons.

We were starting into October and all the tourists had gone. I was amazed that despite all the problems encountered, the new hotel was really coming along quite well. Last night, Molly and I lit a fire in the new lobby fireplace to test it out. It worked fine, never smoked the least bit. We shall complement Dickens on it tomorrow. Now that things have calmed down a bit, Dickens has regained favor with Molly and my job as a peacemaker has become somewhat easier.

Just as it seemed things couldn't be going better with our construction, the weather dealt us a low blow. It has been snowing off and on for the past two days. Presently we have about eight inches on the ground. The wagons that were carrying the plaster materials up from the station at Lagan had been unable to get up the mountain. As a result, the plaster operations have ground to a halt. Of all the years to have winter start early, this is not the one.

The weather has also prevented a number of the workers from making it up the mountain. As far as I am concerned, a little snow is not a good excuse for not coming to work. Fortunately, many of our workers are residing in a tent city behind the hotel so they certainly have been able to make it to work. If this weather doesn't break soon though, most of the work will stop, waiting on supplies.

As if the weather delay was not enough to worry about, Molly had just received word that the Prince was coming in June to take part in the grand opening celebration for both the Chalet and the Banff Springs addition. Almost immediately after the visit was announced, nearly all of the new rooms were booked, a few rooms have even been booked for dates in May.

I guess there is nothing like working under pressure. At least we don't have to worry about all the bureaucratic red tape. There will be no hoops to jump through to get permission to occupy the new building.

The original goal was to complete all construction before the really bad winter weather set in. The plan was to then come back in late April to fit out the rooms for a June 1st opening. With the weather screwing up our schedule, Molly was quite worried. In a recent plea for help she lamented "Logan, I just love it when you come up with solutions to the most difficult of problems. Now would be a real good time for you to do that, don't you think?"

Though I still felt most of the construction could wrap up before December, I doubted the rooms could be furnished, what with paint and all. One major thing we had going for us was that Dickens finally got the heating plant working properly. The only way I could see to pull off the opening was if we were to work through the winter to finish and set up the rooms. As soon as I convinced Molly that my plan of winter work was feasible, she set about feverishly trying to expedite the furnishings. It was critical that they be brought up to the hotel before the winter snows made the road from the station in Laggan too treacherous.

We both agreed that in order to set up the rooms over the winter, we would need some help. Molly had a hunch that the young married couple Sarah and Tom Dash who had worked at the Chalet over the summer would help. They had recently left to winter in Calgary. She promptly sent off a telegram to them promising them good pay and a fun winter. Fortunately, they responded back that they would be glad to help out.

In addition to the furnishings, we would have to bring up supplies to last the four of us for the winter. Having wintered in Laggan, I knew sort of what to expect from old man winter. Though the winter weather was typically a bit better in both Calgary and Banff than Lake Louise, the scenery there by the lake all covered in snow was just spectacular. I was really looking forward to a winter's worth of it.

I talked to Gray Ogle, the Laggan Stationmaster, and

arranged for the loan of a team of his huskies and a good sled. I figured we could use the sled to get about a bit and to bring small items up from the station over the winter. For me, dog sledding had always seemed an exciting form of transportation ever since I first tried it. Molly loved dog sledding as well. She felt the dogs would be good company over the winter.

It was to be a while though, before we would need the dogs and sled. After that snow in October, we didn't have any appreciable snow again until December 8th. Despite a few problems, surprisingly, Dickens had most of his work finished when the December snow hit. That snow signaled the end of the years' work for him. He has now knocked off work until April. Hopefully he would return as scheduled to complete the porches and a few other odds and ends.

We were blessed by having received most of our furnishings prior to the December 8th snow. The crates of furniture are everywhere, filling much of the lobby as well as some of the back rooms. These rooms were going to be the last to be set up. Our little group was settling in for the winter. "Logan, I must confess, despite the hard work we have ahead of us this winter, I think this will be one of the most fun winters I have ever had. I have always wanted to experience Lake Louise through winter and now I am to have my chance. It will be so special to have this magnificent place to ourselves, well almost," she said.

"You know I believe Tom and Sarah will be good company, don't you think?" Molly asked.

"Yes, I think they will be. I must confess, I have been hankering to spend the winter up here for a long time. It's great that our work is giving us the excuse to do it. When I think of all the fun we shall have, well just let it snow, let it snow, let it snow," I cheerfully announced.

"I second that," she added with a big smile.

The biggest concern we had now were the beds. Originally, they were to come by mid November. When they hadn't arrived, we began to worry that we wouldn't get them that winter. It would be hard to set up rooms without the beds. After several frantic telegrams, we finally got confirmation that the shipment would be in on the December 12th train. Hopefully we won't have another big snow within the next few days so we can get them up the mountain. I teased Molly, telling her that we might have to tie the beds to the dog sled. We tried to picture the scene of us mushing the dogs while atop a mattress.

It was December 17th and as I told Molly, the luck of the Irish was with her. We now have beds. It had been a struggle though, taking a crew of CPR rail hands several days to haul all those beds up the mountain using only two wagons. Getting the bed frames and mattresses into the rooms will keep Tom and me busy for a few weeks. As soon as we get a few rooms done, Molly and Sarah can start bringing in the smaller furnishings and then putting out the blankets, bedspreads, and pillows that have already arrived and are stored in the lobby.

Christmas of 1899 was without a doubt the best one I have had since being back in these times. A couple of days after the beds arrived, I thought we needed a bit of a break, at least my back did. "Enough work for the day," I said, "Molly, we have more important things to do," I said.

"O yah, and what might that be, kind sir," she quipped.

"Well I mean we must go and collect a Christmas tree and a Yule log as well."

"But Logan, Christmas is a week away," she said.

"Don't care, can't ever get a tree too soon. You know we must get to the Christmas tree lots before the trees are all picked over," I quipped.

She laughed even though she obviously had no idea what a Christmas tree lot was.

"You are serious, you are really going out and cut a huge log and drag it back?" she asked.

"Oh yes, great tradition, we shall find a nice dead tree for the log while we are out getting the Christmas tree, then I will go back and cut her down and size up a suitable log.

"You must let me pick the Christmas tree, Logan," Molly admonished as she wrapped her scarf tightly around her neck.

"Long as it's a nice big one, my Irish lass, it just wouldn't do to have some puny tree in a Dining Room as grand as ours."

"Logan, you know me better than that, when did I ever skimp on anything," she said quite felicitously.

"Hop on board the sleigh for Santa land," I joked as I hitched up our reindeer dogs.

After some, and I do mean some, looking we found what she considered to be just the right tree. It seems the time it takes for a woman to pick out a Christmas tree is one thing that hasn't changed in a century. The tree was a 10' blue spruce. Just as I had told her, I found a suitable dead tree for the Yule log. The next day I would drag it back and cut it up for a nice Yule log.

Arriving back at the Chalet, we found Tom and Sarah waiting with some great hot cider, which really hit the spot. The cider was especially good after I spiked it with a little bit of rum from the gentlemen's parlor. The happy four of us spent the rest of that afternoon and well into the evening decorating our tree with all sorts of home-made decorations that we could conjure up.

We made popcorn and strung it. I had heard of this vintage decoration, though I had never used it before. We played a game of who could come up with the most unusual decoration. Sarah won, having taken a salt shaker and turned it into a snowman. My decoration was pretty good as well though. It was an owl made out of a pine cone. Molly deemed it quite suitable to me, allowing as how she said I looked a lot like an owl.

"Well, Logan, it's Christmas Eve now, when are you going to light that huge Yule log? You surely will give Dickens fireplace a good test with that huge log. Mind you don't burn the hotel down with your big fire stick," she added.

"Never fear, my dear. Before you is a fine burning log which I shall use to christen this grand fireplace," I said while maneuvering the four foot long log carefully to the back of the great fireplace. "Yes sir, this baby should last all Christmas day," I pronounced upon lighting the great log.

"Boys and girls, shall we sing Christmas carols?" I quipped while launching into a rendition of Winter Wonderland, (so what if I was a bit ahead with this song, it felt right, so I sang it) the others listened to my wretched voice singing one of my favorites. Knowing this lovely melody was about forty years early, I brushed off their requests to teach them that song.

I was especially looking forward to Christmas morning. I had picked out one special gift for Molly. I couldn't wait to see the expression on her face as she discovered it, since it was especially big. The large crate had arrived back in November, along with the other furniture for the new hotel. I had planned it that way so that it would be easy for me to conceal. I placed it there with the other crates stored in the lobby. I had to get Tom to help me move the crate in by the tree after Molly retired to bed. I had decided that the crate was just too large to wrap so I just put a big ribbon and bow on it with a little note: To Molly, From Santa.

I had positioned myself in the door to the kitchen so as to have a good view of the tree and Molly as she made her way through the parlor to the dining room. "Logan, what in God's green earth is that huge crate doing by the tree," Molly asked. "Logan, what have you done?" she exclaimed as she read the tag.

"Not me, says it's from some fellow named Santa," I mused.

"Santa my hinder, what is in this monster of a box and how did you ever get it in here?" she quizzed.

"You know, Molly, I have heard that Santa has this big, I mean, huge sled…," I joked.

"I have never had such a big present," she exclaimed while imploring me to get a pry bar and help her open it.

"Yes, my dear we must open it at once as it may be something you might want to use on this special day." I had prepared the necessary tools; a hammer and pry bar were stashed behind the box. By now, Tom and Sarah, having heard Molly's shrieks had arrived for the big opening. After removing a few boards, Molly recognized what it was. "Oh, Logan, an organ, how wonderful!" she exclaimed while hugging yours truly in a most gracious manner.

"My dear, I just knew when I heard you play that little pump organ at the Congregational Church in Banff, that you would like to have one of them for your own and now you do," I explained.

"Craig, yes this is yet another strange twist of fate, as you are aware you and your mother have just such an organ, an antique 1890 model that I bought from my uncle and refinished years ago. In this incredible insane world, I can only wonder if somehow the organ you now have and this one might be one and the same, God only knows."

We played the organ for hours. When her legs got tired of pumping, she set in my lap and played while I pumped it. Between organ renditions of about all the songs we knew, we watched the snow gently drift down, removing the last evidence of sleigh tracks from the day before. As for me, Molly gave me a new Kodak for Christmas. Certainly, this was no camcorder, but it was a fine gift and one I enjoyed. I took a number of photos that day that I hope will develop well.

New Year's Eve found us toasting the new century with the finest champagne in the hotel. At midnight we did the traditional thing of opening the door and letting the New Year in. New Year's Day I was a bit hung over from the champagne the night before. I did a bit of snow removal, though not too much. The spirits from the previous evening as well as the desires of a certain young lady had taken their toll on my body. By late afternoon I had recovered enough to suggest a skating party with Molly, Sarah, and Tom on a little spot I cleared on the lake. Though Molly and I are not bad skaters, Sarah is a great one, easily skating rings around the rest of us. A spot of hot buttered rum and delicious dinner finished off a wonderful first day of the new century.

We'll all play and no work gets one in trouble and so it's

back to the work of getting the rooms ready for guests. As we set up each room, we decided to name them. The four of us took turns choosing names from the natural surroundings. One of my favorites was a name Molly chose, Lakes Lure. Again, I marveled to myself at the uncanny coincidence of the name and thinking back to my days in the mountains of North Carolina by another Lake Lure.

To say the year 1900 was like any other year was far from the truth. In fact, 1900 was a year where it seemed anything was possible. The sky was the limit. With everyone having thoughts like that, you can only imagine what was happening in our already booming mountain setting.

Besides our grand new Chalet, other big news was announced in February. It was finally decided that the park boundaries were being expanded to take in all of Laggan and Lake Louise. Hopefully that will help protect the game from the increasing number of big game hunters. Perhaps the prospectors that I fear have been sniffing around my digs will now have to look elsewhere.

With the coming of spring, Dickens returned to finish his work as promised. Molly made sure all was to her liking. At last he came to the final portion of his work. It was the sad task of tearing down our beloved little Chalet. I made sure we had plenty of photographs to remember it by. As I keep telling myself, it is now a new century and with it, out with the old and in with the new as time marches onward.

13. Bankhead

Craig, I have been a real slacker about keeping up this diary these past couple of years. Hopefully I can do better in the future. A lot has happened since I wrote about the new Chalet, too much to tell you all. I will just start by telling you it is now 1903 and many changes are taking place in the park.

It was one of these changes that led me to Bankhead. I well remembered visiting this intriguing spot on one of my last trips in 1978. Then Bankhead was a ghost town. All that remained were the ruins of an old mining operation. Oddly, back then, the old concrete walls and rusty metal scattered about held a strange fascination for me. The town had been placed on a beautiful site below mighty Cascade Mountain, just a short distance from the outfall of Lake Minnewanka.

As I found myself being swept up in building this mining operation, I had very mixed feelings about it. It was a great disappointment for me to see such a lovely site spoiled with an ugly mining operation. Then too, I knew the mining operation and the town itself were destined to have a very short life. Helping to build a place I knew only from the ruins was a strange and somewhat sad adventure.

But let me back up and explain how Bankhead came to be. At this time the railroads were all important, not only in the Canadian Rockies, but just about everywhere. They were our airplanes and more. Nearly all long-distance travel and commerce depended on the iron ribbons with their smoking iron horses chucking across the countryside. Rapidly the railroads were being improved. One major improvement was the transformation from wood burning locomotives to those using the more efficient fuel, coal.

These great iron horses had a ravenous appetite for coal. Obviously, this led to a huge demand for the black stuff. Coal deposits or seams had been discovered on the flanks of Cascade Mountain in the early 1890s. It seemed perfectly natural for the CPR to set up a mine there, even though the site lay squarely in the middle of the newly created National Park. What a sacrilege this would have been in the 1970s, but at this time the mining operation was ok. It was even considered to be a viable tourist attraction.

A small coal mining operation was started a couple of years earlier in Anthracite, a little town ten miles or so away from Banff, going east towards Calgary. The mine there couldn't produce enough high-grade coal. From the geologist's reports, the quality of coal at Cascade was superior to that at Anthracite. The CPR's vision was to create a large modern mining operation, complete with a modern little town to support it. This mining operation was to be called Bankhead.

Having known about Bankhead from the 1970s, I had thought about it from time to time, wondering when and how it would come about. The first I heard of Bankhead back in these times was during a fireside chat at the Chalet during the fall of 1902. "Logan, what do you think about that mining town going up down near Banff?" Bill Armbrush asked.

Bob Hamilton responded before I got a chance, "Sure is a shame to spoil that beautiful little lake there with a dirty mining town."

"You mean Lake Minnewanka?" I asked.

"Sure, they are going to cut timber all along the South side of the lake for mine shoring and heaven knows how many buildings they are going to build; I hear a whole town. Say, Logan, how come you aren't down there hammering nails?" Bill asked. "Lord knows, they could use someone as good at building as you are," he added.

Bob then offered his thoughts, "They say it is going to be the biggest and most modern mine in all Alberta. I think they want to show it off to tourists. The CPR is trying to recruit people to build the town and the mine buildings next summer. They say the town and mine will be called Bankhead."

I finally responded that it all sounded rather interesting to me.

It wasn't long after that evening that I received a telegram from my buddy, Tom Orchard, a would-be contractor, who had gotten in good with the CPR. He asked me to come to a meeting in Banff. Sure enough, the subject was Bankhead. Tom wanted to enlist my building skills in the construction of some of the mine buildings.

Concrete, then a relatively new material, was going to be used for some of the buildings. Tom asked me if I had ever worked with concrete. I couldn't help but laugh. He asked, "Logan, what's so funny?"

I couldn't help but have a little fun with the question and so I responded with, "Do you really think concrete will be strong enough to last?" All the time knowing full well that concrete would be about all that would last at Bankhead.

He said he hoped so. I just smiled.

I was sure that Molly would have a fit at the idea of my being gone for six months, especially during the summer season. This project seemed like such a challenging thing to do that I determined to do my best to convince Molly. Much to my surprise, she thought it quite exciting as well. Like me she was not pleased with the impact the project would have on the land. I think one reason she was so willing for me to get involved with Bankhead was her belief that I could help limit the damage to the environment. That was certainly one of the reasons I wanted to participate.

Molly promised to come down and visit me frequently. Likewise, I told her that I would line up a good crew chief, who could take over occasionally so that I could sneak off to Lake Louise. With her blessing began my Bankhead adventure. It was to be an adventure filled with hard work, excitement, and tragedy.

A small mining operation had been started there the past year. The site was about five miles from Banff on the West bank of the Bow River. A single, main shaft had been driven into the East face of Cascade Mountain, just below Lake Minnawaka. With the rapid expansion of the mine, living accommodations were needed for the miners. A modern little town was quickly being planned.

The mining operation was to be different from that in most mines. The veins of coal ran up the mountain so the shafts were to proceed upward with the coal seams. In most coal mines, shafts led downward to deeper depths. The coal was to be mined above the main shaft in chambers or rooms as they were called. The coal would then be allowed to fall down on a wooden bulkhead, which could be opened to fill the waiting mine cars below. In theory at least, it sounded like a pretty efficient way to get at the coal. In reality it was highly dangerous.

When I arrived, a few small buildings such as a machine shop, dining hall, and lamp-house building had already been built. Little houses were springing up like so many prairie-dog mounds. My assignment was to put together a crew and to build the powerhouse. While I worked on the powerhouse, Tom Orchard's crew was to build the boiler house. The boilers were essential to provide steam to run the generators. The plan was to have them both complete and in operation by the end of the summer of 1903. Both buildings were critical to the mining operation since it would be impossible to advance the shafts very far without the power for ventilation and to run the breaker machinery.

Tom and I decided to challenge our crews to a race to see which building could be finished first. Our start date was April 3, 1903. My crew consisted of four stone layers; two sawmill workers, about twenty railroad workers, and four good carpenters. Poorly trained and inexperienced as my crew was, I felt they were better than Tom's crew. I was confident my crew could win the challenge race.

Bad luck plagued us early in the project. No sooner had we finished digging the first footing than an April snowstorm dumped six inches of snow in the footings. The warming temperatures over the next few days allowed work to resume quickly. It was also good fortune that I had some strong laborers. The mixing and placing of the concrete was a hard task. The cement, aggregate, and water were mixed in mortar boxes by the Cantonese laborers. The concrete was then transported by wheelbarrow to the point where it was poured into the footings or forms. Reinforcing steel for the concrete was largely unheard of and I refrained from suggesting we use it. As crude as the concrete was, I knew it would stand the test of time pretty well.

Amazingly, the large generators and other large equipment which had to be placed early in construction arrived by rail right on time. All was going well. This changed suddenly on May 8th when a careless worker let a trash fire get out of control near the main lumberyard. The new lumber burned rapidly in a spectacular fire. Even the pumper truck that had been quickly summoned from Banff did little good. Soon smoldering gray ash was all that was left where the lumber had been.

Even before the ashes had cooled, I sent men to the sawmill near Castle Mountain to scavenge up what material they had. This was of some use, but I had to wait for a full re-supply and to have some special sized timbers re-cut. In less than a week though, we were framing once again. Soon everyone recognized that our goal of generating power by August 1st probably would be bettered by a week or more, in spite of the fire. Spirits again ran high.

Arriving with the generators was a young man named Robert Collins. Robert came from Ottawa, where he had worked as an electrician, a new trade at the time. I had met Robert the previous year while he was on assignment in Banff working on the Banff Springs Hotel. He was involved in correcting some faulty wiring put in by an unskilled tradesman. I was quite impressed with this twenty-two-year-old lad. After chasing the summer girls (a term given to the single young tourist ladies) last year, Robert found someone special.

Robert was sweet on the daughter of the manager at the Banff Springs. Molly and I thought that they made a wonderful couple. They were so young, so happy, and so much in love. At the town fair the past month, Robert and Ginny had won the couple's sack race. I had never seen two people more perfectly matched than this pair. Just being around them made me feel young again.

One Saturday in mid June when Molly came down from Lake Louise. I suggested to her that we invite Robert and Ginny to join us for a picnic. We took them to our favorite spot near Banff. It was a wonderful meadow on the east side of Stony Squaw Mountain. The meadow presented a grand view of the Bow Valley and the little village of Banff below. I fondly remembered camping along the edge of the meadow. One special remembrance of camping there was hearing the wailing of the trains at night as they made their way through the valley below.

Following a most delightful lunch that Ginny and Molly had prepared, Robert and Ginny opted for a walk up to the top of the little mountain. Molly and I chose to relax in the sun. About two hours later we lay there dozing on our blanket, with Molly's parasol shading the sun from our faces. Suddenly we were wakened by yelling. We saw Robert and Ginny running toward us. At once we envisioned the worst, some mad bruin in hot pursuit. Such a prospect quickly panicked Molly who set about fleeing down the mountain. Not one to panic quite so quickly, I opted to set eyes on the beast before fleeing.

We were soon to learn that it was not a grizzly. No, it seemed that Robert had taken the opportunity to propose marriage to Ginny. She was overcome with excitement. Anxious to tell us the news, she took off running. Robert asked Molly what she thought Ginny's father, Roger, would say when he asked for her hand in marriage. Robert was well aware that Molly had known Ginny's father for a number of years. Molly's comment was so typical of my spunky lady; "Well, if the old chap isn't tickled to death, I will kick his hinders," she said. Molly's wit with words never failed to floor me.

Molly and I were delighted for the couple and eagerly looked forward to the excitement of the wedding. They set the date for September 5th. The wedding date was to coincide with the completion of our work at Bankhead. With the power house well underway and the little town of Bankhead taking shape nicely, everything appeared to be going great.

It was a few days after that picnic in June that I was approached by Reverend Gray, the minister of the Congregational Church in Banff. He wanted to know if I would help in building a church for Bankhead. I quickly volunteered, realizing quite well how important a church would be to the fledgling community. I also told him that I knew of an ideal spot. The site I remembered was from the remains of Bankhead as I explored in 1978.

A beautiful spot it was too. The knoll had a commanding view of the valley. You could see mine buildings below and yet be separated by distance from the dirt and grime that went with coal mining. The site was an outpost of the former forest where many large trees still remained. Due in no small part to my efforts, the grove had been reserved from the fate of becoming mine timbers. I vowed to continue my efforts to preserve the trees around the building.

Above the site was the first of the residential part of the town. The church would sit near the road running from the mine to the town. Reverend Gray's comment on exploring the site with me was, "It will place God in the middle, linking the town and the mine in a divine plan." The comment about a divine plan had me wondering if I was making a mistake using my future knowledge to frame the past. When Robert heard of my new project, he quickly volunteered his services. In addition to being an electrician, he was also quite an accomplished carpenter. For the next few weeks, in our spare time we became church builders.

As we began the church, Robert made the comment that he hoped we could finish it by September. I was soon to learn he and Ginny wanted to be the first to be married in the new church. This goal caused all the workers to work even harder to make sure it got finished by then. Our crew thought of Robert as a kid brother. Piratical joking and funning with him was the order of the day.

It was July 21st when the first lights came on, some two weeks ahead of schedule. Our power house was completed and we were producing power. I thought to myself that even with modern technology we probably could not have achieved such a schedule in 1978. Union work rules, government agencies, inspectors, etc. would have mired down the process.

The power plant was first rate. It was the most modern

in the area, with ample capacity for not only Bankhead but Banff as well. Lines had already been strung and soon much of Banff was lighted by our little project. Previously, only the Banff Springs Hotel had lights, with power provided by their own power plant built a couple of years earlier.

Suddenly there was a great demand for electricians such as Robert. The existing buildings in Banff and Bankhead all needed to be retrofitted for electric lights. As you might imagine, many were clamoring for the new-fangled electricity. There were, however, plenty who were scared to death of it. At this time there were few electric appliances and lighting was the main interest.

In order to earn extra money for his upcoming wedding, Robert began working long hours on several jobs at a time. To this youth with unending energy working all the extra hours seemed like nothing. It was not uncommon for men with families to work two jobs to make ends meet. We all soon would wonder at the real cost of all those hours. No one, myself included, realized the potential risk.

By August 10th it appeared that the church too would meet its completion date. The first Sunday service was held in the new church two weeks later. Thirty people from Banff came up in addition to the eighty from Bankhead, this being nearly the entire Christian population of our new town. Reverend Gray personally thanked Robert for his hard work and announced the wedding that was to be held two weeks hence. Everyone was excited and happy for the couple.

The work for which I had originally been commissioned was about finished. By then many new projects had started. It seemed that houses were being built all over the mountainside.

Quite frequently I would be asked to help with another project and if it was small and not extending beyond early September, I might accept. The work had been interesting, but now I longed for the restful life back at our Chalet. I had resolved that as soon as the wedding was over, I was going straight back to Lake Louise, back to my beloved Molly, who I missed so very much.

Two of the first mine buildings that had been constructed in Bankhead the previous year were to be among those yet to be wired for lights. The buildings were the machine shop and the lamp house. The lamp house was a relatively small innocuous structure. It had concrete walls and a tin roof. It consisted basically of two rooms. In one room the miner's lamps were stored. In the other room the lamps were refueled with calcium chloride.

For about a week, Robert had been working on the wiring of both these buildings. He had gotten the lights working in the machine shop and on August 29th he was ready to energize the lamp house building. When he threw the switch that afternoon to light up the lamp house, nothing happened. As darkness approached, Robert and Jim Stamps, his helper, continued to trouble shoot the problem.

It was near nine o'clock in the evening and getting dark when Robert finally discovered the culprit, a loose wire in a junction box in the lamp storage room. Jim was stationed at the main switch on the pole outside the building. Robert would yell to Jim when he wanted the power turned on. Robert was using a test bulb with leads. The room was then only dimly lit by the last rays of sunlight.

I had just crawled into bed in my cottage up near the

church. Suddenly the walls were shaking. The deafening roar left little doubt that a terrific explosion had occurred. This was quite different from the muffled rumblings that accompanied the normal blasting in the mine. Quickly I dressed and ran outside. The evening sky was ablaze. Flames shot over the tree-tops in the direction of the mine.

As I rushed down the hill toward the mine, the mine whistle began to wail. Had the mine exploded, I wondered? It certainly appeared it had. Surely it was a mighty blast. From one hundred yards away the source of the explosion became evident. It had not been the mine after all. Where the lamp-house had stood now was the center of the mighty fire. A section of the concrete wall was gone, along with the roof. Flaming debris littered the area.

"What the hell happened?" I shouted as I ran up to the scene. "Was there anyone in the building?" I yelled. Then Carl Best, an old miner gave me the fateful news, "Lamp-house blew up, Robert was in it, Jim is over there, and he's pretty banged up." I shook my head and began to weep.

"Jim what happened?" I pleaded to know. He was barely able to speak. He had a broken arm and was in a state of shock. Apparently, the blast had thrown him some ten yards or so. He was lucky to be among the living, though I doubt he felt so lucky at that moment. "Have they found Robert yet?" Jim kept asking in a feeble voice. We calmed him down enough to learn of the fateful work that had led to the tragedy. I wept as the reality of the loss of my dear friend became certain.

I knew that word of the accident would spread quickly to Banff. Knowing Ginny was sure to hear about it soon, I decided to go straight away to Banff. I stopped just long enough to send a wire to Molly for her to catch the first train in the morning to Banff. My telegram read: "Molly. Stop. Terrible accident in Bankhead. Stop. I am ok. Stop. Catch first train to Banff. Stop. Meet me at Banff Springs." On arriving in town, I went straight away to the Banff Springs and broke the news to Ginny's father. He and I had the dreadful job of telling Ginny.

What was to have been such a joyous occasion was now one of immense sadness? I write this with tears in my eyes just thinking about it. Instead of a wedding, that last day in late August; the little church Robert had helped build had its first funeral. Death, although a more frequent visitor in these years, was still seldom expected, especially for someone so young and so full of life as Robert. Reverend Gray was even moved to tears as he conducted Robert's funeral. As for me, since the accident I have probably wondered as much why God took Robert as I have about my own fate.

How could Robert and I have known that the grassy clearing behind the church, where we often took our lunches, would become his gravesite? It was such a beautiful and peaceful spot. It was sheltered on all sides by giant firs and larches. From his grave the church could be seen on the right some fifty yards away. The Bow Valley and lower Bankhead lay through the trees to the left. He would rest eternal in a truly beautiful spot.

Standing there by Robert's grave, my thoughts drifted back to you and your mother, Craig. I wondered if you might already be lying in some cold ground somewhere far from me, a whole lifetime away, and a world away in another time and place. I prayed out loud that was not so. In those sorrowful hours, I once again came close to telling Molly about my own tragic past. Again though, I stopped short of telling her.

Ginny's father took her back East to Ottawa for a month to get her away and try to help her over her loss of Robert. She would remain in Ottawa, not returning to our mountains again for several years. I don't think she ever fully recovered from Robert. When next I saw her, she had lost the youthful smile and the joy that made us all feel so young being around her.

I would return to Bankhead on a number of occasions during the next few years. Sometimes I would help with a new building, but mostly I just went to visit with the good friends I had made there. A terrific bunch they were; the carpenters, the inexperienced miners, the town leaders, and of course Reverend Gray. I never failed to visit Robert's grave on my return visits to Bankhead. I would offer a little prayer to my departed friend and pray that you, Craig, were healthy and happy.

After all that had happened, it was good to get back to the Chalet that September. Molly and I found time for a horseback trip up the Pipestone River and into the Skoki Valley, another place I had grown quite fond of. When we passed my old mining site, I couldn't resist asking her if she wanted to pan for some gold. Not surprisingly she responded, "Why Logan, surely you don't think I would waste time on such a foolish endeavor. No one has ever found gold in these parts." I just laughed, thinking so little did she know.

Well Craig, thinking back on the year 1903, I had helped build a ghost town and endured a dreadful tragedy. Bankhead, the town born to die, was prospering. I can honestly say that my experience there gave me an appreciation of the people of this era that I had never known before. I guess it was then that I fully realized that I was now one of them. I wish you could have known those wonderful people. Life in this era seemed to have so much more meaning. The harsh existence coupled with the wild beauty all around us heightened the senses beyond description. This was truly a time where every day was precious.

Bankhead

14. Exciting Years 1904 — 1910

Damn these mosquitoes. I thought this would be a great place to catch up on my writing. Today is July 20, 1906. Yes, I know, I have been poor at keeping this diary up, seems as though I am destined to do this reporting in spurts. Presently I am seated on a large rock outcropping in the middle of the otherwise flat meadow at Red Deer Lakes.

This is really one beautiful place this time of year what with the blazing red Indian Paintbrushes and the lakes almost as blue as the cobalt sky. Adding the finishing touches to this picture are the lingering patches of snow hiding under the shadows of the trees around the edge of the meadow. The only detraction from a perfect experience here is these pesky mosquitoes or sketters, as this old southerner is prone to call them upon occasion.

What brings me out here today is scouting out an adventure for the Brock family. Last year I took them on a quick trip into the Skoki Lakes. They seemed to really enjoy the experience and they are returning this year with the desire to do a bit more exploring in the same area. So, I am up here getting a look-see at the land before bringing them in here two weeks hence. I sure hope these sketters die down a bit by then, otherwise I fear they will not fully appreciate how wonderful this place can be.

On our last trip, we came no further into the backcountry than Skoki Lakes. We camped there between the lakes for a most pleasant few days. Those lakes are very special to me as I consider their beauty second only to that of Lake Louise. The place is so majestic with towering peaks surrounding the two small lakes. The lakes themselves are near perfect, what with the upper lake a bright blue green color and the lower lake a darker blue color. They are also unique in the way the upper lake outfall tumbles down a narrow canyon to the larger lower lake. Quite by coincidence, these are called the "forget me not" lakes.

Our campsite last year was positioned just high enough to allow us to take in the view of both lakes. The sound of the water thundering through the canyon mixed with that of the occasional hollow sound of rockslides down the backside of Mount Richardson. Mount Richardson is the massive peak forming the backdrop for the upper lake.

During this era, there is still an abundance of small trout in these lakes. These provided a great feast. In addition to the feast for the eyes and ears, our stomachs were rewarded. Last year while we were camped there the group was so delighted, they were already planning their return. They had quizzed me as to what other scenic wonders lay about. I told them the headwaters of the Red Deer River which lay about ten miles to the northeast. Though I hadn't personally explored there, I had been told it was quite lovely.

Craig, for a bit of history, the Red Deer River was one of the primary routes into the mountains from the East. This had long been a favorite spot for trappers. There was good hunting and trapping to be had along the Red Deer. It was also possible to traverse a couple of passes and make it up to Jasper. Jasper was, by this time, already a hundred-year-old trading post. There is still evidence of those early travelers in this valley in the form of their wick-ups and the occasional remains of a cabin. I figure these remains should add a bit of spice to the trip as the Brock's eldest of their two sons is somewhat of a history buff.

I am using my trusty old map that is now quite tattered. With its guidance, I have blazed a satisfactory trail from Skoki up here. I have also marked out some likely campsites I spotted along the way as well as some good critter viewing spots. Last year the young Brock lad allowed as how he was interested in dinosaurs, so I have picked a trail through one area that is especially littered with fossils of various types. The kid should have a jam up time looking for some of these interesting rocks. Mr. and Mrs. Brock though, while seeming to love the Rockies trail experience, don't have the stamina for long treks. As a result, I shall have to limit our travels to perhaps six to eight miles a day on the trail.

The trip I had laid out for them would take them along the route I had followed for the past week. I started from Laggan, going up the Pipestone River. I knew well that this would be the worst part of the trip since the blasted muskeg overgrew the trail each year. I had managed to hack a halfway decent trail through for "Pocket", my horse, and me. After about six miles, I found there was a faint trail leading off to the east up to Pipestone Pass. The trail up to the pass turns off a few miles before my digs. So far, my little spot of gold digging is still a secret, and I hope it stays that way.

The uphill to the pass would be a bit tough for the horses. It had proved rough for my trusty horse "Pocket," but he was a good one and not one to complain. There was still a good bit of snow at the pass. I think with a couple of weeks of warm weather though those remaining patches of snow should be pretty well done for. I sure hope these black flies and sketters are done for by then as well. I can well remember when I used to only come out here late in the season, just to avoid these pests.

Shortly after my descent from the pass, I found a lovely campsite. While camped there I was lulled to sleep by the howls of the neighboring wolf pack. I expect they were after some of the sheep with their young that I spotted yesterday while coming down from the pass. I have also seen a bit of grizzly signs though I have yet to see one of the fierce beasts on this outing. Right now, I would almost rather face a griz than these sketters. I will sure have to prepare the Brocks for the wolves. I must remember to explain to them that there is little danger from these wild beasts.

What with the Skoki, Red Deer, and Pipestone I figure we will have about 30 miles of trail, more than enough to satisfy the group. Since they only want to be out a week, this route should be perfect. It will take them through some mighty fine scenery in that short time. I can't wait to get Molly to do this trip with me.

Since yesterday I made my way back from the Red Deer Lakes and navigated around the little mountain that I knew would one day carry the Skoki name. Tonight, I am camped very near the spot where the Skoki Lodge would someday be built. I vaguely remembered having long ago read a book about the history of Skoki. From what I remembered, there was one log cabin in the compound named Wolverine Cabin. I remembered from the account that the cabin was one of the first structures built on the site and was used initially to store the builder's grub. As I recalled, the name came from the break-in and damage caused by one of those furious beasts.

I find myself looking about to see if I might spot any of the ancestors of that devilish wolverine. It seemed that I also remembered a bear story that happened near here as well. That story was a tale of the young packer who brought supplies up to the lodge. One summer he made a name for himself by making the trip into Skoki on foot in record time. As I recalled it, they said he started running the trails rather than walking after packing in 30 pounds of chicken on his back for Skoki and having to run to stay ahead of a bear. This was undoubtedly a tall tale as the likelihood of outrunning a griz with 30 pounds on one's back was just too improbable.

This area is not really even named Skoki yet, it is merely referred to as the Red Deer Mountains. I have to watch myself and not refer to it by the name Skoki. While sitting here by this lively fire tonight, the devil in me has me thinking about leaving one of my 1980 vintage coins for builders of the lodge to find. Alas, I have done so well over the years leaving history alone; I shall once again refrain from such mischief. Oh, what the heck, what harm can just one-coin be?

I wonder at the grand adventures that await all the guests who will come to spend time in the little remote lodge that can be reached only by foot or horse. This is sure one wonderfully wild and beautiful site. I think one reason why I always enjoyed the Skoki area so much is that over the years it has seemed impervious to man's changes. I hoped it would always remain so.

Today I passed back by Ptarmigan Lake and yes; there were Ptarmigan in the meadows at lake's edge. These fool birds, as most call them must be kin to the possums. Possums would freeze in the highway when frightened by automobile lights. These well-camouflaged little fowls likewise would freeze when approached. This action may have helped protect them from some predators but caused many of the creatures to end up as a man's dinner and lead to their nickname. On occasion I had killed a few for a meal. I hated doing so but they were easily dispatched and were mighty tasty.

While I have resisted talking about a lodge at Skoki, I do believe I shall refer to this lake by the correct name of these fowls, Ptarmigan. It only seems fitting to name it for these little critters that have inhabited its meadows for at least 100 years. It is so comforting to know that these little fowls shall survive man's taming of this land.

I have been away from the Chalet a week and can hardly wait to get back to some of Cookies great eats. Of course, I miss Molly a might as well. I suspect she will have a long shopping list of projects for me to take care of during the next couple of weeks before I am scheduled to start my guide duties.

Craig, I do so love being out in these wild surroundings. It is special seeing a place where there isn't a single sign that man has been before. I guess the Indians have been here but somehow that doesn't seem to count. Besides, they didn't seem to mess up the landscape as bad as the newcomers what with their tin cans and all. Even where white men have come this way in the Red Deer Valley and Skoki Valley, their presence is not to be found save those few little quaint wick-ups. Myself, being somewhat of a history buff, finding these little signs of earlier mankind has been interesting for me. I always wonder about their builders and who they were.

Had to stop my writing long enough to get one of those porcupines away from my rump sack. As for porcupines, I have never had a quill in me but I have been told it isn't much fun if you get stuck with them. I gently coaxed this fellow away with a six-foot stick. These pests seem to frequently show up around camps. I understand they like the salt in clothes and consider leather a delicacy.

It is now a week later and I am back at the Chalet and quite satisfied with my trail blazing efforts. I do believe over the next little spell, the route I have blazed through Skoki and Red Deer should prove out nicely with my adventurous clients. I told Molly that before year's end, I intended to take her in to see my forget-me-not lakes (the translation for the Indian name for the Skoki Lakes) and the lake of the fool birds. She laughed when jokingly I told her I had named it Fool Bird Lake. Only after having a bit of fun with and her admonishing me for the name, did I agree to call the lake Ptarmigan instead.

The jig was almost up with Molly yesterday. Over the years I have done pretty well at hiding these scribbles from her. Usu-ally, I would do my writing when I was up at the Teahouse or while out on the trail. Late yesterday while she was showing 'what was what' to a new housekeeper, I decided to sit down at a writing desk in the parlor and pen a few lines. I guess I must have been daydreaming about when Molly and I climbed Temple while I was penning the above. In any event I did not hear her come up behind me and start reading over my shoulder.

I had to do some fast-talking. Luckily, she believed me when I told her I was just writing up an account of the climb to send to the Cosgroves. She thought that was a very nice thing to do. It continues to be very hard not to tell her the truth. Perhaps I will soon.

Guess I better backup a bit again, as it has been a couple of years since I last wrote any scribbles here. I should mention a few events of the past couple of years. Reading back over my last writing about Bankhead brought back a lot of memories, too many for that matter. I think that is probably why I haven't written since. Robert was sure a fine young man and I still miss him today. As for Ginny, she has yet to come back to Banff from her trip back East after Robert's death. So sad.

Well enough of that, like recent years, 1904 started off with another bumper crop of tourists. I knew from the reservations we had received that there would be a several climbing parties that summer, the first being the Abbott party who were set to arrive in June. What little I knew about Abbott was that he was an acquaintance of Mr. Wilcox whom I had taken into Paradise Valley back in '97. Just prior to getting the Abbott reservation, I had been asked by Roger Cane if I would take charge of showing a well-connected German family around. As it turned out, this assignment was at the same time as the Abbott party was to be in the area.

Anyway, the Abbott group consisted of John Abbott, Bill Prince, Conrad Davis, and Tom Longstreet. They arrived on the 17th of June. At my suggestion, Abbott had arranged for Bruno Angle, a new outfitter from Banff to be their guide for the four weeks they would be climbing in the area before moving on to the Selkirk's. Abbott was a studious looking young man who I took to be maybe 30 years old. I thought him a Brit due to his accent. Curiously, he allowed as how he was from New York.

My first impression of Abbot's climbing partners was that they seemed clearly to be stuck up northeastern aristocrats. I even wondered if Abbot's British accent was an attempt to appear more aristocratic. They seemed very put off by my southern dialect. I was thinking to myself after meeting them how glad I was that I had been previously committed to the German party. It was to be Bruno who drew them to guide rather than me. Oh, how little did I know how lucky I was?

After climbing for a couple of weeks in the mountains around Moraine Lake, the Abbot party set their sights on Mount Wyeth, the mountain to the left of Mount Victoria at the end of Lake Louise. Bruno and I both knew that depending on the weather this could be either a moderate climb or a very difficult and dangerous one. Since the weather was fine though, there seemed little concern for the scheduled climb.

The morning of June 22nd the group set off for Mt Wyeth. That same morning, I took my German couple over Saddleback and into Paradise Valley. We camped overnight in my usual spot up near the giant steps. We had a most pleasant experience with the best weather ever in the valley. I showed them the usual sights, the Giant Steps and the Hoodoos.

The next afternoon we made our way back over saddleback and down to the Chalet. As we approached, I immediately became aware that something was going on there. From the trail coming down from Saddleback I could see a larger than usual crowd gathered by the lakeside. We soon learned that Abbott had fallen to his death.

Bruno had led the survivors down and was organizing a party to go up that evening to bring Abbot's body down. Abbot had fallen on the col between Mt Wyeth and Mt Victoria. He had come to rest at the head of Victoria Glacier. Bruno appeared to have the recovery effort pretty well organized. Even though I offered my services, I knew that he felt a great degree of responsibility and he insisted that he was ok and with the four others he had recruited felt he could handle it. I felt sorry for poor Bruno, and had pangs of guilt for getting him the assignment.

The CPR became quite alarmed over the Abbott accident. As was typical of this fine institution, their main concern was what affect the accident might have on their booming tourist business, in particular, thongs of would be climbers. After a couple of meetings in Montreal, they decided that it would be a wise move to import some experienced guides from the Swiss Alps. Though I agreed with their plan, it certainly was a slap in the face for guides such as Bruno.

By June 1905, the first of the Swiss guides had arrived. With their arrival came a new project for me, namely the design and construction of a separate building to act as their quarters. This was a very special project because I knew that, unlike a number of other projects I had worked on to date, this building would survive largely unchanged until modern times. It would later become the Chateau manager's residence.

The design of the guides chalet was to be that of a typical Swiss style Chalet which was thought to complement the

Tudor style of the recently enlarged main Chalet. I was told to plan for quarters for four guides. It was sort of a large house with four bedrooms, a separate kitchen, a large parlor storage closet, and a large bathroom fitted with the most modern in indoor plumbing fixtures. One very important feature was to be a large covered front porch upon which the guides could sit and talk to clients while taking in the air and grand view.

I recruited a crew of carpenters that I had worked with the past year in Bankhead. We started the GH as I called it that August and had it largely completed by the first major snow that November. The project was not without its share of obstacles. A sudden gust of wind that came up as we burned some construction debris almost destroyed our work. It was fortunate that the ember landing on the wooden porch did not go unnoticed very long, leaving only a slightly burned area. We scraped and sanded down the spot to where it was hardly noticeable. Craig, I imagine those scorched floor boards have long since been replaced.

The deal the CPR made with the guides was that the railroad would pay to bring their families over, but for some reason their employer didn't want their families living up the hill at the Chalet. Most settled their families over in Golden, British Columbia. Golden was on the CPR main line and an hour by train. This arrangement allowed the guides to live outside the park in the off season and to travel home to see their families whenever they weren't working. Getting back and forth to Golden was easy. At this time anyone who was in the employ of the CPR had free travel.

The Swiss guides Ed, Walter, and Stan have been pretty busy with the climbing crowd. The climbing craze slowed down a bit after John Abbot fell to his death last year. These guides have a healthy respect for the dangers, which the novices lack. The guide's services have been much in demand. I am grateful for them as well since I am not too keen on a lot of climbing at my age.

The guides are a bit eccentric and can be cantankerous at times. Generally, though, I get along just fine with them. I think they respect my knowledge of the area as well as my affection for this place. Likewise, I respect their climbing ability and the caution they exercise. When climbing, they seriously calculate every move. The guides are also good with our guests, though there is a bit of a language difficulty. It can be very amusing, especially watching the Americans trying to converse with these chaps, what with their limited and elementary English.

I had the opportunity to go on a climb with Ed and Stan shortly after they arrived last year. I really enjoyed their company. Understanding their German dialect was a bit difficult. I am sure my southern drawl was a hoot for them. Molly thought it would be good for me to go along with them when the Cosgrove couple was here, since they wanted to climb Mt Temple. Obviously, she knew that I was familiar with the route and since the guides were not, it seemed to make sense.

I was afraid that my leading the expedition would be insulting for the guides, seeing as how they are known to have such great self-worth. Fortunately, I was wrong. They seemed more than happy to have me lead. I guess Molly probably had a hand in this because they said she had told them she "thought" I had climbed Temple before. I chuckled and thought how much fun I could have telling them she had been the first to summit the beast of a mountain that lay ahead of us.

It was a beautiful July day, without a cloud to be found. All in all, it was nearly a perfect climb, though it was a bit more of a struggle for me than when I did it with Molly a few years back. I guess my age is telling on me. At the summit, I sure had my fun. When they went to place their names in that cairn, the one Molly and I built, they found that napkin that Molly and I had left there back in '96. I just smiled and played dumb.

1907 will go down in the books as the year of the great fire. Even though forest fires are a more or less regular thing in these parts, the fire we just finished with was the fire to end all fires. The conditions that led this fire to being such a bad one probably started last winter. The past winter had been rather mild, with little snow.

By spring, the usual rains of the season had not developed. As we progressed into summer, it was apparent that it would be a really dry year. About a month ago, in mid August everything was bone dry with the pines dropping needles like they were dying. In addition to the usual fire hazard of the trains spraying their sparks, we had more and more groups of inexperienced campers venturing into the backcountry.

It was just inevitable that fires would occur. No one knows, or at least no one is telling, how this one got started. All that is common knowledge is that when the morning west bound stopped in Laggan, the conductor reported seeing a small fire burning west of the Bow River near Castle Mountain. That was the morning of August 16th. I got a call from Mitch Small, the park superintendent, that same afternoon asking if I could come and help. He wanted me to try and round up a few guys in Laggan as well.

I took David from Lake Louise and found a couple of track

hands who were laying over in Laggan and the four of us hopped on a speeder (one of those hand operated contraptions that run on the rails) and hightailed it to the Castle Mountain siding.

Initially we thought perhaps the crews that were working a logging operation over near Castle might have been responsible for starting the fire. With good fortune, our speeder arrived ahead of the East bound train. I had been a might worried we might run headlong into it. I was very uncomfortable about riding one of those contraptions on the main line. When we arrived at Castle, we found many of the logging crew there ready to help fight the fire. This was indeed fortunate.

In these days, without modern firefighting equipment, namely aerial support, about the only chance at controlling a fire was if it was caught very early. We were lucky to have favorable terrain, with cooperative weather. As for equipment, Mitch had sent up two new steam pumpers, hose, and several teams of horses. We attacked the fire with axes and saws to clear firebreaks. The pumps were of little use due to difficulty getting the bulky carriage mounted devices close enough to the fire. It quickly became apparent to me that we were facing a doomed effort.

For a little over twenty-four hours, we attempted to stay ahead of the fire by cutting a series of firebreaks. Without chainsaws though, this work was too slow to stop the rapidly growing fire. Looking down from a ridge where I was surveying the advance of the fire, the crew of loggers looked like a few ants trying to battle a flood of red tongs.

I guess about the only good thing to come out of that day's effort was that not one of us was killed. That in itself was remarkable, considering how quickly the fire grew and changed directions. By Thursday night, it was obvious that the fire would set its own course, despite our efforts. Though our humble efforts failed to stop the fire, it did appear initially that the Bow River and all the logging that had been done around Castle Mountain might allow it to burn its self out there.

With a change in the wind, the beast took on a new appetite, running up and down the valley. In the days that followed, there was some fear that the fire would burn all the way south to Banff, some fifteen miles. For me a worse concern was that it would advance north the ten miles and consume Laggan and Lake Louise. Since Molly was at the lake, I worried for her safety.

Our only salvation was a sudden cold front that arrived on September 8th. The front brought heavy rain and even a little snow. It was all that saved Laggan and Lake Louise. By the time the fire was out, it was less than two miles away from us. Likewise, by then the fire had driven south within a few miles of Banff.

I know it will be years before the black eyesore is gone in our otherwise lovely Bow Valley, but at least our homes and lives have been spared. As with most disasters, some good has come from it. For one thing, the park superintendent has announced that a series of fire breaks will be created. These should help with any future fires. There will be a better chance of perhaps stopping a fire before it consumes the entire valley. There is also talk of some fire roads to help get equipment in to fight fires, perhaps even a good wagon road from Laggan to Banff.

It is now 1908 and automobiles have arrived. Yes, with the

start of the season this year the first tin lizzy rolled into Banff. It was an exciting event for the town's inhabitants. I imagine it was some difficult trip getting that fossil of an auto over the pothole filled coach road from Calgary. Most certainly this momentous event is bound to bring improved roads between places like Banff, Lake Louise, and Bankhead. Alas, the day of luxury family motoring is still a ways off, I do believe.

As one might expect, our granddaddy, the CPR, is none too happy to see these new gadgets. I can only imagine there is someone up the food chain in the organization with enough smarts to see the potential competition these four wheeled beasts will give their rolling fire dragons. Bet the CPR will be none too happy when asked to pay for the roads for the new automobiles. As for me, while I have longed for modern things, I have come to feel that trails and buggy roads are more natural and a bit romantic.

Today is August 14, 1908. So far it has been a quiet summer. Other than the first car, there have been a number of other firsts this year. For several years now the larger hotels such as the Banff springs, the Sanitarium, and the Chalet have had some sort of indoor plumbing. At the same time, homes of the town's folks haven't had that luxury, even most of the new ones up at Bankhead lack indoor plumbing.

One of the main reasons is that we don't have a proper water or sewer system. Since June, work has been underway to change all that. Both Banff and Bankhead are getting a sewer and water system. While people in general seem to have reservations about automobiles, most are overjoyed at the prospect of the new in-door plumbing.

The added benefit of the water system will be to help

with fighting the numerous house fires like those we have had the past winter. To me, the construction buff that I am, I have enjoyed watching the antique steam shovel and wheel digger work. It is a wonder though that no one has been killed with all the blasting accompanying the work. Little effort is made to contain the blast rock from the trenches. Frequently rock showers the town's buildings and those inhabitants unfortunate enough to be on the streets where the work is occurring.

Accompanying the water and sewer project is a number of related projects such as a new bridge over the Bow River opposite the Sanitarium. The new bridge is a more substantial modern steel structure to replace the old pontoon one. This new more rigid one was needed to provide a means to carry the water line over the river. It is also wide enough to allow the carriages and automobiles to safely pass. The horses are still a bit unsure about being too close to their noisy replacements.

Molly is thrilled by all the changes and is especially fascinated by automobiles. I have been giving a lot of thought to cashing in a bit of my gold fortune that I have stashed away and buying one of these marvels for her. Perhaps in another year, for her birthday, I may surprise her with one. Bet she would be one reckless speed demon behind the wheel of one of these babies, doing a whopping 45 miles per hour.

As I sit here writing now, I am somewhat apprehensive of what this winter has in store. The past few years Molly and I have enjoyed wintering at the Chalet. Even though it will be many years before winter business will provide incentive to keep it open year-round, we enjoy it there year-round.

Over the years, for a number of reasons, I have never

ventured far from these mountains, with Calgary being my longest journey except for that trip to Ottawa a few years back. This winter Molly says she would like to go to New York. She has never been there and I led her to believe I haven't been either. For some reason I am extremely hesitant to leave this place that I have become so willingly imprisoned in. I have told her that I would go, so I guess we will see if I disappear upon leaving Canada. In any event I did want to give this diary another little bit of writing before heading off into the unknown of the Big Apple.

15. *Let It Snow*

Time continues to get away from me. To think it has been nearly a year since I last put pen to this paper. Now that I am confined with this incredible winter weather, I no longer have any excuse for not writing, that is, other than having to hide this from Molly. I am none too sure if I would even mind her finding me writing at this point. Without a doubt, the most outstanding thing to report this past year has been this incredible winter weather.

The winter started bad and quickly got worse. It was as if the wild critters knew what was ahead. Us human types didn't seem to have a clue. Thinking back, I remembered that the Ptarmigan put on their winter white coats early. The past few winters we had relatively little snow and no bone chilling cold. When I say little snow, I define little being about three feet. As for cold, these past few years it didn't stay bitter cold, more than 15 degrees below zero for more than a few days at a time. Well, that all changed this past winter of 1910.

This year we wintered at the Chalet, as has been our habit these past few years since the new hotel was finished. We love it here in the winter because it is so peaceful. This year it was especially so since we had the whole place to ourselves. A couple of the Swiss guides who had stayed in the guide's house last winter have gone back to Golden this year to be with their families.

I guess, our first sign that this was to be the winter of all winters came on October 5th. Molly and I woke up to a gray day with a few snow flurries. That afternoon we planned to meet the three o'clock train to pick-up our supplies as we usually did every Thursday. While we were sitting at the staff table in the kitchen having our breakfast, we heard what sounded like thunder. Without getting up to look out, we decided it was just a large avalanche on Mt Fairview. A couple of minutes later we heard the sound again. This time we ventured out front to see if we could see signs of an avalanche. We were surprised to discover the sound was not an avalanche but appeared to indeed be thunder.

Back in Georgia, it had not been too unusual to have thunder storms the year around. Here though, it was sure unusual to have them this late in the season, especially now that it had turned so cold. What followed was a snow thunderstorm. By lunch, when I should have been getting the wagon ready to head down to the station, we were furiously bringing in more wood from the wood yard and stacking it by the fireplace. By the time we finished, we were trudging through nearly six inches of new snow that had quickly accumulated.

Any hope of making it to Laggan that day was dashed. Since blizzard like conditions had now set in, we wondered if the train would even be running. The storm lasted for three days, giving us nearly a whole year's worth of snow in one

October dose. When the storm was finally over, it took us another week before we could get a sled to bring our supplies up to the Chalet. It was fortunate that we had enough provisions on hand so that the two weeks we went without re-supply was not too bothersome. It was also fortunate; I correctly took that as a sign of more severe weather to come. We quickly got well stocked up for the rest of the winter.

We were to find that large snowstorms seemed to come about every couple of weeks this winter. I feel Molly and I fared better here, isolated in our wonderland than many of the town's folks. The Chalet had always been its own little self-sufficient outpost. Our life was filled with a bit of work, a lot of fun, and a chance to just relax by the fire and read. We went through just about all the books in the hotel's library over the winter.

After a couple of months, we had sort of accepted the year's harsh winter environment. In early February, during a break in the storms, Molly and I, suffering from a bit of cabin fever, took the train down to Banff to visit with some friends for a few days. I remember that it was February 7th and the weather was grand, probably the best all winter. We had sent a telegram to Roger at the Banff Springs notifying him of our visit. He had the tallyho at the station to meet us. While we were there, we stayed in one of the vacant rooms in the hotel. Having such accommodations available was a great perk of working for the CPR.

Of all years to have a booming winter tourist business, this was not the one, but that's just what Banff had. Though the Chalet was not open, the Banff Springs and a couple of other smaller hotels in Banff were. They were doing a brisk business.

Roger allowed as how the Banff Springs alone had over one hundred guests. He even hinted at putting us to work, as he was short on staff. We were not too keen on that idea.

When we arrived that February morning, snow was still covering everything from the last big storm of two weeks before. The visitors were out and about, sliding and snowshoeing. The Brusters had a couple of sleighs they kept busy giving rides around town, they also took folks up to Bankhead and to Lake Minnewanka. This lake was a great destination for ice-skating. The snow was removed from a spot on the lake and the ice there was usually quite smooth.

All in all, everything and everyone seemed to be dealing with winter pretty well. That changed two days later on Feb. 9th. That afternoon snow flurries turned to serious snow. By the afternoon of the 10th there was an additional 18 inches of snow. The wind had picked up, causing terrific drifts. Just before the telegraph and phone lines went dead, a message came in that a large avalanche had taken out the main line near Canmore. We knew it must be even worst to the west. Getting back to the Chateau any time soon was out of the question.

It quickly became apparent that Banff w ould be cut off from the outside world by train for a number of days. Since many of the guests at the time were not Canadians, a lot of them had never experienced much snow. I do believe most got their fill of it in Banff this winter.

Roger Cane was struggling with how to keep all his snowbound guests pacified. He came up with a capital idea. I never really knew that the idea had originated with him, but I credit him with pulling it off. He asked his staff to organize some winter games and exhibits to entertain the guests. Quickly the plan expanded to include many of the townspeople and a few of the Stoney tribe.

The event was called a winter carnival. It was to take place on Saturday, February 15th. Considering the short time for planning, it became truly an amazing and grand thing. Though Molly and I had planned to return to the Chalet at the first possible moment, we were quickly drawn into the activities. It sounded like a lot of fun and took ones mind off the difficulties the weather presented.

Of all things, Molly and I were put in charge of an igloo-building contest. Now if that was not an absurd thing, having an old Georgia fart in charge of an igloo-building contest. I thought to myself this should sure be good for a few laughs. Molly went on about how she was going to really show me up in the contest. I just told her not to count her igloos so fast.

Before I tell you about our igloo-building, let me mention some of the other crazy going-ons. Dr. Brett provided his two ice racing boats for everyone's use up at Lake Minnewanka. As skiing had yet to take hold, Brett's ice sailing was about as crazy a winter activity as we had. The Banff Livery provided free sleigh rides up to Minnewanka. The sleigh they rigged up for this event was one amazing contraption. It was a long wagon on runners with a canvas top. The Brusters, not to be outdone, connected two large sleighs into one super sized one and mounted a small potbellied stove in the center. Riders could surround the smoke belching stove for warmth on the six-mile ride to the lake.

Jim Bruster's son, Ben, was the driver of this super sleigh. He promptly dubbed it the fire ball express. Jim's three sons and Dr. Brett's two boys were always pranking each other. This time was no exception. Ben Bruster was really lauding it over Tom Brett about how lucky he was to be driving the super sleigh. Almost predictably, Tom Brett had to set Ben back a notch or two. Most assuredly he came up with a plan to do just that. After a couple of runs, when Ben stopped by the woodpile to replenish his stove fuel; he unwittingly loaded a couple of special sticks of wood that Tom had laced with firecrackers.

Unfortunately, I didn't witness the event and must only rely on second hand accounts. By all telling, it was quite a spectacle. While Ben was driving up to Minnewanka, he asked a passenger to stoke the stove. According to a group following close behind in Tom Brett's sleigh, shortly after the stoking all hell broke loose on the fireball express. As the old potbelly began to give off distinct sounds of a major explosion, several passengers were reported diving off into snow banks.

Quite fortunately, none of the passengers were severely injured. It was a wonder Ben didn't kill Tom right there on the spot. Only concern for his passengers was probably all that kept quite an altercation from taking place. The incident surely did provide a good laugh for many and will be a story to be retold for some time, I imagine.

As for other events, there was skating on the Bow River. This followed a major snow clearing effort by about a dozen of the locals. There was to be a men's and women's ice-skating contest. Many of the town's folks loaned their skates so the tourists could have a go at the adventure of skating. It was comical to watch those who had never been on skates before. Of course, I couldn't but help by offering a bit of my hard-gained knowledge to the novices. I advised a number of gentlemen and ladies to consume a large quantity of alcohol prior to skating, allowing as how it relaxes them and greatly enhances the experience. It surely did enhance it for those of us watching the drunken fools and probably helped at least temporarily diminish their pain.

For the younger souls, there was a snowshoe race up Tunnel Mountain. For the kids there was tobogganing. The children around town had constructed a great collection of snowmen. The snowmen were judged. The winner was given a new toboggan which had been donated to the cause by Dave White. Watching the kids was by far the most fun of all. Oh, but to be a kid again. As I watched I couldn't help but regret that Molly and I didn't have kids.

Another favorite event was the ice sculpture contest. This artful activity was under the direction of the Banff Springs chef Gary Roberts, who created some great works with chisels and a saw. Surprisingly, some of the fellows from the carpentry shop up at Bankhead placed very well in this event. My favorite was Gary's sculptor of old man Van Horn, the granddaddy of the CPR and the Banff Springs. I can't say he would have been flattered by the likeness, still, knowing the old man, I found it quite amusing. I told Gary that his carving would make a great statue to sit beside the Banff Springs entry. He allowed as how he felt his statue would rapidly decline to unsuitable size come spring.

But now, I will tell you about our igloos. To start with, our venue was near the boat dock on the Bow. We decided to use coal scoops to cut and lift out the blocks of pretty well frozen snow from the riverbank. We had debated actually sawing blocks of ice from the river, but seeing as how the snow was of a good consistency and considering how much easier and safer this was, it was our choice. Dave White furnished eight shiny new scoops.

There was a real mixed group of participants. As you would expect, those from more southern climates seemed the most interested. Not surprisingly, they were the most unskilled in making these creations. Molly and I organized four teams of four people on a team. Over the past few winters I had seen a few of these structures built by some old trappers. Though those were probably more snow caves than true igloos, I guess that qualified me as an expert.

One team was made up of kids. Molly was their leader. Perhaps not too surprising, the kid's team scored very high. The only team to beat them was the "Pro" team, a name given them since they had one member who actually had built an igloo before. It wasn't too hard for all to agree who lost. The loser's igloo provided all with a spectacular collapse, with all four team members inside, immediately following its completion. All judged this an unquestioned sign of failure. Their igloo was however, voted the most entertaining.

Though our Igloo building was wonderful fun, I wish we could have been able to get up to Lake Minnewanka to see the ice boat races. From all reports, the women racing the men was a sight to behold. Dr. Brett reported that despite his claim that his boat couldn't be overturned, the men's crew managed to do just that. No one was badly injured, that is other than their pride. Their disaster gave the women's team a win.

That night a few of us sat around a roaring fire in Mt Stevens Hall up at the Banff Springs. We laughed till we hurt over the comical scenes we had witnessed that day. All agreed that the Winter Fest must become an annual event to be held every year; not just when the tourists were held captive by the trains being out of commission. Roger thanked us all for our efforts and vowed to commend us to Ottawa. We were sure the CPR would want to advertise this as an annual event they provided.

Within a few days, the tracks had been cleared and the train's whistle was again echoing down in the valley. With the return of the trains, it was time for us to get back and check on the Chalet. Upon arrival back in Laggan, we found that there was still too much snow for the horses. It was fortunate for us that Gray had his dog sled which we used to ferry our supplies up to the Chalet. It took two trips, but then we were set for a few more weeks.

Other than having to shovel a path to the lobby entry, everything seemed generally ok. We discovered that the storm or a search for salt had led several big horn sheep to take up residence next to the stone wall at the hotel's rear entry. We welcomed their company. We quickly learned that their presence had a disconcerting side to it though, that being wolves.

Despite some limited efforts up until then to eradicate wolves from the park, there was still a healthy population. They preyed on the elk and sheep primarily. Molly seemed quite concerned at the presence of the wolves. I assured her we were quite safe and after a time I got her to enjoy their howls at night.

It is now near the end of March and, one can only hope, near the end of this blasted snow. With all the snow we have had, the peaks will surely look like winter all year. Guess we will be sleeping to the sound of avalanches year-round as well. Such is life in these wonderful mountains.

16. Our Son For A Summer — 1911

It looks as how this summer may be an interesting one for us. Molly received a letter yesterday from her sister Jean. It seems that she has asked if her son Ben could spend the summer with us. She felt it would do him good. Molly is going to respond that we would love to have the lad. I expect Ben will arrive next week. We have not seen Jean or Ben too much these past couple of years. Ben, now thirteen, is old enough to really enjoy getting out into the wilderness. Having a youngster around should keep us hopping.

Ben has arrived and he is one live wire. He is certainly a handsome kid what with his blond hair and blue eyes. He does not have the red hair of his mother's heritage. Ben has expressed a desire to see some really wild country and as he put it "some ferocious beasts". I am not too keen on those "ferocious beasts," but I have determined to take the lad for a few adventures into the back country, starting with an overnight over to the Lake O'Hara area. I guess that should be a good test to see what the boy is made of.

Molly's sister said she would like for us to put Ben to work for the summer at the Chalet. Now that he is old enough, she wanted him to see what the lodging business was about. I certainly think there will be an ample supply of tasks for a spry young lad. I will take him on the O'Hara outing before the big rush of guests arrives. After that adventure, we will line him out some tasks.

I had considered taking Ben along on a trip with a group of greenhorns that just arrived but. after one short outing with the bunch, I did not particularly enjoy their demanding ways. I told them I would not be available to guide them next week. I would rather spend some time alone with Ben. I have worried about Ben ever since he lost his father a year ago and I have wanted to try and be a bit of a father to the lad.

I had asked Molly if she wanted to join us, but she allowed as how there was still a hotel to run and besides it should be a "manly" trip. "Manly ha, well I guess you fairer sex just can't cut a little rough living," I added in jest, knowing full well she could rough it with the best of them.

Molly has not been the death of me yet, but this crazy kid may be. When I mentioned a trip to Ben, all he could talk about was whether he could shoot a grizzly. I explained that I really hoped that would not be necessary. I tried my best to explain how wasteful it would be to kill such a magnificent one of God's creatures. Unfortunately, I am not too sure I convinced him of that. I also reminded him that since we were now part of the national park, hunting was forbidden.

Ben's arrival has made me a bit melancholy. He is now about your age, Craig. He will have to fill in the role of my son, if only for a brief time. Perhaps I can show him some of the places his father will not be able to show him, some of the places I was not able to show you, Craig. As you read of the things Ben and I do together this summer, please know that, he is you in my heart.

For our outing, I had decided that we would take the horses. I would ride Burgess and let Ben take Molly's old favorite, Tail. We would also take along a pack pony to carry the tent and grub. Since packing for such a trip is an important thing to know about, I got Ben involved as I sorted through the gear. I told him about planning meals for a pack trip, things like how many tins of various canned goods, as well as dried foods and perishables.

Surprisingly, Ben is pretty fair with these causes (horses). I wasn't too sure if he could even stay on one or if he might have to ride with me. After the first mile, he was doing just fine. The weather was grand when we started out that morning for the twelve miles around to the O'Hara, or as I call it, the other side of the mountains. Truly that is where Lake O'Hara is since the O'Hara valley lays directly behind mount Victoria, the lady that proudly guards the end of our beautiful Lake Louise.

There is no short and direct route. Over the last few years others have blazed a pretty fair trail there. The trail circumnavigates the base of little beehive and Mt. Saint Parin, past Ross Lake then up O'Hara creek to the lake. It usually takes one long day to make the trip from Lake Louise. In this case we will do it in two days to allow for an easier pace.

After the first mile or so, we came to an area where most of the trees had been stripped, allowing for a wider trail. This allowed us to ride side by side. It gave me a chance to point out some of the more important natural features such as the muskeg, and various animal signs. Like most kids, he had great curiosity. Soon we had to stop for water to quince my throat which had dried from answering all his questions. With all our talking and noise we were making, I knew there wasn't much chance of spotting game.

Despite all our noise, there are always some creatures about. "What are those?" the lad piped up.

"You mean those crazy birds the horses about stepped on?" I asked. "Those are fool birds, least that's what everyone calls them, though their real name is Ptarmigan."

"Wow, I like the fool birds," Ben piped up. "Uncle Logan, how did they get the name fool birds?" he begged.

"Well didn't you notice that the horses near about trampled them, you see they don't know to be scared."

"Maybe they should be called fearless birds," he quipped. We both enjoyed a good laugh and every time we spotted one of them, we called it a fearless bird.

We over-nighted in a pretty little clearing, not far from the stream that flowed down from Lake O'Hara. "Uncle Logan can I set up the tent?" Ben asked as we arrived at the little clearing.

"Sure, you can, son. Ever set a tepee before?" I queried.

"Well…no I haven't, but I think I can do it," was his confident reply. I told him that I too believed he could do it and I would show him how. When planning our trip, I had decided on a teepee as it seemed more Indian like and I thought more exciting for the kid.

With only one packhorse, I had not packed tent poles. I also wanted to give Ben the full experience, including cutting poles. "First, we must select, cut, and trim our poles," I instructed. I showed him a nice group of young larch's and we set about cutting six 12 footers. When we got them trimmed, I showed him about tying the tops together and wrapping the canvas around the poles.

He did a pretty fair job, though I am sure some of my old Indian friends would mock the tent's appearance. I showed him how to ferret out the rocks and roots to make for better sleeping and to cut fir boughs to place our bedrolls on. Afterward, we set about preparing our campfire and dinner.

We crafted a nice pot of stew from the dried beef, a tin of potatoes, and onions I had brought. Based on Ben's comments, it must have turned out pretty fair. I guess I have become a pretty good trail cook, though I still miss the simple pleasure of freeze-dried instant foods. After a good dinner and the dishwashing task, my young camper was showing the affects of a full day of adventure, so it didn't take much prodding by me to get him in his bedroll.

Could this kid ever snore? I started to kid him about it the next morning but remembered that kids his age sometimes take things too seriously so I didn't, though I did make a mental note to stuff something in my ears the next night. As we ate fried ham and biscuits for breakfast, we discussed our plans for the day. We marveled at the beautiful sunrise. A noisy whisky jack showed great interest in joining us for breakfast. It quickly made off with our scraps. "Ben, do you want to learn how to pack a horse?" I asked, feeling it was some knowledge that might serve him well in the future.

"Sure, that would be swell," he responded. I showed him about distributing the pack goods and how to tie the diamond hitch.

I was quite pleased with the boy's willingness to learn and help out. One of the tasks that Molly and I had discussed for Ben was helping out with the horses. So, there was a bit of purpose to my guidance. Ben asked if he could take the lead. I quickly gave my OK but cautioned, "Don't go too fast, remember, grizzlies don't like being surprised." That comment definitely slowed him down. I didn't have to worry again about him getting too far ahead after that.

By mid morning we had arrived at Lake O'Hara. The only sign the area had been visited before were half a dozen fire hearths and a few piles of tins left by previous tourists and their guides. In the interest of minimizing the impact to the terrain, I chose a site for our camp that already had a hearth. I also instructed Ben that it was always proper camp etiquette to bury one's trash. From the lakes edge on the western shore, we had a great view of the backside of Mount Victoria. I commented that old Victoria's backside looked nigh as good as her front. Ben laughed and agreed.

We had selected a nice spot on a little knob sheltered by a grove of pines. It was about a hundred feet from the water's edge. After we un-saddled and unpacked our horses, we started setting up camp. Soon it was time for a lunch of some hardtack and bread. I told the lad that this was true trail fare. "Uncle Logan what is hardtack, really?" Ben asked.

"Well to start with, another common name for it is Pemmican, but what it is really is dried meat. It is usually elk, deer, or beef that has been salted and dried in the sun," I explained. He seemed pleased at having this new knowledge.

I sent Ben to the lake to get water. He hadn't been gone long when he let out a yell. Panicked, thinking he had spotted a bear; I grabbed my rifle and ran toward him. It turned out he was merely excited by seeing some trout in the water. I asked how big the fish were, he held his hands about eighteen inches apart. I was sure it was the usual fisherman's exaggeration of double actual size. I decided that we would attempt to make some of these fish our dinner for the night.

Though I had been over to O'Hara a couple of times before, I had never been beyond the lake. I was anxious to explore a bit to the south. After lunch we cached our grub, tied up the horses on a line, and set out afoot around the lake and up the valley beyond. The going was a bit rough but the lad didn't complain. Shortly we emerged from the wooded lake vegetation onto a rock strewn clearing. Upon looking about, I spotted half a dozen goats on the slope about 50 yards to our right.

Ben and I sat there on the rocks watching them for some time until they got behind a large outcropping. "Uncle Logan, have you ever shot a goat?" Ben asked. I responded that I had hunted for game to eat occasionally, but I had never killed a goat. I had actually eaten goat before and found it to be quite tasty.

My view of hunting was a bit hard to reconcile in these times, having grown up hunting as a kid. Over the years though, I had come to feel that unnecessary killing of animals was wrong. My views were very much out of step with present day thinking which favored killing all predators and any other animal if it proved good eating. I tried to explain to Ben that God's creatures should be left alone whenever possible.

I quickly violated my own teachings as we fashioned some crude fishing gear and set about attempting to catch a mess of fish later that afternoon. After an hour of dangling a piece of string with a bent pin baited with a piece of cheese in the water, I was in doubt we would have the tasty dinner I had promised. Fortunately, while playing with some rocks set in soil, Ben discovered a few worms. Sure, enough the old faithful worms did the trick. We ended up with three nice trout for our two hours effort. I showed him how to clean them and cook them over the fire. Ben declared it to be the best fish he ever ate and consumed the better part of the two smaller ones.

That night in our tent, Ben and I had quite a talk covering every subject from mountain climbing to a bit of the birds and bees, the latter subject proving quite a challenge for this old man. I kept telling myself not to be too liberal about the subject. I knew that views on the subject were much more conservative during this time.

I asked Ben if he had a girlfriend, he said no but I gathered that there was one girl he met at school the past year that he had a bit of a crush on. He blushed quite a lot when I asked if he had kissed her. He allowed as how he had wanted to but had not had the nerve. I told him not to worry; there would be a right time.

When I asked his favorite subject in school, his reply was history. "Well that is a surprise," I commented, wanting desperately to engage him in some real history education.

"Yep, we were studying the Roman History last year and I thought those gladiators and emperors were kind of interesting," he added.

"Well Ben, did you ever think that what you are doing is sort of adding to history?" I posed this question to get him thinking.

"What do you mean?"

"Well, there will likely be books written about the exploration and adventures of kids like you in the wilderness exploring this new land. Have you ever thought about writing about your adventures?" I asked. "

No, I haven't, but that sounds kind of like a good idea," he responded.

"Ben, you should consider keeping a diary of your adventures this summer," I suggested. "But don't wait too long to start as you will forget the little things that will make it interesting to read."

"I will do just that, Uncle Logan. I will start tonight if you have a piece of paper and a pencil," he replied quiet excitedly.

"That I do," I responded and so began another diary.

We made it back from our camping trip none too worse for the wear. Much to Ben's disappointment, we didn't see a single bear. I promised him he would see one before summer's end. After our little trip, Molly wasted no time putting Ben to work. She assigned Ben to work with Sandy, one of our housekeepers. He will help her clean the rooms and carry up the linens from the laundry. I think this will be a good experience for him for a week or two until I can get him on with the stable crew. Molly and I figure that we should get the lad exposed to a variety of work, thereby keeping him from boredom that so often occurs with kids.

Ben has been with us now for two weeks and he certainly is a pistol. Though not bad for mischief, he has managed to get himself into some real situations. Sandy is a great housekeeper who keeps right with her work. That said, she has a real thing for one of the coachmen and she is occasionally away from her assigned tasks when he arrives with the coach. It was Ben's second day working with Sandy. She was off visiting with her flame for a few minutes and that was just long enough for Ben to get into it.

All the housekeepers know to always knock and wait before entering a guest room. Unfortunately, our rambunctious lad had to learn the hard way how important that was. Fortunately, the newlywed couple that he burst in on was very understanding.

I guess we are really providing him a complete education this summer, I told Molly. My birds and the bees talk last month probably seems a bit elementary to Ben now, especially after he asked me if Molly and I did what that couple were doing. I expect that question to me gave me about the reddest face ever. I had to explain that it wasn't polite to ask a question like that. When I told Molly about that she about died laughing. "Well, old man, what did you tell the kid? Huh, huh," she kept kidding me, causing me to again turn a bit red faced.

Shortly after the housekeeping incident, I was able to convince Molly to give Ben a try at helping with the horses. It soon was clear that Ben had found his favorite job for the summer. He was just great with the horses, so much so that we have started letting him take the two pack ponies up to the Teahouse each morning to carry up supplies.

The guests were really taken with Ben as well. He and I took several short outings with guests. On these trips he was not only a great help, but provided entertainment for the guests, taking some of that burden off me. "Son, you would make quite a trail guide," I complemented him after one outing when the clients gave me a handsome tip. I gave a good share of it to Ben, telling him to save it to help with a college education.

Ben's mother may be in for a surprise. It seems the kid has his heart set on getting his own horse. I have tried to explain to him that since his mother and he live in a city, that might not be possible. I did tell Ben that I would have his favorite bay here for him whenever he could come and visit. Bet that brings the kid back, I sure do hope so as I expect I will miss him a lot.

Over the past couple of weeks, Ben has been spending quite a bit of time over at the guide's chalet, listening to the stories and boasting of our two Swiss guides. As a result of their tales of climbing adventures, Ben has voiced his intention to climb mountains. I am not real keen on this and am pretty certain his mother won't be either. Since he continues to persist and since the Swiss guides are kept busy taking paying guests out, I said I would take him for a bit of climbing.

For a starter I have chosen Mt. Saint Piran. It is close and with its 9,000-foot elevation, a relatively easy climb. In addition, it offers a grand view. Much to my surprise, Molly has hinted at coming along. Even though Molly has done a bit of climbing, the most notable being Mt Temple, she usually is not too keen on it. I have wondered if the reason for her wanting to tag along was that she doesn't trust me with her nephew's safety. I really doubt if that is the case. I will be glad to have my lady tag along.

It was a perfect crisp late summer morning as we set out for our climb at 7:00 am. Cookie as usual had us well taken care of for food. As we started off, the guides, who were waiting for their clients, made fun of us saying we should leave before sunrise if we were to be "real" mountain climbers. I shot back with, "If it took us as long as them to reach a summit, then I suppose we would need to leave before sunrise as well!" They made some remark in German that I couldn't understand and am sure I wouldn't have wanted to.

Considering the short distance, we had to travel to start the climb, I elected not to use horses. Instead we hiked the two hours to where the trees thinned and then began scrambling. The route took us up to the Teahouse, then across the slope toward the Little Beehive, past Craig's rock, yes Craig, I named the rock where this diary resides for you. A short distance beyond the rock we headed straight up the talus-laden slope.

The smaller loose rock proved a minor challenge but considering that all three of us were in pretty fair shape, we made good time. Despite the difficulty, I didn't hear a complaint from my partners. The exertion of the climb upward kept us warm. After starting out in perfect weather, the weather that greeted us at the summit was some of the strangest I had ever experienced. Clouds had built up as we gained elevation. The weather was becoming more threatening and for a moment I thought about that fateful morning on the tram, now years past. I wondered if we should abandon the climb.

As we summited around 11:00 am, it was surprisingly cold and started to snow. We quickly ate our lunch, concerned we might have to make a hurried descent before conditions became slippery. Soon the sun peeked out, but not for long. Then we experienced a sleet storm. In the distance we heard what I was pretty sure was thunder, then the sun again, but not for long as a mini blizzard ensued and we scrambled to pack up the remains of a quickly eaten lunch.

Just then an amazing thing occurred. The sun reappeared and with it the most spectacular double rainbow I ever witnessed. The weather was once again quite nice for our descent. The three of us vowed to from that day forward refer to this as rainbow peak. It had been a great first climb for our lad.

The summer is flying by. It seems like there is another adventure with Ben starting as quickly as the last one ended. The night we got back from Mt Saint Piran; a new guest arrived at the chalet. He was not one of our usual Easterners; no, we had as a guest a real sure enough mountain man. He never said why he was there but I guess he just wanted to spend a few days seeing how the other half lived. He seemed a bit out of place, a real odd bird. He was, however, a decent fun-loving chap full of tales of living in the wilds. His name was Steve Dugan.

Steve had just returned from the Yukon where he had been successful with a gold pan. I longed to swap tales with him about prospecting but refrained. At dinner he was telling his tales and quickly caught Ben up in a web of gold fever. As a result, Ben was all hot to try his luck in the streams thereabouts. I attempted to discourage him and Steve did likewise. We told him that we had never heard of any good show in the southern Rockies. Obviously, I knew different. The last thing I needed to do was upset the apple cart with starting a gold rush in the park.

After my attempts to disinterest him had failed, I finally agreed to take Ben gold panning. Molly again allowed as how she wanted to be a part of our adventure. That next Sunday afternoon we packed our gear and set out on a two-night camping and gold panning trip on up the Pipestone River a mile or so. I must confess I was a tad worried that we just might be too successful. I knew that could be really bad. I worked stealthy to ensure that we didn't find much. All the time thinking what a ridiculous situation this was with me trying not to find gold.

We found a beautiful spot for our campsite late that afternoon. I enticed Ben to tend to the horses and help set up camp. By then it was too late to do any panning, much to his disappointment. I promised Ben that we would get an early start the next day. To my surprise, Molly was as anxious to get to panning as Ben was. While Ben and Molly had been getting camp squared away, I secured four nice sized trout. The three of us had a grand dinner that night cooked over the fire and turned in rather early, expecting an early rising the next day.

What a beautiful day it was. We had a gentle breeze and surprisingly few sketters to contend with. Our quick breakfast consisted of some cooked bacon, rolls, and jam. After cleaning up from breakfast and putting our bedding out to air, we headed down to the stream. I had procured an additional gold pan from our prospector guest. My story about how I came by my pan was that I had found it while on one of my adventures. I couldn't bring myself to admit that I had also been bitten by the fever years before. I gave them minimal instructions and my two eager gold hunters were about their adventure. I watched from my comfortable position reclining against a large pine near the stream, occasionally offering words of encouragement.

After a couple of hours without any success, the pair was starting to lose interest, just as I had expected. I started feeling a bit sorry for them. I did want them to have a little fun and so I opted to show them a bit about how to pan. Soon I was pointing out a few grains of sparkle in their pans. As far as they were concerned, it might as well have been the mother load.

At days end, the pair had collected enough grains to perhaps equal a quarter ounce. I was able to convince them that they had maybe a couple of dollars worth at most and that it would not prove a very profitable endeavor at that rate. I think I was successful as they both allowed as how it had been great fun in spite of the limited financial success. We arrived back at the Chalet that evening in time for dinner. Ben told Cookie all about his adventure.

It was turning out to be one jam-up summer; I really didn't want it to end. Ben was supposed to leave on August 20th, but since his school didn't start until September 6th, he wrote his mother and begged to stay two more weeks. Molly and I certainly didn't mind, especially as we still had one more, large group of guests coming in. We knew he was such a hit with the guests and he made our jobs easier.

Our last party consisted of a group of ten old Scotchmen. I was somewhat apprehensive as the few Scotts I had met had a rather unpleasant disposition. Fortunately, these were not as I had expected. As they disembarked from the tallyhos it was clear where they hailed from. They came fully decked out in their finest kilts. I thought to myself how in the hell can a man sit a horse in that garb. As I amused myself with these thoughts, Ben had enough sense not to comment on their looks.

It seemed that the head of their clan had recently passed away. Some years before he died, he had heard of this place in Canada named Banff after his Shire of Banff in Scotland. He had wanted his entire clan to visit the place and so when he died, he had left passage to Canada to each of the men in the clan. Quite a strange thing to do, I thought.

Their accent took a bit of getting used to but all in all they were quite a pleasant group. They also loved their music. Now in the evenings when Molly played her organ, she had bagpipes to accompany her. One of the old guys even gave our Ben a go at the pipes. Like about everything else, he took to it like a duck to water. I kidded him, saying I was going to nickname him little bag of wind.

I promised Ben that he would see a bear before summers end. And his bear adventure was to be a classic one, for sure. The group of Scotts had wanted an adventure in the backcountry. Molly, without a moment's hesitation, told them that I would be glad to guide them. I told Molly I would get even with her for that. When I started rattling off a few spots we might visit, I mentioned Lake O'Hara. I should have known their response to that. "Sonny", imagine them calling a sixty-five-year-old man sonny, "That sounds like just our kind'o spot; let's go there," the elder most of the group piped up.

It seemed I was to make a second trip back to O'Hara that summer. Ben asked if he could come along. He allowed as how since he now knew the way, he could lead. I thought to myself that will likely get these gents dander up to be guided by a kid just turned fourteen years old. It all seemed like a real dejavu kind of trip. We would camp where Ben and I camped, maybe do a bit of fishing, and give these gents the taste of some great trout.

Usually I am pretty good about picking campsites; however, when Ben and I went in June the bear berries weren't ripe. When we set up at the same campsite, now late August,

I stupidly failed to equate the abundant crop of berries around there with the bears. Apparently, every bear in those parts was quite aware of our berries. When I added a few trout remains, those bears had one hell of a banquet spread out. We were camped right in the middle of their banquet table.

About eight o'clock, right after dinner, before it even got fully dark, one of the old Scotts was returning from a visit with nature and spotted a large bear near his tent. The old man started yelling as if he was being eaten alive. Of course, by the time the rest of us got to his tent there was no sign of the bear. That didn't last long, however. While we were discussing the matter over by the fellow's tent, the bear and his friends out-flanked us. We heard a racket and the horses' started carrying on. Sure, enough we spotted two of the beasts near where we had cleaned the fish.

Ben was really excited, so was everyone for that matter. I grabbed a couple of pans and succeeded in scaring them away. Fortunately, they were black bears, not grizzlies; regardless, none of us slept too well that night, knowing they were near about. Needless to say, we moved our campsite the next day and once we got away from those berries and stopped eating fish, they didn't bother us for the rest of the trip. I suspect that was the first time and perhaps only time ever that Lake O'Hara has echoed with the sound of bagpipes, but it just somehow, seemed quite fitting. All in all, I think they had a great time.

It was finally time to take Ben to the train. Molly and I gave him fifty dollars for his summer's help. We made him promise to save it. He vowed as how he wanted to come back next summer and that winter too. We told him he was like our son and was always welcome. You know I think the lad now has a bit of what this place is about in him. I suspect he will be back; I sure hope so as Molly and I will miss him. We were both about in tears when that train pulled out.

242

17. Goodbye Sweet Molly

I guess I first became aware something was wrong in January of 1912. When I look back on it though, the symptoms probably were there in the fall of 1911. We had enjoyed such a wonderful summer with Ben that I guess I was still expecting something like that again the next summer. I wondered at first if it was just the let-down from all that fun. Molly was certainly never one to complain when she didn't feel well. She had always been so healthy and full of life that it was hard to comprehend anything different.

We wintered at the Chalet the past winter. In January, Molly came down with what I thought might be pneumonia. It had been very cold and damp. She blamed her illness on catching a chill when she went down to Banff shopping. Molly was dreadfully sick for two weeks. Try as I might, I couldn't convince her to go and see Dr. Brett. I did the best I could to care for her. I fed her plenty of liquids and did my best to keep her in bed.

By early February she was quite a lot better but still didn't have the energy that she formerly had. Just watching her walk it was easy to tell that the hop, skip, and jump were gone.

Our favorite winter pastime of ice-skating on the lake would tire her quickly. Previously she had been able to skate circles around me and do so for hours at a time.

At the end of February, when her strength still had not returned, I finally prevailed in getting her to go see the doctor. I accompanied her to Banff to see Dr. Brett. She kept telling me that all he would do was to give her a bottle of his own brand of elixir. After Dr. Brett examined her, I had the uneasy feeling that he knew something was wrong but he refrained from saying so. He recommended that she go to Calgary to see another doctor. This was most unusual for the town doctor who always insisted he could diagnose anything.

On March 14th we took the train to Calgary to see Dr. Grant. That night we stayed with Molly's sister. Jean showed great concern at Molly's pale appearance. She urged Molly to rest and told me in no uncertain terms to see to it that she did. I guess she acted as any doting older sister would. Sharing her concern, I agreed I would see to it that Molly got the rest and care she needed.

The first thing the next morning we went for her appointment. After the examination, Dr. Grant wanted to make some blood tests, saying that she might be anemic. He told us that he would send us the results in about a week. Jean had wanted Molly to remain in Calgary, but she had refused. We returned to Lake Louise, still not knowing what the problem was. My diagnosis was that she was just anemic and therefore needed rest and a better diet. I made it a point to pick up a batch of fresh fruit for her before we left Calgary.

We received a telegram from the doctor in Calgary on April 1st. What a cruel April fools joke it turned out to be. Dr.

Grant's telegram asked how she was doing. It also requested that she come back to Calgary for another visit. While the telegram gave no clue of anything being wrong, I felt it odd that he wished her to return without giving a reason.

By now Molly was feeling somewhat better and didn't want to be bothered with another trip back to see the doctor. She was busy working at replacing the linens in the Chalet. Since I had to go to Calgary to purchase some pipe later that week, I decided to stop and see the doctor. Even though Molly was now insisting she was fine, I had a troubled feeling that all was not right.

"Mr. Bristol, I am so glad you stopped by. I was concerned about Molly and hoped she might come back. She is doing better, yes?" Dr. Grant asked. I explained that she insisted she was fine. The doctor said he certainly hoped she would stay that way, but he feared she might not. He then told me his terrible diagnosis. His words pierced me like so many dull knives. It seemed the tests had indicated that she had a cancer.

In those days, not much was known about cancer other than it was nearly always fatal. The wonder drugs, chemotherapy, and the bone marrow transplants that I knew of were so many years from where we were. In a trembling voice I asked the doctor what the outlook was…"Grim, I'm afraid," was his answer.

"How…how long does she have?" I finally was able to get those words out.

"Honestly, Logan, I don't know. Sometimes people live quite some time and experience little pain, other times there can be a swift and painful death," he responded. "She is young and hopefully her body will fight a valiant fight with the disease."

Numbed and in tears, I boarded the train at dusk, completely forgetting about buying any pipe. I was losing my sweet Molly. How could I tell her? I just couldn't. I longed to get back to her. I wanted to hold her and treasure every moment. I am sure Molly thought my excessive affection that night was strange. Maybe she even knew. I had to excuse myself several times to hide my tears. It was impossible for me to keep my mind from replaying the wonderful times we had and thinking of how few we might have left. What was I to do without her, I kept thinking? I just couldn't bring myself to tell her, at least not yet. Perhaps Dr. Grant was wrong.

With the onset of spring, Molly was much better. Dr. Grant's diagnosis now seemed more like just a bad dream. Even so, I knew too much about cancer for that. I could no longer take even one day of life for granted. As close as we had been, we became closer that spring of 1912. I kept my mind occupied with thinking of fun things for us to do, not wanting to waste a minute.

Pulling her away from her duties was sometimes difficult, but she usually yielded to my gentle prodding. During those weeks of spring we took hikes in the low country where the snow had receded from the meadows. We visited the hot springs a couple of times. I guess I had a glimmer of hope that the hot springs might help her. In any event, those trips helped my spirits a bit.

The first of May, when Molly caught a cold, the symptoms were much worse than usual. She had a fever and soon became very weak again. I tried to get her to go to Calgary to see the doctor. She stubbornly refused, instead using just about every home remedy available at that time. Oh, how I wish I had some wonder drugs to give her.

In the time since I first got the fateful diagnosis from Dr. Grant, I had confirmed what I already knew to be the truth; at that time there was simply not an effective treatment for cancer. I had written to prominent doctors in Philadelphia and New York. Each response shattered my hopes for some way to stop the ravishing beast of death. It was shear agony to know that only a lifetime away lay treatments to forestall the demon and perhaps even a cure. If only I could travel back in time once again to get help, I thought.

The season was starting and by mid-May, Molly's symptoms were again a bit better, though she was still weak. I had been agonizing over whether or not to tell her what the doctor had said. I had now come to some conclusions: first, yes, I must tell her; secondly, I determined to fill each day she had left with all the joy and happiness possible. Yes, and one other thing, I also decided to tell her my story, the story I had kept to myself all these years.

I would tell her of my journey through time, how I came to be in this place at this time. I felt the timing for telling her my story was very important. I decided to wait until I felt she needed a lift. Surely if anything would lift her spirits, my wild story was bound to do just that. At the very least, it was bound to get her mind off her situation.

"Logan, if I don't regain my strength soon, I don't know how I will be able to keep up with the hotel now that the season is starting," Molly lamented over dinner, a dinner she ate little of. That evening, May 24th, I decided the time had arrived when I must tell her about her disease.

After dinner we retired to our cabin. I built a little fire in the fireplace; I poured each of us a spot of brandy, and asked her to join me by the fireside. She willingly obliged, as this was one of our favorite pastimes. "Molly I have to tell you something," I stopped.

"Yes?" she pleaded.

Then I blurted out, "My darling, Dr. Grant thinks you have cancer." It took a few seconds for these words to register with her. She looked up at me with wide eyes, which had now lost their sparkle and were sad.

"Is he sure?" she asked.

"I am afraid so," I managed to choke out. She grabbed me and hugged me tighter than I ever knew she could. She obviously knew what these words meant for us.

We remained silently embraced several minutes. Finally, she let go and again looked into my eyes and said words I will never forget. "Logan, your eyes tell me this is true. Knowing that I must die soon makes me so thankful for the happiness I have known with you. We have had so much. You must not be sad when I go. Few people have had what we have and…we will be together in heaven someday.

"Always remember, though I may be gone, you will have this wonderful special place of ours. I feel this land is us and it will always remain."

How could she be taking this so well I thought. This was certainly not what I expected. I wept shamelessly and embraced her with all my strength.

Molly never reacted to her illness and impending death the way most do. She seldom seemed sad and hardly ever complained, despite the pain I knew she had. It was her great strength that enabled me to get through those days that summer of 1912. As the days rolled by, the cancer began to really extract its toll. Molly became weaker and had dizzy spells occasionally. Her stomach was also frequently upset. Never one who was overweight, she now became emaciated.

Our walks by the lake, canoeing, and travel were now limited to only brief sessions. By now she had pretty much handed a lot of her duties over to her senior housekeeper, Betty Cannon. Molly had tried hard to get me to agree to take over for her and while I agreed to help in any way I could, in my heart I knew I couldn't stay there when she was gone.

One day in mid July when it became obvious the end was nearing, I decided the time had arrived to tell her everything. She was having one of her better spells. This was important as she needed to be well enough for me to spring the surprise I had planned.

"Molly, since you seem spry and chipper today, let's plan a picnic up to the Teahouse tomorrow, what's yea say?"

"That would be lovely, Logan," was her reply. "I only hope I will feel this good tomorrow," she said.

"You will be fine; I just know it. I will set you up on old Aspen and he will give you a most gentle ride up the trail," I said. I knew the idea of riding her favorite old mare would help convince her to do it.

She was doing ok the next morning and with the outlook of great weather we were off right after breakfast. Immediately she became suspicious, "Logan, why did that sign say the Teahouse is closed for today?" she asked. "Didn't you see that sign, it said Teahouse closed for repairs today, will reopen July 17th." "What repairs? I should have known if there was a problem," she went on to say.

Seeing how upset she was getting, I piped up with, "Oh I

am sure it is nothing. We will find out soon if there is a problem," I said in a comforting tone.

My senses were in a heightened state, recognizing every bird sound and relishing in the scent of the fresh balsam. I wanted so much to fully capture every moment and all the sensations that went with it. I felt I would be replaying this time in my mind as long as there was life within me.

As we neared the Teahouse, she shot more questions my way, "Are Mary and Robert going to be up here if the Teahouse is closed today?" Again, I said not to worry if they weren't there, I was sure I could make us some tea. Soon we were inside and I was stoking the stove with some lick log, preparing to make tea.

It wasn't long before the kettle was whistling away. We poured our cups full of tea and went out to sit on the porch. Having the place to ourselves, we chose to sit on the corner where we had the best view of the valley and our lovely Lake Louise, far below. Looking behind us up toward the North end of Lake Agnes, Molly commented that nearly all of the winter's ice was gone. "I wonder if I shall live long enough to see ice again on this lake," she said wistfully. With uncanny and chilling timing, a lone dark cloud obscured the sun as if to provide a crushing answer to that question.

As the sun reappeared, I could see the tears forming in her eyes. I quickly turned away, vowing to myself to be strong for her and not breakdown. Gathering all my strength, I tried to cheerfully respond by saying, "Molly my dear, you shall have the unique opportunity to see ice on this lake sixty-five years from now."

Molly looked confused and hurt, like I was playing some

cruel joke on her. "I wish I could, but alas my love, you know that can't be."

"Don't be so sure. You asked earlier why I closed the Teahouse and gave the staff the day off, well now I shall tell you. You see I have a secret to tell, a secret only your ears may hear.

"Molly, the answer is really quite simple, I wanted this place to be all ours today. I have an amazing story, something very special I want to share with you. Through all the wonderful years I have known you, I have kept one huge secret from you. In fact, I have kept this secret from every living soul for eighteen years. Now I want to share that secret with you," I said.

It was obvious by the serious look she gave me that I now had her full attention. "What I am about to tell you will likely cause you to question my sanity, but I will assure you it is all true. This crazy incredible story is true, but…Before I tell you my story, it is vital that you know that my life with you these past seventeen years has been so wonderful that I wouldn't have traded it for anything. I love you dearly.

"I hope also by telling you this you will even better understand how very much you mean to me and that you will come to believe that almost anything is possible. What I am going to give you now is a first hand look into the future. You see, there is a land over the rainbow, and I have been there," I said.

Having sat quietly, wide-eyed Molly now piped up with, "Logan, what on earth are you talking about? You are frightening me."

"No, no, don't be frightened. There is no reason for that."

"Listen to my story now. I will show you things to prove it

is all true." Having said that, I began the account of the morning of August 26, 1982.

"Molly, when I arrived in Laggan on August 26, 1894, I arrived not from an ordinary place…no, I arrived from the future, I was born in Knoxville, Tennessee. I lived in Atlanta, Georgia, was married and had a wonderful little boy named Craig.

"Logan!" Molly started to admonish me.

"Please wait…let me continue," I begged. "I had visited the Canadian Rockies several times and loved it out here. I loved it so much that starting about 1974 I came every summer.

"Did you say 1974, Logan?" she asked, in a very excited voice.

"Just listen," I implored her. "I would spend a week hiking and camping. The summer of 1982 was to be like that of the previous years. Most definitely it was far from that.

"On the morning of August 26, 1982, I decided to ride the tramway (a modern device to transport people up mountains, I explained) up Mt Whitehead. About one third the way up. a large thunderstorm hit. I think the tram was hit by lightning and at just that moment I was staring at an old 1894 gold coin.

"When I came to, I was laying in the forest with no sign of the tramway in sight. Only a charred piece of metal from the car that I had been riding remained. I was all right other than being confused and sore. My pack that I had with me was also ok. Search as I did, I could find no sign of the tram, or for that matter, the trail that ran beneath the tram. The gold coin I had been holding had also vanished. I started down the mountain through dense woods. Upon my arrival at the Bow River, I found the railroad line, but to my horror, there was no highway or any man-made objects that I was familiar with.

"Making my way up the tracks, I came upon Laggan. The place I knew as a modern tourist center was now nothing more than a railroad station, a few shacks, and little else. I found the trail going to Lake Louise and made my way up to the lake. Everything seemed as if a dream. I still did not understand what had happened.

"When I finally arrived at that beautiful the lake, that same lake down there, the reality of it all finally hit me. The lake was unmistakable, indeed. It was the beautiful Lake Louise, but instead of the huge grand Chateau that I knew so well, I was greeted with a quaint little structure with a sign saying The Chalet.

"I realized then, as I collapsed there, that I had somehow traveled back to an earlier time. It was a time I found strange and frightening, yet so amazingly wonderful. My excitement was short lived and gave way to despair. The loss of my family, my little boy; it was almost too much to bear. I nearly went crazy that first winter trying to figure out how to get back. Had I not met a wonderful Irish lass that next Spring, I surely don't know what would have become of me.

"Quite likely, Molly, you saved my life. Never could I have survived that great a loss without your love. You can never know how badly I wanted to tell you all this back then. I didn't tell you because I was terrified that by doing so I might somehow change the future, possibly preventing Craig from being born or causing some other terrible event in the future. I was also sure you would view me as completely crazy.

"Keeping this secret has been an awful burden at times over

the years, especially when events like when the terrible Titanic sinking occurred three months ago. Now you know why I have seemed secretive about my past and why I have seemed to be keeping to myself at times.

"I am sure you have some doubts about my story, but just you wait, I have proof. I am going to show you some amazing things from the future. I have selected several of my treasures from my pack that survived the journey. Take this coin for example," as I handed her a 1976 US dime. "Check the date," I said.

Shaking her head, she gasped, "Logan, this…this is incredible. Are you sure this is not some joke? Please tell me the truth!"

"No, Molly, it is all very real, just as real as you and I being here right now. Here let me show you some modern camping gear," I said. With that I produced my single burner Gaz stove that fits in the palm of the hand. "That little stove will burn four hours on that little tank of gas," I said.

"Amazing," was her only comment.

"Molly, do you remember that time when we climbed Mt Temple and I knew the route so well? I knew it well because I had climbed it before. And do you remember later that night when I fixed that seemingly elaborate dinner in ten minutes? I told you then that some day I would share my secret with you, well my dear, you experienced freeze dried food. Just add hot water and wala.

"There is so much that I want to tell you about the future. Things are so grand, so exciting, and I guess a few not so nice. Why they have jet planes. I could travel from my home in Atlanta, twenty-five hundred miles away, up to Calgary in just six hours."

"Logan, that can't be possible," she responded.

"Oh yes, Molly, and space travel is a reality. Men have actually walked on the moon," I went on to explain.

"Logan, you are surely crazy. This can't be true…can it?" she asked.

"It sure is true," I reassuringly stated.

"If it is true then Logan, tell me more," she pleaded.

"Well, let me start right here by telling you about this place that we love so much today. Oh, some things have changed. Thank goodness there are thick forests where the blackened slopes are now. One big change is our Chalet has been replaced with a grand structure and is called the Chateau at Lake Louise. Though the Chateau is indeed a grand thing, losing our Chalet is sad, just as it was when we lost the original little Chalet ten years ago.

"But, just wait a moment, Molly. I have an even grander surprise; you see I don't have to just tell you about the future, oh no…I can actually show it to you. Stay here, I must get out a few things," I said as I got up and walked toward the door under the Teahouse porch.

I emerged from under the porch carrying a wooden ammunition box covered with a piece of canvas. Returning to the storage space again, I came out with yet another heavier box. I then carried both boxes up to the porch. Molly was like a little kid anxiously awaiting candy.

I opened the heavier box first. "What is that? It looks like…is that a battery?" Molly asked.

"Good guess," I responded. Now carefully I proceeded to open the other box. I withdrew a plastic bag, which, in itself was an object of wonder. From that bag I took out one of my most treasured possessions, my camcorder with its miniature color screen.

Predictably, Molly quickly asked what it was. "Well," I said, "this tiny gizmo will show you color pictures of my past and the future of this place. Just watch," I said as I continued to hook up the equipment. "If everything works, not only can you see the pictures, but you can hear sounds from the future as well."

Knowing that I was going to be putting on this show I had, over the past couple of weeks, checked out the equipment and tested the battery in an attempt to make sure all went well. The battery had been the biggest obstacle. The rechargeable camcorder battery had long since expired and there was not the correct current to recharge it. The large storage battery that I had obtained seemed to work ok, but it was not very portable.

From the second box I now withdrew another smaller plastic bag. From this I took three small cassette tapes. I had these three tapes with me when I arrived here back in 1894. It was very amazing that they had survived the travel and all the time since in such good condition. It must surely have been some divine plan, I thought.

One of the tapes was an unused blank tape. The second tape was about half shot and was in the camera at the time of my travel. The third tape was an older one of the previous year's trip. I had never been able to figure out why I had brought that particular tape along on a backpacking trip. Again, some divine destiny…? I wondered.

"What is all this?" she continued to ask.

"Wait you will see in just a minute," I responded as I

inserted the half-shot tape in the camcorder. I paused before pushing the play button. "Molly, what you are going to see now are pictures taken around Lake Louise in August 1982. You will see what the hotel looks like. You will see trails and animals. You will even see a modern cabin at Moraine Lake, but enough of my talking. Open your eyes, here comes the future." As I pressed the button the oddly familiar whining of the little motor began. The tiny screen sprang to life with flickers as the speaker produced static. Suddenly as if by miracle, a beautiful color panorama shot of Lake Louise appeared.

Craig, I will never forget that surprised look on Molly's face as she viewed those first scenes. Her face looked just like yours when you, as a baby, first tasted ice cream. The sound of a Canadian Jay and some tourists talking in the background added a perfect touch to the tape. Shaking her head and looking back and forth from the screen to me she finally said, "This is so beautiful, so wonderfully beautiful." After a minute the scene changed. The images were now of a late afternoon scene in front of the Chateau by the water's edge. "Oh no, that can't be! "she exclaimed.

"Oh yes, it can and is, my dear," I interjected.

"Yes, Molly, that is the Chalet all grown up, or as it is now known, The Chateau," I stated. "It is so huge", she exclaimed, "and … Just look at that lovely lawn with those gorgeous flowers! Are they, are those, really Icelandic Poppies, after all these years?

"Yes, they are the flowers you chose still gracing the lawn here," I responded.

The scene of the hotel that had so charged us with emotion ended. With the next picture she let out a gasp, for there in unmistakable clarity in the lower left-hand corner of the scene was the date and time "August 23, 1982 7:05 PM". Equally shocking was the subject matter of the scene. The picture was that of a group of hotel employees clad in swimming suits, draped in coats by the water's edge.

"What on earth is going on?" Molly exclaimed. "Why…just look at that girl, she hasn't enough clothes on. No, no Logan, don't look!" an obviously embarrassed Molly again exclaimed. I went on to try and explain what she was looking at was a modern version of the swimming suit called a bikini. It was easy to tell she was not ready for that part of the future.

"But Logan, whatever are they doing?" she asked again.

"Well, can't you guess?" I teased her, "They are just carrying on the tradition that you and I started. It is the annual end of the season Polar Bear Plunge," I added. This was a bit of craziness we had started the end of the season in 1900, the century mark when crazy acts were the norm. Molly and I announced to the staff that we would jump into the lake if the staff got through the Prime Ministers visit that season without incident. This having occurred, we made good on our bet and were joined by several other foolish souls.

"How magnificent!" Molly exclaimed, "I can't believe they are still doing that foolish thing, Logan. Tell me again that this is all real?" she begged.

"Oh yes, and there is much more," I answered, releasing the pause button so the action continued with the shrills of the young men and women as they encountered the icy water. "And this, Molly, is the cabin I was staying in down at Moraine Lake the last night before my adventure," I said as the picture changed.

"My dear, does this look familiar?" I asked. It was the same Teahouse we had created and where we were now. "Can it be our special place has survived all these years?" she said while crying.

"It sure is and I had visited this same spot many times before 1894. You see, I knew what to build here. I was however, a little concerned about being the one to build it," I added.

Suddenly the picture ended with white fuzzy flickering and static. "What happened?" she shrieked in a surprised and disappointed tone. I quickly assured her that was just the end of that tape and that I had another. Eager for more, she implored me to use great haste in changing the tapes. While engaged in switching the tapes, I prepared her for the next adventure.

"This tape was made a year earlier in Banff and Bankhead and if you thought that last tape was unbelievable, wait till you see this one," I stated proudly. The tape started with a shot of a metal plaque which contained a brief history of Bankhead and a picture of the town circa 1910. "Why that picture looks just like Bankhead today, but ... but why does it have the dates 1903 — 1923?" she asked, quite perplexed.

As I began my explanation, the timing of the scenery change was perfect. The picture began with a panorama of the grassy field that lay down the hill upon which the plaque stood. All that protruded above the grass were concrete foundations. These were the foundations and skeletons of the buildings I had by then helped build.

Molly gasped. She now realized that it was all gone. "Logan, what on earth happened?" she begged. Before I could start to answer, a picture appeared so chilling as to send goose bumps over my body. Molly did not immediately realize what she was looking at, I hesitated a moment in telling her, concerned at her reaction. "Molly, that is all that is left of our church," I added.

"No,…you can't mean it. Tell me it isn't true. Surely, they didn't tear down the church too," she said, almost in tears. "These steps are now called the stairs to Heaven" I added.

Stopping the tape for a minute, I tried to explain what had happened to Bankhead. "You see Molly, by the middle of the 1920s, people had begun to realize how inappropriate it was to have a mining operation in a National Park. The final nail in Bankhead's coffin though, was a labor strike in 1921. When the mine closed during the strike, it never reopened. Two years later, the Park Service decided to remove all of the buildings from Bankhead and let nature reclaim the town. And so, you see the work of nature for the last fifty odd years."

"You knew this would happen when you helped build it?" she asked.

I replied, "Yes, yes, I did and I had a real hard time dealing with it."

"Logan, I think it is so sad that the town is gone, but I guess I never did think that mining had any business in the park. After all, the preservation of the park is the most important, don't you agree?" she asked.

"Yes, I sure do."

"Let's see some more," she pleaded. The pictures rolled on, showing the grassy field where upper Bankhead once stood.

"Stop, Logan, what was that?" she asked. What she had just seen and wanted to know about was a monument beside the road.

I didn't think about the implications of the picture as I started my explanation. "That is a monument that was erected to the memory of those men from Bankhead who died in World War I," I said, immediately realizing I had opened a Pandora's box.

"What World War? Who fought? Who died?" she begged to know.

I went on to explain about the war with Germany and skirted the issue of who died by saying I didn't remember, though I knew I could probably freeze the film and we could read the names. It would be too great of a burden knowing that among those who would die were surely friends of ours. Knowing when and where these people would die gave me the shivers and I was thankful Molly didn't press me about it.

Suddenly the scene changed again to something lovely. "Oh, what beautiful gardens," Molly exclaimed. "Look at all those flowers. Where is this picture?" she asked.

As I again paused the tape, I answered saying, "Do you know where Dr. Brett's Sanitarium is just across the Bow River Bridge in Banff? That is the site of the Park Headquarters and these lovely gardens."

"It is too grand, Logan, much nicer than Dr. Brett's tacky hotel," she added.

"Even more eerie, Molly, those gardens are called The Gardens of Time," I explained.

"Amazing," was her reply.

"Can that be?" she exclaimed.

"It sure is," I said with great pride. The picture on the screen now was of the magnificent Banff Springs Hotel. The camera captured the unmistakable West flank of Mt. Rundle as it lay behind the hotel. The next scene was similar, but even more spectacular. It was a scene of what the CPR referred to back then as the Million Dollar View, the mountains, Bow Falls, and river behind the hotel.

"What wonderful green lawns," she added. "Oh, you mean the golf course," I said. The camera had picked up the spectacular course that lay behind the hotel alongside the Bow River. "Golf," I explained, "is a sport that soon will become very popular with both men and women. I will tell you more about that later, but now let's continue," I added, anxious for what was to come next.

Adding to the spectacular effect of the scenery, there was now beautiful music in the background. "Where is that music coming from, Logan?" she asked. I explained that I was taking the picture inside the Rundle Lounge in the hotel looking out through the window. The camera panned the Bow Falls and river below as I explained that a pianist was playing music for patrons during afternoon tea time, or happy hour as we Americans came to call it after substituting alcohol for tea.

"Logan, what is that music? It is quite nice," she added. Chill bumps again broke out all over me. Surely nothing on earth could have been more ironic than that, I thought as I answered her simple question.

"Molly, the music the pianist is playing is called 'Somewhere in Time,'" I said.

"Logan, you are joking, aren't you?" she asked in a very unbelieving tone.

"No, my dear," I said. "I know this is unbelievable. It is music from a film about time travel. Somehow I was always very fond of the music from the first time I heard it." Truly I could never have comprehended how profound it would be for me. We both agreed that there must surely have been some divine destiny to that particular music being on that particular tape.

Of all the pictures on the tape, that scene of Mt. Rundle catching the afternoon sun as seen from the lounge of the Banff Springs Hotel was the most spectacular. I replayed that scene with that incredible music again as we became mesmerized by it all.

Sadly, the tape ended and the present reality returned slowly. We embraced, holding each other very tightly, lest we end as the tape. Molly broke the silence, "Logan, I am so happy that this place we love so much has stayed so beautiful. It is really wonderful to know that the generations that follow us can enjoy the same wonders we enjoy. You know, Logan, showing me this is the most wonderful thing anyone has ever done for me."

On the way back down to the Chalet, we walked quietly, holding hands. As we neared the Chalet, Molly asked him to tell her more about the future. "I want to know as much as you can teach me before I go," were her haunting words.

I responded with, "My dear, I will tell you everything."

The days and weeks that followed were filled with happiness and excitement as I painted Molly a canvas of things from the future. Her days were not always good now. As summer drew to a close, pain and weakness kept Molly from the places we loved so much. No longer could we go up to the Teahouse or venture into Paradise Valley.

On good days we would sit by the lake and I would tell her of some exciting future adventure. Sometimes after I coaxed her into eating a little dinner, I would wrap her in a shawl and we would go canoeing on our lake. Sometimes she would hum that haunting song 'Somewhere in Time'. At other times we would just listen to the soothing sound of distant waterfalls echoing from the mighty mountain walls that surrounded us.

The end came with loving peacefulness. My sweet Molly passed away in her sleep on August 27, 1912. The significance of that date was lost in the pain I felt at the time. I was able to summon my last bit of strength to carry out Molly's final request.

She had wanted to be buried in Paradise Valley near where we had camped when we climbed Mt Temple, those short few years ago. Paradise Valley welcomed her with beautiful weather. Such a lovely place she had picked to linger for eternity. I wanted so bad to lay down with her in that grave. I prayed to someday join her there for eternity.

The funeral was the way I think she would have wanted it. Reverend Gray, now up in years, came up and said the prayers. Roger Cane gave the eulogy. I was too broken up to say much. All the staff from the Chalet, every last one, made the trip into the valley to the funeral, as did many of her friends from Banff. She had touched so many lives with her happiness during her short twenty years out here. All came out that day with tears in their eyes to say goodbye to my sweet Molly. Craig, I must end this now. I can write no more.

18. LOST YEARS / A FINAL DIARY ENTRY

Craig wiped away tears as he paused to think of the moving words he had just read. As he turned the page of the diary, he immediately noticed that the paper was different. The writing also seemed somewhat more erratic. The explanation was soon found as he read on.

August 28, 1918

"I am writing this on August 28, 1918. It has been six lonely years since Molly left this world for a better one. No one can know the pain of losing loves from two lifetimes. It's been hell. Well, enough of the melancholy. Craig, I couldn't leave you wondering at my plight so I have decided to update the diary for my "lost years".

Shortly after I laid Molly to rest, I left Lake Louise and headed north into the wilderness. It was September of 1912. I didn't have a destination in mind; rather I just traveled into the wilderness with reckless abandon in hopes of finding a short path to join my Molly. My will to live had departed with her. Despite all my carelessness, I continued to survive.

My wanderings took me up toward Jasper. I passed the Columbia Ice Field, tramped up over Gresham Pass, and down to Maligne Lake. I then went up a stream leading out of the lake up toward Red Deer. Winter's early snows were harassing me by the time I arrived in the little settlement of Jasper. At the time, Jasper was not in the park. It was still only an outpost for trappers, hunters, and in the summer an occasional hardy tourist. I found an old abandoned trapper cabin a few miles from town on the shore of the Athabaska River. The crude abode fit well with my mood and outlook on life at that time. It was in this simple shack that I settled in for a long lonely winter.

Having not enough provisions, I was faced with either hunting or trapping to supplement my nourishment for the winter. Trapping had never been an endeavor I took much pleasure in. Most of my winter meat came from good fortune with my rifle. There was an abundance of wampi. My sojourns away from my cabin in search of meat and firewood gave me a much-needed activity to relieve my melancholy. A diet, largely of meat, left me yearning for fresh fruits and vegetables. My thoughts turned to my long-gone Southern cooking. How I missed Christmas dinner back home, my mind kept creating the wonderful dishes, I could almost taste them.

I dreamed of picking strawberries on your great grandfather's farm and of defending the tomato patch from the squirrels and crows. Aside from daydreaming and hunting, I took to writing. I wrote about things I did each day. These writings included an expanded version of this diary's ramblings and when I felt particularly literary, I even penned some poetry. Fortunately for the literary world, all these scribbling were lost in a misadventure of a river crossing near winter's end.

Why I survived, I don't know. I must assume that there was still some destiny I had yet to fulfill. As Canadian winters go, that winter was about as bad as they get. My thermometer broke so I don't know for sure how cold it got. The cold made me feel the pangs of my 63 years, despite my previous remarkable good health. By winter's end, I guess that I had lost thirty of my previous one hundred seventy pounds. Along with the pounds, I lost the ends of two toes to frostbite that winter.

By April 1st I had come to the realization that I was destined to survive, despite all the foolish things I had done. My spirits were raised with the first signs of spring. The wonderful renewing power of the awakening season brought me back to life. Feeling a need for people, I decided it was time to rejoin civilization. I headed south toward Banff. I walked all the way back to Laggan. It took over a week to make the trek. I still couldn't bring myself to stop at Lake Louise and I caught the train at Laggan for Banff.

On May 1st I had arrived back in the booming town of Banff. Over the past few years this once quaint little town had spread like wildfire. All the advertising that the CPR had done must have paid off. The word had spread that the Canadian Rockies was the place for adventure. There were people from all parts of the world journeying here, but mostly from the United States and Europe.

The booming sister town of Bankhead, what with its mine, had helped keep Banff energized, even in the winter. Automobiles were another thing that had occurred the past couple of years that was to change everything in the coming years. After the first cars had arrived in Banff, better roads were to soon follow. The cars would ultimately lead to the demise of rail travel. But lest I get ahead of myself, let me get back to Banff.

For the past two years, the Banff Springs Hotel had been booked solid, even before the season began. Other hotels, such as the Prince Albert, had recently sprung up and they too were doing a good business as well. Dr Brett's sanitarium was doing a land office business for those with ailments. The Sanitarium by now had gained just about as big a reputation as the Banff Springs Hotel itself. Still the Banff Springs remained the king of lodgings. Its continued success led to a grand expansion of the hotel that started in the spring of 1913.

Tom Gunter had taken Roger Cane's place as manager of the Banff Springs Hotel a year earlier. I had hated to see Roger retire, but Tom was a good guy, not stuffy as some of that CPR crew were. He was sure a lot better than others they could have brought in. I think I first met Tom back in 1910 when a group of CPR managers appeared one day out of the blue at the Chalet. I showed him around and we seemed to hit it off pretty good. All of Molly's bragging on me probably had made an impression, especially since by then she had almost as much clout as old man Wilson himself.

Tom, having learned that I was in town, invited me to join him for dinner a few days after I arrived. It was over dinner that he asked me to help him in supervising the work on the addition to the hotel. The offer was too tempting to pass up. Working on one of those grand hotels always was a special treat for me. I willingly accepted the challenging year-long project. I figured at least it would keep this old man out of trouble.

Our task was to replace the West wing that had been part of the original 1888 wooden building. The new addition would be seven stories and built with stone masonry, concrete, and steel. It was sad to tear down such a large part of this grand old hotel but I kept thinking that we were creating something more substantial, something that would last. As I helped build those walls, my thoughts and hopes were that one day, Craig, you would look upon them.

The order that came down to us was "do whatever it takes to create the most spectacular hotel in North America," a pretty ambitious goal, don't you think? With all the money flowing into the CPR's coffers, no expense was to be spared. I will refrain from boring you with all the details of the construction as I doubt you share your father's interest in this line of work. The workers were a joy. Of particular note was their eagerness to perform quality work. They were a great bunch of guys with great work ethics, so much better than I had experienced in my career back in the 70s. With that crew and the blank check, the CPR gave us to make it happen, nothing seemed beyond our ability.

As I got to know the men, I found most came here looking for a better life in a clean invigorating environment and a good place to raise their families. Each seemed to have a special pioneering spirit, just as my long-lost friend Robert had. They acted as though they were doing some important work, creating something special. I shared their enthusiasm and pride in what we were together creating. The building progressed well and I can say now that it was some of the most rewarding work of my years.

We had our challenges and then there were the amusing times as well. I guess one of my favorite memories was the time when I realized the workers had closed in a guest room, leaving no door. Surprisingly, the Architect had not noticed the error. I pondered the situation. Should I leave it that way for a bit of added mischief and mystery? I had a hard time deciding. My mind conjured up thoughts of hidden passageways and the like. What do you think, Craig, is there a missing room still in the hotel today?

In August of that year (it seems that every significant event in my life continues to occur in August), while I was up to my neck with the new construction, Tom came to me in a panic. His problem was that two of his best guides were quite sick and he had a group of affluent tourists (by coincidence from the Southern US) expecting a guided tour of the area. Tom said his first thought was me. He said I would be perfect and begged me to help him out of a spot.

I explained to Tom that I had not worked as a guide for several years and was quite suitably occupied with his construction work. Tom, realizing the importance of keeping his guests satisfied, wouldn't take no for an answer. He finally got me to agree to help him as a guide. I agreed to do it for only one day though. In return he said he would always have a room for me at the hotel, whenever I wanted it. I figured that might be a pretty good thing to count on down the road.

Playing guide for a day proved to be a surprisingly pleasant relief. For the outing I led my group of greenhorns up the backside of Sulfur Mountain, pointing out fossils in the rocks along the trail. A number of my charges were about done for by the time we got to the top. A group of mountain sheep that made their home on the summit put some life back into the bunch. Coming down, I shared the secret location of a couple of other hot springs that existed around the base of the mountain.

At one secluded location the group took off their boots to soak their weary feet in the soothing hot water. While the guests were having a great time soaking their feet, I was having a bit of regret for bringing them there. It brought back memories too painful for me. I couldn't help but remember back to the wonderful times Molly and I had spent at that seductive spring in the years following our first night in the cave. After a bit though, I realized that Molly would have wanted me to share that special place with others, just as we had with the Teahouse.

After a day of showing my group the sites, much to my complete surprise, they seemed eager for more. I decided I would conclude the day with a little evening entertainment. I thought about giving a little talk on the history of Banff that evening. For this program I decided to use a format that I remembered fondly from my youth. The spot I selected was a clearing behind the hotel near the Bow Falls. With the help of a couple of the stable hands from the hotel, I placed some logs to form a large circle. In the center of the circle, I formed a fire pit. We piled up an ample supply of firewood to last an hour or so. The fire would take the chill off and hopefully drive the sketters away.

It was in this setting that I conducted my first fireside program. I told the story of the discovery of the Hot Springs at Banff, the development of Lake Louise, and the early years of the Canadian Pacific Railroad. I also threw in a couple of adventure stories of my own. Much to my surprise, after an hour and a half, my audience, who by all rights should have been exhausted by the day's activities, still were asking questions.

The success of this first campfire program spread quickly. What I later learned was that one of those in attendance had sent a telegraph to a relative who just happened to be on the CPR board. They had described my program and gave glowing praise for it and its value to the visitors. In a matter of a few days, my old friend Bill Wilson who was still the general manager of hotels at the CPR home office, sent a wire to Tom Gunter. In the wire to Tom, he instructed him to immediately employ me to conduct similar programs for the guests on a regular basis, and give me whatever I wanted. Needless to say, I was somewhat shocked by all this. I had never considered myself to be a historian, much less a lecturer.

As the season was nearly over, and since my work on the new addition was far from over, I managed to forestall this new line of work until the start of the season the next year. I gave the new job a lot of thought that winter of 1913. I spent a number of evenings jotting down some notes to use in talks that upcoming season. The more I thought about the idea, the better it set with me. I didn't do too badly on the compensation either. For this gig I was to get a whopping $150 per month, and nice new cabins in both Banff and Lake Louise and free train travel whenever I wanted it. This will be a pretty good pension for an old man.

I did not consider myself to be much of a speaker, I worried about being boring. I tried to remember some of the gimmicks I had seen rangers use at some of the many campfire programs that I had attended as a kid. What I finally decided to do was just simply to tell the story of life in the wilderness and not worry about my speaking abilities. As I thought back on some of the experiences I had enjoyed, I began to realize that some of them had really been pretty exciting and others might just enjoy the tales a mite.

By June 1st of 1914, the addition was finished and ready to be occupied with early guests. My evening talks started on June 5th. I worried that the especially large crop of skitters would eat up my audience before we even got started. Despite the little pests, the reviews were good, much to my amazement. I thought to myself, if they find the history of the area that interesting, boy…could I give them some history. Tempted as I was to spice up the talks with the future, in the end, I chose to keep my long-kept secret just that.

It now appeared that I had fallen upon a job well suited to my advancing years. I moved into my new cabin on the shore of Vermillion Lakes in the township of Banff. The evening programs left my days free for exploring in the mountains or just sitting on my front porch watching the few remaining beavers repairing their lodges in the marshes of the lakes. As good as things seemed to be, there were clouds on the horizon, dark clouds.

As 1914 drew to a close, the event I knew as World War I was raging in Europe. Soon the effects of the conflict could be seen in Banff. Many of the locals were going off to war. My age gave me an excuse not to go. I am glad not to have remembered much about it from my history class, other than we won, that is. With the war, many things were to change. The most dramatic change was that the tourist business dried up. The CPR decided to close the Banff Springs for the duration of the war. The CPR's main mission now was to keep goods for the war effort flowing.

My career as a speaker was put on hold. I now occupied my time helping in the machine shop at Bankhead. The mine was now working around the clock to produce coal for the war effort. It seemed the Bankhead coal produced less smoke than other coal and was in high demand for her majesty's ships. The coal helped them avoid detection by the German U-boats.

Since housing was at a premium in Bankhead, I decided to reside in Banff while working in Bankhead. Each morning I would saddle my new horse "Campfire" and ride the five miles up to the mine works and then ride back in the evening. Getting back in the saddle was good for me. I quickly formed a strong bond with my new steed. The work wasn't really that bad and I enjoyed the opportunity to renew my acquaintances there.

Bankhead was still such a great little mining town, but my how it had changed. Once this was just a hand-full of buildings and village to one hundred souls. Now it was a town of some seven hundred, with all the amenities of a modern little city. Dave White had opened a store there. The town even has a fine curling rink, one even better than Banff's. Before the war took all the young men away, the Bankhead curlers had won a bonspiel with Calgary the past year.

Finally, the war was over. I felt good about having done my part there for the war effort. I guess knowing the outcome in advance helped me a bit, still like any war, the loss of life was awful. Bankhead and Banff both had lost men, two of which were friends of mine. Regretfully, one was Tom Orchard, my old building buddy.

I now longed to get back to the more leisurely work that would allow me time to be out in the wilds of nature again. The hotel was reopened again for the season of 1918. The reservations poured in and it quickly filled up. With the return of the tourists, my employment as a campfire host at the Banff Springs resumed and was soon in high gear. Once again, I was surprised at how well my talks were received.

Not to be outdone, the manager at the Chalet, David Notel, did some lobbying with the CPR home office, pressing them to make my campfire programs available to the guests there at Lake Louise as well. The offshoot of all these negotiations was what turned out to be a rather hectic schedule for me. I would spend one week in Banff, then the next in Lake Louise that whole season. Since I had already sort of planned for this when I first agreed to do these programs, I had negotiated the use of a cabin at Lake Louise as well as one in Banff as part of the deal. With all this travel back and forth, I quickly began to feel like a regular modern-day commuter. I couldn't help but ask the conductor to be sure and credit my frequent rider account. He just laughed.

And so it was, that beginning that summer of 1918, I once again returned frequently to my beloved Lake Louise. It seemed strange to be back there after nearly six years, and oh how sad it was without my Molly. But, still…this was after all my little corner of the world. This was always the place my heart longed for, ever since I first laid eyes on it as a kid two lifetimes ago. It is here in Lake Louise that I have spent many days relaxing up at the Teahouse. It is here that I have written a lot of this diary over the last number of years. Sitting up here looking down on the miniature landscape below must surely be a preview of heaven.

The programs at Lake Louise were held by the lake's edge near the boat house. The boat house has changed little, but of course we no longer need the ice house, what with the new electric coolers. I often thought that in such a spectacular setting, I could have spoken on any subject and been successful. The scenery did the charming, not me. The well fed and quite tame ground squirrels and jays frequently joined us early in the evenings before sunset. As the sun went down, the crackling fire added wonderful sounds and aroma.

Today is August 27, 1919. It was twenty-five years ago today that I started my life here. Still after all these years, Craig, hardly a day goes by that I don't think of you and your mother and wonder what kind of life you both have. Little has changed with me these last few years. I can't say that about the world or this place. As for Lake Louise, things keep changing.

One of the latest things to occur here at the Chalet over the past couple of years is the addition of our own little railroad. We have a little miniature railroad. The narrow gage rails extend from Laggan Station up to our little depot just the other side of the lake's outfall. It is about where you would find the public parking today. This new way of getting folks up the mountain has been quite popular with the guests. They can now arrive in an open rail carriage in lieu of a disgusting wagon road, which regrettably I must report is still unsuitable for the new motor cars.

Jean's son, Ben, has been a real delight to me. Ben returned to Banff last summer after finishing his schooling in Montreal. Of all things, this young lad of 21 wants to be a writer. I expect he can find plenty to write about out here. Even more surprising, he wants to write a story about this crusty old guy's life. Maybe I will let him have a go at helping me spruce up this diary...no, my secret is too old by now. I guess I will take it to my grave.

Ben is like a sponge. He takes in everything and seems to always long for more. He reminds me much of yours truly many years ago. His love for the outdoors is second only to his yearning for the "summer girls" as they still call the eligible lasses around here. Ben has even tried to get this old man interested in courting. Alas, I fear my courting days have gone the way of the wolf.

I have, however, taken great pleasure in counseling Ben in the fine points of courting. Having had a good part of two centuries exposure to the fairer sex, I guess it should make me a bit of a point of reference. I must confess though; women are always a challenge for a man. Just the other day, Ben made a real blunder. He remarked to June, his girlfriend of the day, that he thought the clerk at Brewster's was cute. You would have thought that kid would have had enough brains to realize that all women want to feel that they are the only one their beau has eyes for; well I guess he will know better next time.

It is now May 27, 1921, and I am writing this at my camp on the Red Deer River. Ben came along with me on this camping trip up here. Presently he is off clambering up Skoki Mountain. I told him there were lots of fossils up there. That was all the curious young man needed. A few years ago, I might have enjoyed the scramble up there, but I fear my years have caught up to me. Actually, I am enjoying being alone for a bit to ponder my thoughts. In any event, this seemed like a good time to catch up a bit with this diary. Soon my summer campfires start and I fear I will get too busy to write.

With the recent completion of the new automobile road from Banff to Lake Louise, things are certainly becoming different. No longer is the train the only means to get to Laggan and Lake Louise. It won't be long before the CPR starts to lose its grasp on this place. There is also a new road being built to Moraine Lake. That lake is destined to be its own special place of splendor. Though not too many locals have automobiles, a surprising number of rich tourists seem to have the noisy machines. I still miss my 1977 T-Bird. Boy, would Ben enjoy driving that baby. Bet he could really catch the eyes of the summer gals with one of those. Oh well, I expect his handsome looks will serve him just fine in that regard.

Tomorrow we plan to camp by the Skoki Lakes, those two beautiful spots of water that in my way of thinking rival Lake Louise. These sky-blue specks are surrounded with the most rugged and spectacular peaks to be seen anywhere. Craig, you must see these someday. Many a time I have camped on the little neck of rock that separates these two blue jewels. My special place is just high enough to see both lakes at the same time but close enough to hear the roar of water pouring through the little canyon connecting them.

Guess I will have to knock off writing for a bit to get under cover from this blasted sleet that has started to fall. It has been one sure enough backward year so far. We didn't have much snow for the winter, but it has sure made up for it this spring.

I am wondering if the bears are still hibernating what with all the spring snow. I am not too worried about the weather right now though. I can still see a patch of blue sky and that is always a good sign.

March 19, 1935 — Craig my string of good health may be about played out. At eighty-six, I guess I am due a few ailments, don't you reckon? Ailments one might expect, but an accident? Like the old fool that I am, I let myself slip on a bit of ice at winter fest and broke my leg. To make it even worse, I fell right in front of my friends, guess they were thinking this old fool should not have been out on the ice. I told the doc that I expected he better shoot me because if I couldn't hike the back country any more, then I didn't want to go on.

While I am laid up with this leg, I decided that I might give this old diary one more update. I only hope I can make it up to the rock to put it in your jar. As I look back, it has sure been a long time since I penned any lines here for you, Craig. The past now sometimes only seems like a misty dream. I do still remember your cute baby face and your mother's smile as if you were both right beside me. Perhaps I am to be with you again soon, who knows, nothing seems impossible to me, all in all though, it has been one hell of a ride for me. I dream of you and Ben meeting some day in the future.

So much has changed these last years it is hard to even start telling about it. One thing that hasn't changed is that the good old CPR still seems to want me at those campfires this season, Lord only knows why. I hope I am off these dam crutches by then. Can you imagine an old mountain man like me on crutches? Well, doc has assured me I will be able to hit the trails again soon. He had better be right.

19. THE END OF THE TRAIL

As Craig closed the diary, he slowly began to emerge from the trance of his fathers writing. The sun was rapidly declining behind the Little Beehive Mountain. The breeze that had earlier been warm was now cool. He reached for the jacket he shed earlier in the day. As his senses again began to function, he suddenly realized he heard someone calling his name.

Craig awkwardly arose, his back wincing with pain from sitting too long on the rock. As he looked around for the sound of the distant voice, he realized that it was probably Bill calling him. He picked out a figure some distance below his location. "Up here, Bill," Craig yelled. The figure immediately turned and looked up toward Craig's rocky perch. Craig waived his arms, motioning for Bill to come up. During the minutes it took Bill to make his way up to him, Craig decided not to tell him of the diary, at least not just yet. Ever so gently, Craig placed the diary in his pack. He carefully placed the now empty jar back under the rock and concealed it with stones.

"Man, where have you been? I have been looking for you all

afternoon," Bill chastised him as he approached. "I was headed down to the Ranger Station to report you missing," he added.

"I am sorry, Bill," Craig responded sheepishly, reading the disgust in Bill's face.

"Man, I was seriously worried," Bill lamented.

"Sorry, Bill, I guess I was so exhausted I must have drifted off to sleep or something." This was the best excuse Craig was able to muster.

"Well…did you find it?" Bill asked. Rather than respond, Craig merely reached into his pocket and produced the film container. In a deliberate casual manner, Craig tossed the container to Bill without saying a word. Bill immediately snapped off the lid, revealing the shiny twenty-dollar gold piece. "Man, this is great, really special," Bill said, sounding quite envious. "Yes, it sure is," Craig managed to say, turning away and fighting back tears.

It didn't take Bill too long to realize that Craig was not yet ready to talk about finding the coin. Silently they walked back toward the Chateau. The cool evening breeze blowing on their backs added to the strange coolness between two ordinarily very close and talkative friends.

The events of the day were largely ignored during dinner conversation between the two that night at the Chateau. Bill told Craig that he was going to try and come back to the Canadian Rockies next year and bring his girl friend. Craig agreed that he too would like sharing this wonderful place with Julie. They compared their girl friends and how they might take to hiking and camping. They decided that both would probably love it.

Craig's appetite was far from normal. He even passed up

the dessert that came with the meal. Noticing this strange behavior led Bill to inquire, quite seriously, "Craig, are you alright. I mean no dessert, that is so unlike you." Craig responded with the excuse that he was just really tired. Bill didn't pry any further.

After dinner, Bill wanted to walk through the lobby and check out the girls. "Bill, I will let you go cat'in alone tonight, I think I am going to turn in," Craig said. Bill just shook his head and wandered off. A short time later when Bill arrived back at their room, Craig could no longer hold back. "Bill…there is something I need to talk to you about," Craig nervously blurted out. "You see the coin was not all I found…I mean there was this book…or…diary. The diary belonged to my father. I know, I know you are not going to believe this," Craig said, his voice quivering as he spoke. "My father apparently traveled back in time and lived here from 1894 to 1935."

The obvious impact of this preposterous statement was as one might have expected. "Man, do you know what you just said. You are sick. You were out in the sun too long today," Bill quipped, obviously thinking that Craig was joking.

"Bill, I am serious," Craig shot back.

Craig then reached into his backpack and produced the diary. Gingerly he handed it to Bill saying, "Here, read this, but be careful of the pages. It is very old. Read it. Read it and you will see for yourself. I think it really happened." Before Bill could say a word, Craig added, "Bill, I have to find out what finally happened to him, the last entry was 1935. I wonder if he died then."

By now Bill had become absorbed in reading the first pages of the diary. Craig started collecting his thoughts and trying to decide how to find out what happened in the end. There must have been some record of Logan Bristol, he thought. He wondered to himself where any records of that time would be kept. Suddenly he remembered a sign he had seen in Banff. The best he could remember the sign read Museum or Archives of the Canadian Rockies.

The archives would probably be a good place to begin the search. As Craig pondered leaving for Banff in the morning, another idea came to him. Why not ask some of the older employees there at the Chateau if they knew anything about Logan Bristol? He thought about that and decided to explore that idea the first thing the next morning.

During the wee hours of the morning, while Bill was still absorbed in reading the diary, Craig's exhaustion finally claimed him and he drifted into a much-needed sleep. The knocking on the door and the call "housekeeping" finally awakened the pair the next morning. As they looked at their watches, they discovered that it was already after 9:00 am. Though surprised by the late hour, that was nothing to the shock that they felt as they began to remember the previous day. They began by asking each other if the diary was for real.

Their excitement multiplied as they discussed it over breakfast. One thing they both agreed that at the very least it was an amazing story. Frequently their eyes would scan the dinning room to see if anyone was eavesdropping on their wild conversation about time travel. Bill kept asking Craig if he really thought the whole thing could possibly be true. Craig, normally the skeptic of the two, acknowledged that he believed it all. "Craig, do you understand how this could have happened?" Bill asked. "If your father could do it perhaps, we could as well," he added.

"Would you want to, Bill, if it was one a way trip with no return?" Craig asked.

"Well, I don't know about that," Bill commented.

"Bill, I want to leave right away for Banff and see if I can find out anything more about my father in the Archives there," Craig said.

"That's a great idea," Bill chimed in, eager for more of the exciting mystery. "First though, I am going to see the hotel manager here. I want to see if he knows anything about my father or if there is an old employee who might," Craig said.

Craig was soon to learn that no one at the Chateau knew of Logan Bristol. It seemed that the manager had only been there for two years and that the oldest employee at the hotel had been there for a mere fifteen years. Though not surprised at this dead-end, he was, never-the-less disappointed. Craig gazed at the old photographs of the old Chateau and its predecessor, the Chalet that hung in the hotel corridors. His mind tried to picture his father; the father he couldn't even remember now from the old photos he had seen of him. He soon concluded the photos did not help him find out what happened, so the pair departed for Banff.

It was past lunch time when they arrived in Banff. After locating the Archives Building down by the river, they decided to have a quick picnic lunch in a park nearby before venturing into the building. Craig decided to go alone to the Archives. Meanwhile Bill went down the street to get grocery's and for supplies. The plan was for Bill, once he completed shopping, to go up to Tunnel Mountain and get a campsite. After setting up camp, Bill was to join Craig back at the Archives. Craig wondered how long it would take to do his research. Since the building didn't close until six o'clock, that should give him plenty of time he thought. While desperate to confirm the diary and find out what happened to his father, he was also apprehensive of what he would find.

"Ma'am, I wonder if you could help me. I am trying to find some information about an individual who lived in this area in the early 1900s," Craig asked. The librarian was a spindly middle age lady who seemed to be well fit for the place. In an eager to please voice she asked for more specifics. "Well, the man's name would have been Logan Bristol. The last account I have of him was in 1935," Craig added. The librarian started energetically flipping through a card file.

"What did you say his name was, son?" she asked again.

In an apologetic manner, Craig said, "Logan Bristol. You probably won't have much on him," Craig said speculating, yet hoping he was wrong.

"Well, let's see," she said, offering some encouragement.

"We can start with references in books, which would be listed in these card files," she said, motioning at the cards she was looking through without any apparent success. Or we could try periodicals such as newspapers," she said as she motioned to another bank of card files. After some time when no reference had turned up in the books, Craig's hopes had dimmed.

After a few minutes with no success, she piped up with, "We might get lucky and find a newspaper obituary."

This suggestion, especially the gleeful way she made it, shocked and offended Craig. He hadn't really considered the possibility of finding his father's obituary. Craig rationalized that she had no way of knowing how emotional this was for him. That word 'obituary' though just cut like a knife. "Sure, that's a good idea," he finally responded.

She took over the search for him. "You are in luck, son, here it is," the librarian piped up. Craig's heart skipped a beat. This couldn't be real. The dream continues, he thought to himself. She read from the card: "Bristol, Logan,—1936; Banff Chronicle, Newspaper, 1936. Must have died in 1936," she said. The date she read was by far the most shocking thing she had said yet. As chills ran through him, Craig heard himself saying, "July 24, 1936." "Well, young man, oddly enough it doesn't give the exact date, but you can look through the micro-film for that year and maybe you can find it. Say I thought you said you didn't know when he died," she commented.

Craig responded to the librarian's question by merely saying, "Now I feel I know that."

"We will see if you are right," she commented. As she scurried off to the back room to retrieve the roll of micro-film, Craig continued to stare at the card that bore his father's name. He had not known a lot about his father but one thing he did remember for sure was his birthday. . . July 24, 1936. Died July 24, 1936, born July 24, 1936; impossible! Incredible! This whole thing just kept getting even more bazaar. This just couldn't have happened, could it, he wondered?

His hand was quivering noticeably as he reached out to take the roll of microfilm she offered. She then instructed Craig on how to use the film reader. The instructions, though quite simple, seemed to go over his head. By now the librarian had become somewhat wrapped up in the search and asked a rather obvious question, "Son, who was this person and what is your interest in him?"

Craig, now in a complete daze, answered honestly, "He was my father."

She laughed and quickly said, "You mean your grandfather, don't you?"

"Oh … oh yes, that's right … my grandfather," he managed to mumble, while thinking how absurd this conversation had become. There is no way I can tell her this story, he kept thinking to himself.

The tension mounted with each crank of the film reel. He quickly turned through 1935 and then slowed down as 1936 started. April 6th, May 30th, his heart was pounding. Finally came the day, July 24th. With the eye of an eagle, he scanned every printed word. When nothing was found, he felt both relieved and at the same time disappointed. Maybe he hadn't died on his birthday after all, he reasoned. With hope of finding anything plummeting, he slowly realized that the obituary might have been published a day or two after he died.

The search ended abruptly as he cranked to July 27, 1936. It was not what he expected. He didn't have to look far on that date. There it was on the front page in the lower right corner. The little headline quickly etched itself forever in his mind. It read, "A Sad Day at Lake Louise — Logan Bristol Joins Molly in Paradise Valley."

Tears rolled down his cheeks. He rubbed his eyes and looked away briefly, unable to continue. After a few deep breaths, he forced himself back to the screen and read on. "Logan Bristol, who nearly everyone knew and loved, passed away at his home at Lake Louise on Tuesday, July 24th. Logan was believed to be about 80 years old, though no one really knew for sure, him being secretive about his age. Little is known about his years before coming to the Valley. This reporter can testify to his reluctance to discuss his early life, having several times tried to interview him during the past few years.

"It is thought that Logan arrived in the Canadian Rockies some time in 1894. He spent the better part of the last forty odd years around Lake Louise, though he was also a frequent visitor to Banff. Logan was one of the pioneers of the area, having helped build many buildings, roads, trails, and more recently he had become a popular lecturer. Above all, Logan loved this land and vigorously undertook to protect it. He enjoyed showing off his "Diamond in the Wilderness," as he referred to Lake Louise. The thousands of tourists who were fortunate enough to meet him were given a taste of his special insight into this land and will long remember him.

"Bob Anderson best summed up Logan in the touching tribute he gave at last night's campfire program at Lake Louise. 'Tonight, I have the great privilege and face the great challenge of carrying on a tradition started by a great man, Logan Bristol. As some of you may know, it was Logan Bristol who started these campfire programs both here at Lake Louise and at Banff some twenty-two years ago. I am saddened to tell you that this great man and good friend passed away Monday.'

"Logan, while not a Canadian by birth, so loved this land that he chose to make it his home. He charmed and entertained many with his tales of the early years, tales of Bankhead, of Lake Louise, and of Banff. I first met Logan in the summer of 1913. He had just returned to Banff after living in the back country for a number of months following the death of his wife, Molly. Though I never met Molly, those who knew her and Logan back then said no two people were ever more in love. But, equal to their love for each other was the love they shared for Lake Louise.

"When Molly died, Logan nearly died of loneliness. He was still in much pain when I first met him. I was a green assistant manager at the Banff Springs that summer. Logan was put in charge of the construction of a large addition to the hotel that year. I believe it was his affection for that grand hotel and the excitement of working on it that helped him pull through that tough year of 1913.

"The hotel addition was nearing completion when one day Logan was asked to entertain a group of tourists from the Southern United States. Logan gave a talk that night around a bonfire down behind the Banff Springs Hotel near the Bow Falls. The response was tremendous. The rest is history. He started a tradition that I am continuing here with you this evening.

"Until his recent illness, Logan gave these talks nearly every night during the season. He had been doing this ever since that first night in 1913. Those who had the privilege of hearing him speak remember the excitement he stirred up while talking about the early pioneer years. He told tales of the early mountaineers, of greenhorn's misadventures, tales of the wildlife, and of just living life to the fullest in his paradise on top of the world.

"Over the years, many had wondered at his uncanny physic predictions of the future. More than once did he correctly predict a significant event before it occurred. This odd and strange talent added to the mysticism that surrounded this man. Those of us who really knew him knew to take his predictions seriously. Was he a physic? We shall never know.

"Logan gave a lot to the park. He left a legacy of trails he blazed. He left many buildings, including the Teahouse up the way at Lake Agnes. Of all the things he did, leading others to love and respect our beautiful land was probably his greatest achievement.

"Logan had requested permission from the Park Service several years ago to be buried in Paradise Valley. This last wish was granted today. He was laid to rest in an unmarked grave in the valley. It was in that same valley where he buried his beloved Molly back in 1912. He often said that paradise lay there beneath Mt. Temple, the mountain many old timers used to say Logan and Molly first conquered together.

"Tonight, Molly and Logan are together once again. Together in the valley they explored, where they loved and laughed, so many years ago. Their love story is now complete. Goodbye Logan, we will miss you old friend."

Craig's eyes could no longer hold back the flood of tears. He was barely able to speak as he asked the librarian for a copy of the article. The librarian was clearly shaken by his outpouring of emotion. She asked again and again if he was all right. He nodded and walked out of the museum.

Through blurry eyes he looked up to the West. The sun was sinking low over the snowcapped peaks. So now he knew. Now he knew the father he had never known. Now he knew how marvelously he had lived and loved, and how he had died. His father had truly been a part of these mountains, these mountains that now Craig knew would always be a part of him.

ABOUT THE AUTHOR

Trails Through Time is Larry Engels's first novel. Engels has a background in construction management and has been in charge of everything from subways and hospitals to high-rise buildings. Though it probably seems strange that an author from Georgia would write a novel set in the Canadian Rockies, Engels became enamored with the area many years ago, visiting no less than twenty times.

About fifteen years ago, he started visiting the Whyte Museum & Archives in Banff and found himself spending hours reading old newspaper articles about the history of the early days of the park. He even had the good fortune of meeting Ken Jones, probably the last of the true old mountain men.

It was while learning about the area's history that Engels got the idea to weave a fictional story through the exciting past, a story told through the wonderful people who lived there. There really was a "Molly," and there really was a father who hid gold coins for his son.

Perhaps equally strange is that Engels completed Trails

Through Time ten years ago and is just now having it published. The simple answer? "Brain tumor and a miracle recovery."

Engels leaves it to the reader to separate facts from fiction.

Acknowledgements

Though a work of fiction, I wish to acknowledge the help, history, and inspiration from the following.

The Wythe Museum and Archives of the Canadian Rockies for their assistance in my research of the history of the era.

To all the great writers of trail guides and the wonderful historians whose works I have enjoyed are too many to mention here, thanks.

And especially to Ken Jones, the last of the old-time mountain men. It was my pleasure to have had Ken regaled me with his tales of old on a trip into Skoki many years ago.

Another person I wish to thank for her inspiration was Petra Pauw. She was an immigrant to Banff from the Netherlands, arriving in Banff years ago, similar to 'Molly' of this work. As a long time Banff resident, she showed me sites most tourists seldom see.

And to my wife Cynthia, who found the manuscript for this book while I was in the hospital undergoing brain surgery. Without her discovery, this book would not have happened.

And to my old friend Alice Murry whose literary expertise and encouragement proved invaluable.

Finally, my thanks to Bob Babcock and the team of Deeds Publishing who had the courage and patience to take on a first-time writer.

www.ingramcontent.com/pod-product-compliance
Lightning Source LLC
Chambersburg PA
CBHW051644180726
48284CB00006B/1860